A Fresh Start on the Bridle Path

Margaret Amatt

LEANNAN
PRESS
INDEPENDENT PUBLISHER

LEANNAN PRESS

First Published by Leannan Press 2025

Book Cover designed by Margaret Amatt

eBook ISBN: 978-1-914575-47-1

Paperback ISBN: 978-1-914575-36-5

PROLOGUE

Dagmar

Sixteen Years Ago

The bell rang and Dagmar Ingenfeld gathered her books together, her fingers fumbling with the worn edges as she shoved them into her bag. Her head and ears burned with the stares and whispers that followed her like shadows.

'Hey, Horse Girl, got any carrots in your lunch today?' a sneering voice called out from the back of the classroom.

Dagmar didn't turn around. What was the point? After four years of High School, she was used to this. It wasn't exactly going to change, was it? She kept her head down as she headed to the door.

Another giggle, another snide comment. 'Maybe she's trotting off to the stables.'

'*Neigh!*' Someone whinnied loudly and several others burst out laughing.

'With teeth like that, she could eat an apple through a letter-box.'

Dagmar's cheeks flamed, but she kept walking, her steps quickening as she made her way along the hallway, now bustling with students, changing classes. She joined the throng, hoping to disappear. Why did she have to go through this torture, day in, day out?

She rounded a corner and froze, almost colliding with James Charlton. *Oh god. Not him.* She'd crushed on this boy since primary school. He'd seemed ok when he was little. For a while anyway. Then he'd stolen her favourite Schleich horse, the Friesian stallion – a toy that wasn't just collectable and very realistic, but very expensive – and she'd lost it forever. That was when his true colours had started to seep out. She wouldn't forgive or forget, especially now. Not when he was always going about with horrible friends, who teased her relentlessly about her extremely long hair and her sticky out front teeth, which were now caged in ugly braces.

As with all the other friends she'd had at primary school, they seemed to have forgotten they ever knew her, made new friends and moved on. Now she had no one. Not at school anyway. The horses were her friends and some girls at the pony club were ok, though they usually came from families with a lot more money and status than Dagmar.

James's easy smile faded slightly when he saw her. She went to skirt around him, but he caught her eye.

'You had Mr Duncan today?' he asked. And his voice was normal, like he was talking to one of his friends, not her.

'Um… No.' Her heart raced. James's bright blue eyes were still on her. Not only was he good looking, but he was the brainbox of their year, and everyone suspected he'd be head boy in a couple of years' time. Dagmar knew better than to think this seemingly friendly chat meant anything. Why would it? She'd heard one girl in his group saying just the other day, 'Who knows what Dagmar's problem is? All we ever do is try to be sociable. And she's just so rude.'

Ha! Rude? They were being sociable! That was a laugh. If sociable meant being constantly teased and talked about, then she wanted nothing to do with them. This little chat was more than likely another chance for them to claim they were being sociable when they just wanted further reasons to dislike her.

'Lucky you,' James said. 'He's—'

'Hey, James, watch out! Horse Girl might kick you,' a voice shouted from behind Dagmar.

Her face and neck were so hot it was like someone was pushing a branding iron into her skin. She glanced at James, expecting to see a smirk or a laugh, but his expression remained neutral.

Without another word, she hitched her bag higher on her shoulder, put her head down, and almost ran down the corridor.

'Guess Horse Girl's got a new jockey!' the loud voice shouted.

Her eyes stung, but she kept running, wishing she could get away from it all. Away from school, away from nasty comments, and away from James Charlton.

CHAPTER ONE

James

James swirled the wine in his glass, watching the ruby liquid catch the light from the modern chandelier above his parents' sleek, minimalist dining table.

'Sales are up another fifteen per cent this quarter,' his father, Laurence, said, slicing into his steak. 'The new artisanal cheese is a real hit. People can't get enough of those truffle-infused gouda wheels. They are delicious, mark you. I've got one in for later.'

'It's delightful to see such enthusiasm for local produce.' Sherri Charlton beamed at James, her designer dress sparkling under the lights. James smiled back at his mum, who was so perfectly turned out she might have been dining with the royal family, not her husband and son on a Thursday evening. 'And I love having Genevieve Harrington onboard. Her cookware range is wonderful. Pity things didn't work out there, but I see now she was all wrong for you.'

The open-plan dining room, with its glass walls, seemed to close in on him a little. The heat was stifling. His parents' conversation topics were two-track, they either talked shop – literally, because they owned Duchan Fayre, the famed country shopping centre near Glenbriar – or they discussed his love life, which they micromanaged with the same precision and attention to detail as they did with the business. Was there no way to break free without hurting them – or his prospects?

Maybe it had been rash making the promise he had, but at the time – when his father had been in hospital hooked up to machines and drips – it had seemed like the right thing to do. And now he was bound by it.

He turned his attention to his dinner. Roast beef, Yorkshire pudding, and an assortment of side dishes that could feed an army. His parents never did anything by halves and with the produce at Duchan Fayre at their disposal, they always ate well. Succulent beef was a welcome distraction from the mention of Genevieve. James had dated her a few years back, somewhat disastrously, and subsequent relationships hadn't exactly gone to plan either – his parents' plans anyway. The ones he'd promised to go along with for the good of the business – as well as himself. Sometimes he was grateful. It was one less thing to worry about when he was so busy with work; he didn't have much time to meet people himself. The same problem, however, seemed to surface again and again. None of the women his parents set him up with were right for him. Something was always missing.

'Oh, I forgot. She's not Genevieve Harrington anymore, is she?' His mum took a sip of wine. 'She got married, didn't she?

I heard a funny story about her getting drunkenly engaged and going through with it, but I doubt it was true.'

It could well be. Genevieve and James had dated more as an arrangement than anything else. It had kept both sets of parents off their backs for a while. He could do with something like that round about now to save him from what he knew was coming. Something that would keep on coming until he actually settled on one of these women.

Laurence dabbed at his mouth with a linen napkin. 'So, James. You're doing splendidly at work, but we can't help but notice you've yet to make any significant progress in... other areas.'

James stabbed a roast potato. *Here we go.* The way his father spoke to him sometimes, like they were at a review meeting, was so ridiculous. 'Other areas?'

Sherri leaned forward and took his arm. 'You know what we mean, darling? We've found you some lovely young women from good families. And yet, here we are, still waiting for you to find someone suitable.'

'Yeah, but...' How could explain it? He'd met these women, and they'd all been nice enough, but he just hadn't clicked with them. Perhaps the last one, Ophelia Chattan-Blythe, had been the most promising. She'd grown on him, but when he'd sug-gested trying again after a couple of disastrous meetings, she was already in a relationship with someone else, so that was that.

'I wonder.' Laurence took a large swig of wine. 'We agreed that it should be someone of status. An insurance policy, so to speak.'

James gave him a tight smile. This was the promise he'd made after his father's heart attack some years back. Laurence was so worried something would go wrong, and they'd lose the business that he'd made up his mind the only way to secure it would be to link it to some high-ranking family. James, being paranoid that his father might die, had agreed. At the time, it had seemed almost a throwaway thing, but his parents now viewed it like a blood oath. The number of times his mother had thrown the words "remember your promise" at him must be in the thousands by now. And really, he wouldn't mind. If he could just meet someone of status who he actually liked.

'I've been thinking a lot about this.' Laurence tapped his finger on the table. 'Trying to figure out why things haven't worked out. I mean, you have the money, the looks, the charm. What's missing?'

James raised his eyebrows and gave a half shrug, not sure he wanted to know where his father was going with this.

'Maybe it's because you're just not... not posh enough.'

James almost choked on his potato. 'Posh enough? Really, Dad?'

'Actually, that's a good point.' Sherri sat back and covered her mouth. 'We're all guilty of it. Remember last year when we went to the Highland Games and met the earl and countess of Dairvin for the first time? I was petrified.'

'But we're also good at learning and adapting,' Laurence said. 'It's why we've done so well in business.'

'So, what are you saying?' James asked. Where was this leading? Did they want him to buy a title or something? Surely that would defeat the point.

'I'm not sure.' Laurence glanced at his wife. 'It was merely an observation.'

Sherri's eyes softened. 'We just worry, darling. After what happened to your father. It's thrown so much into perspective. If Duchan Fayre was connected to one of the big families around here, it would just give us a sense of security. These families might not always have the money, but their estates have lasted for hundreds of years.'

James ground his teeth. He'd heard this argument repeatedly. He couldn't deny that a part of him liked the idea, but at the same time, he couldn't wholly get behind it. Not when he lived in fear of being forced into a relationship with someone he didn't really like. 'What if, well, what if there isn't anyone? I mean, we've tried. I don't want to settle for someone just because they have an old family name. What if I did that, only to end up fighting for the next several years trying to force a marriage to work?'

His parents exchanged a look. 'No one's forcing you.' Laurence pulled a nonchalant face. 'But I admit there aren't a lot of options. However, I subscribe to the belief that there's no such thing as "the one". It's such a silly idea. If you're at all compatible with someone, then you can make a relationship work. Marriage is almost like business. Obviously, different emotions are involved, but ultimately there are principles, routines, transactions, and compromises that can make the relationship a success or not. If you're holding out for love at first sight, destiny, or some other nonsense, then you're wasting time that you could be using making real connections.'

'Look.' James pushed his plate away. 'That's not what I'm doing, and I appreciate what you're trying to do, but it hasn't worked so far. Maybe it's time I looked for someone on my own. Someone who fits me, not just the family's image.' Though when he would find the time, he wasn't sure... or where to start looking.

Sherri sighed dramatically. 'We just want you to be happy.'

James couldn't help but laugh. 'And do I have to marry someone "posh" to be happy?'

'Not necessarily.' Laurence put his cutlery across his empty plate. 'It's the stability that we need.'

'And the connections wouldn't go a miss,' Sherri said, a hint of a smile playing on her lips.

James raised his glass in mock salute.

'And actually, speaking of connections, I have some very good news.' Sherri leaned forward. 'I recently met the Countess of Dairvin again. She's such a charming woman, which goes to show we shouldn't be worried about meeting people from the upper class. She's quite normal really.'

James stifled a groan. *Seriously?*

'We got to talking, and I told her all about you and Eloise.'

James frowned slightly at the mention of his sister. She'd escaped this circus by marrying her college sweetheart at twenty-five. If only James had been so quick off the mark. But he'd spent his time learning the family business and working at Duchan Fayre – successfully, yes, but it had left other areas of his life woefully empty.

'She remembered meeting you at the Highland Games, which was nice.' Sherri splayed her hand on her chest. 'Then, you'll never guess what she told me. She has a single daughter. And I think she only mentioned her because she saw the potential in a match with you.'

'Oh yeah?'

This was Ophelia all over again. He remembered his parents introducing her in much the same way. They'd insisted on him making plans to meet her and doing all number of silly things to appear like the kind of person she'd be attracted to, including wearing a hideous pair of salmon pink trousers to the highland games to impress her – apparently that was what everyone "in her set" wore. He'd spent the whole day feeling like a spare part and was pretty sure Ophelia hadn't noticed his trousers or given two hoots about what he was wearing.

'I know what you're thinking,' Sherri said. 'We tried this already with the Chattan-Blythes.'

'Exactly.'

'Have you heard who Ophelia took up with, by the way?'

'No.' He lifted his glass with a frown.

'Her builder.'

James raised an eyebrow, recalling a couple of times he'd met the builder. 'Wow. I wouldn't have put them together. He's...' Well, *he* certainly didn't go about wearing pink trousers, that was for sure.

'All very strange,' Sherri said. 'I heard the estate is falling to bits, but I'm not sure shacking up with the builder is the way to save it. Anyhow, the countess's daughter. Lady Victoria Bruce.' She widened her eyes dramatically. 'Is a very promising horse rider. Apparently, she adores horses and always does well at the horse trials. She's even sponsoring a new event at the castle this year.'

Laurence nodded. 'I looked her up; she's rather pretty too.'

James rolled his eyes. 'So, you want me to date her because she can ride a horse and looks good in jodhpurs?' This really was Ophelia all over again. No one rocked a pair of jodhpurs the way she did.

Sherri laughed. 'Oh, darling, it's not just that. I have a really good feeling about her.'

'It wouldn't hurt to meet her.' Laurence added. 'As far as I can discover, she's well-educated, accomplished, and sensible. All the qualities you might admire in a partner.'

James leaned back in his chair, crossing his arms. 'This is exactly what you said about Ophelia.' And she was all those things and then some. She was beautiful, charming, ran a successful business, rode horses and all the rest, but something was missing, not from her, but from him. The feelings, emotions, passion, desire.

Sherri reached across the table, patting his hand. 'There's no harm in trying. Just because it didn't work out with Ophelia doesn't mean it'll be like that with everyone.'

'Look at it as business.' Laurence waggled his finger. 'It'll change things completely. I promise. Approach it in exactly the same way. Look at how you've grown to love Duchan Fayre. The same will happen here, you'll see.'

James shook his head. 'You think?'

'He's right.' Sherri nodded. 'Love is a nice idea, but that excitement surrounding it only lasts a short while. After that, it's more... Well...' She wafted her hands around, but didn't seem to have the words to say what she wanted.

'Let's say I'm interested,' James said. 'How do you propose I meet her? It was easy with Ophelia; her father was desperate to marry her off to anyone with money, but the earl and countess of Dairvin don't need our money.'

'I wouldn't be too sure.' Laurence leaned back. 'These old families often have the title and not the cash.'

'Ooh, I have a really good idea.' Sherri held up her hands and wiggled her fingers.

'Oh yeah?' James had a really bad feeling about this.

'What's the best way to get to know someone?'

'I... er... talk to them, I suppose.'

'Yes.' Sherri wound her hand, as if trying to wheel out a better answer.

What the hell did she want him to say?

'You have to find something to talk about,' she said, as though it was obvious. 'Common ground. And to do that, you have to have a shared interest.'

'But I can't know what her interests are until I meet her.'

'Aha, that's where my plan comes into play. It's so good.'

James sighed, picking up his wine glass again. 'Uh-huh?'

Sherri beamed. 'You need to learn to horse ride.'

'Pardon?' James choked on his wine. 'No way am I getting on a horse.'

'Actually, that's a great idea.' Laurence nodded at his wife, looking very impressed. 'It's like what I said before about not being posh enough. I think part of the problem is that you don't have enough in common with these women. If we'd had the means when you were at High School, we would have sent you to private school and you'd fit in with their set a lot better. But sadly, Duchan Fayre didn't start paying off until later.'

'They all went to schools where riding was on the curriculum.' Sherri pulled a face somewhere between approving and annoyed. 'So if you learn, then you'll instantly have something they can relate to.'

'You see.' His father winked. 'Good business skills. All it takes is critical thinking and we'll crack this.'

Jesus Christ. His parents had lost the plot. But then, what did he have to lose... Assuming he didn't fall off the horse and break his neck?

Laurence raised his glass. 'To new possibilities.'

James clinked his glass against his father's. 'Indeed.' He glugged it back. Now he needed to engineer a meeting with this woman before his parents booked him into an intensive riding course. Wouldn't it be lovely if this time they just clicked? Even better if she was someone he knew already, and they could have a good laugh about this. But his dad was right, he'd grown up in different circles from these people. He'd attended a big high school in Perth and done well for himself, becoming head boy and getting top grades. But it meant he hadn't grown up with the kind of people they now wanted him to be rubbing shoulders with. At thirty years old, he should be further on with his life than this, but still, maybe Lady Victoria Bruce would be the one – or someone he could build a steady relationship with if he followed his dad's rather emotionless approach. But Laurence and Sherri had been happily married for over thirty years. They'd had two children, built a business, and made a name for themselves, so they must be doing something right.

If horses were the answer and ended up being what brought James together with his life partner... He let out a sigh. Well, it could be worse. Couldn't it?

Chapter Two

Dagmar

Dagmar urged her grey mare, Zephyra, into a gallop. The rhythmic thud of hooves against the forest floor vibrated through the woods, a steady beat that matched the quickening pulse in her chest.

'Come on, girl,' Dagmar said. This was what she lived for, the thrill of the ride. If the rest of her life was this much fun, then she'd be the happiest person alive.

Zephyra flicked an ear in response, the other resolutely forward, indicating she was keen to run. They wove through the trees, the path a familiar blur, the breeze hitting her face, the sense of freedom and space, and even the hint of danger highlighting the sheer power surging through her – like she was sitting on a rocket ready to blast off. Dagmar knew every twist and turn; she'd ridden here for years, ever since she'd taken a summer job on the Glenvorneth Estate when she'd left school. How was that twelve years ago? It felt like yesterday. The summers had flown by. Now she was a single thirty-year-old living in a converted trailer, and it didn't sound quite as exciting as it had done at eighteen. These days, it seemed a bit sad, and she had no doubt outsiders had plenty to say about her. As they always had.

Up ahead, the trail narrowed, and a fallen tree lay across the path. It had been there for years. Nothing to worry about; it wasn't huge, but it was a definite obstacle. Dagmar slowed the pace a little, letting Zephyra do the work. Her muscles coiled, then released, launching them both into the air. For a brief moment, Dagmar felt weightless, suspended above the log. Then, with a thud, they were back on the ground.

'Good girl!' Dagmar patted Zephyra's neck.

The woods thinned, the trees giving way to a grassy hill. Dagmar nudged Zephyra on. They crested the hill, the landscape opening up and revealing the sprawling hillside below. The estate of Glenvorneth occupied much of this hill. The manor house was prominent in the centre. Though part of it was covered in scaffolding, it still maintained a grand presence. Since Ophelia Chattan-Blythe, the heiress to the estate, had taken up – rather scandalously – with a local builder, a lot of repairs were taking place. Dagmar had known Ophelia for years. They were a similar age and had been in the pony club together as teens. But they weren't really friends. Then again, Dagmar didn't exactly have a lot of friends. Experience had taught her that people were best kept at arm's length. Getting too close to anyone always caused trouble.

Hopefully these repairs wouldn't threaten her job. Her heart trembled a little at the thought. This family didn't have a great record so far. She'd gone months without wages when they'd been in financial difficulties before. Ophelia had eventually seen to her getting the money she was owed, but trusting the Chattan-Blythes wasn't easy after that. They were pretty base and had even tried to marry off Ophelia to a wealthy businessman for his cash – a businessman Dagmar knew from old: James Charlton. Her insides churned at the thought. That stupid schoolgirl crush still hurt. When she'd found out Ophelia and he might be an item, she'd made herself scarce. How could she watch that? She'd endured enough watching him going about with the prettiest girls in school. And Ophelia had to be one of the prettiest girls in the world, never mind school. Dagmar had never been able to compete with them. Except in the arena. That was where she could show them all.

But in between doing that, she had to do her job. Money didn't grow on trees. Yes, she was a good rider, and she had rosettes and medals to prove it. People often told her she could go anywhere horsey and demand the wage she wanted. But that was easier said than done. Making a living competing was super tough. Most high-level riders came from wealthy families to start with – how else could they afford to travel and sign up for all the shows? She'd need a groom and coaches, not to mention quality horses, which were also super expensive. And at the end of the day, she didn't have that kind of confidence. Staying put and doing the job she knew was so much easier. Adapting to change was something she'd never done well.

She sat up, engaging her core and stabilising her legs, preparing for the descent. Zephyra knew what was coming and braced accordingly 'That's a good girl.'

Dagmar had ridden so many horses over the years. Some she'd gelled with straight away, and Zephyra was one of them. They had a rapport and worked so well together. If only people were this easy.

As they neared the new stable block and the old steading that had been newly done up, Dagmar spotted Francesca, Ophelia's half-sister, carrying a bucket across the yard. Francesca and her friend Caitlin often helped out at weekends. Caitlin's dad was the builder Ophelia was now living with, an arrangement which clearly suited the girls as they got to see each other frequently. Dagmar saw in them the starry-eyed looks teenagers often had when working with horses. Once it became a job, the shine wore off a little. Stealing these moments to ride and enjoy herself was important because looking after other people's horses was bloody hard work and she rarely got a word of thanks. Teaching riders was the same. While she liked working with the students and matching them to horses, she couldn't abide the parental interference. So many helicopter parents just wouldn't back off and accept she knew what she was doing.

'Morning,' Francesca said as Dagmar approached the yard. 'We saw you riding like a demon, as always.'

Dagmar gave her a little smile. 'It's a nice day for it. And we have to use them, while we can. Likely the rain will be back any day.'

Caitlin came out of the stables and looked up. 'I wish I could ride like you.'

Dagmar swung down from the saddle, rubbing Zephyra affectionately. 'Keep up with your lessons and you'll be fine. You did well the last time.'

'Thanks.'

Dagmar scratched Zephyra's forehead. 'Are you two staying all morning?'

Zephyra nudged Dagmar with her nose, desperate for more attention.

'Yeah, I think so.' Francesca looked at Caitlin and flicked her long blonde hair over her shoulder. Like her sister, she had that unmistakable upper class look about her, with her smart clothes and immaculate hair. Dagmar had been around people like that all her life but never mastered the easy elegance. She had the riding clothes; she was tall, slim, and blonde, but somehow, she didn't fit. No one would ever mistake her for one of the Chattan-Blythes or call her the names they called Ophelia – beautiful, glamorous, hot, leggy, stunning, immaculate. The things people called Dagmar hadn't improved much from "horse girl". She often got "stable girl" from visitors and had overheard people calling her awkward, skinny, gaunt, and similarly unflattering names.

'I need to go out for a bit.' Dagmar led Zephyra towards the stable. 'As soon as I've untacked and groomed Zephyra.'

'Cool,' Caitlin said, and Dagmar was pleased she asked no more, because she didn't discuss her private life with anyone if she could possibly help it – not that there was much to say about it – and it always felt insignificant when she heard the things other people got up to.

The drive to Glenbriar, the nearest town, took about ten minutes, occasionally more, if she got stuck behind a tractor, which was always a possibility in this part of Scotland. Most of the farmland was on hills around Loch Briar, but the majority of the landscape was woodland. The trees still clung to their wintery branches, though a few buds were visible on close inspection. But the bright skies surrounding the loch made for beautiful reflections even on a chilly March day. Dagmar might have appreciated it more if the weight on her chest wasn't so heavy.

The message she'd received from her mum the night before suggested that all was not well in the state of The Cosy Bean Café. Her mum had run it for years, since before Dagmar could really remember. Apparently, she'd been three when her mum had taken it on but she had no memory of a time before that. It was as much a part of her life as the horses.

Something about the message set the worry worms to work, eating into Dagmar's thoughts.

Recently, things had been tough for her mum. The bargain house she'd bought in Glenbriar was a cash drain. Money was flowing down it and there was no getting it back. It needed so much work just to keep it habitable.

Dagmar parked her old pickup truck on the road outside the café and took a deep breath before heading for the door. Maybe it was just the mood she was in but the familiar pale yellow paintwork around the door looked tired and chipped. What had seemed like a modern sign nearly thirty years ago now seemed dated. This haven that her mum had set up as a little nod to their Danish roots, serving a slice of hygge to the Scots before it was even a "thing" in this country, didn't look as welcoming as it should.

Pushing open the door, she was momentarily distracted by the warm pastry and cinnamon scents, so reminiscent of her younger days here. But her eyes lingered on the faded floral wallpaper. The wooden floor creaked underfoot. Once-vibrant curtains now hung limp at the window, their colour dulled. A sorry sight really, though not as sorry as the fact that no one was inside. March was still on the edge of the tourist season, but where were the locals that used to pop in on Saturday mornings looking for pastries and coffee?

Her mother, Dotty, was behind the counter, wiping the surface almost manically.

'Dagmar, you're here. So glad. Turn the sign to closed, and lock the door, will you? Not that it'll make much difference.'

'What's happened?' Dagmar flipped the sign and pushed the lower bolt into the floor.

Dotty lifted two mugs and brought them to the table, giving Dagmar a hug as soon as she laid the mugs down. 'Business has been so slow of late.' She returned to the counter and brought over a plate with her trademark mini pastries filled with jam, raisins, choc chips and custard. They all looked delicious. 'There's so much competition in town.' She sat with a sigh and Dagmar followed her, taking the seat opposite. 'The other cafés are more modern. They have the best facilities. I can't afford that. And this building is so old. It has charm, yes. But the landlord doesn't pay for the repairs. Now he wants to kick me out and sell the property. I don't know what to do.' Her mother still retained a little of her Danish accent, though years of living here had dulled it and it could pass for as a slightly quirky Scottish accent if you didn't know any better.

Dagmar frowned and sipped on her coffee. This was worse than she'd thought. Without this café, her mum had nothing except a falling down house. Dagmar couldn't have her living in the trailer with her. It was already too small for one person. 'Can't they give you more time?'

Dotty shook her head. 'Time for what? Even if they do, how do I get more business? I can't move with the times if I can't afford it. Every penny I make goes into the house. I've already used the money you gave me, but it's not enough and I don't want to ask you for more. I know you don't have enough for yourself, never mind me. Everything has got so messy. I should be the one providing for you.'

Dagmar's heart sank. The café meant everything to her mum. It was more than a business; it was a piece of her soul. 'I'll always help if I can. You spent so much on me when I was younger.' Horses weren't cheap, neither was the pony club or the travelling to all the events she took part in. Her mum had never begrudged a penny of it.

'No, no. I don't want you to think you owe me anything. I don't want your money, just ideas about what I can do.'

Dagmar clenched her fists under the table, her mind racing. She had to find a solution, but this kind of thing wasn't her strongpoint. She had no idea how to run a business or raise funds. If she was closer to Ophelia, she could ask her for ideas, but she didn't want it to sound like she was asking for a handout, especially when the Glenvorneth Estate was only just starting to make money itself. 'What other ways are there to raise some money?' she asked.

Dotty smiled weakly, shaking her head. 'I only wish I knew.'

Dagmar tapped the table and sighed. 'Well, I've seen some local businesses on social media asking for community support before. They post in local groups about how long they've been around and how important they are. Maybe we could try something like that?'

Dotty tilted her head and pulled a pout. 'Would that really work? I'm not sure who would care.'

Wasn't that the truth? Dagmar had spent her high school years panicking her unpopularity would filter down to her mother's business, but it hadn't. They hadn't lived in Glenbriar back then. Her mum had bought the tumbledown house here after Dagmar had left school and taken the job on the Glenvorneth Estate.

Back then, the café had thrived, and Dotty employed people to run it at weekends so she could take Dagmar all around the country to events and horse shows. Had anyone at school even realised her mum ran a café? No doubt some people knew. But they'd lived in Perth and Glenbriar had seemed a long way, though it was only about a thirty-minute drive. Dotty had commuted, but it made more sense to live nearby.

Would any of her online acquaintances even be vaguely interested if she posted about the café? They were mostly people from the horse world who didn't all live in the area. She rarely saw people she'd been at school with, and she actively avoided them on social media. Some had the gall to send friend requests. Why would she want to be friends with people who'd taken pleasure in making her life a misery?

If she posted, would the people she avoided see her name and laugh? Maybe it would have a detrimental effect on the café. It wasn't like she was a celebrity or had anything special about her to make people interested.

'I like the idea,' Dotty said. 'If we can do that, it might drag us into the modern world.'

But what would they say? The Cosy Bean Café, while charming, was definitely showing its age. The other cafés in town had sleek interiors, Wi-Fi, and fancy coffee machines.

Dagmar squeezed her mother's hand. This woman had sacrificed so much for her, and this was Dagmar's time to step up. 'We'll get through this. Somehow. We have something these other cafés don't. Heart. Character. And your pastries are still the best in town.'

Dotty chuckled softly. 'You always were my biggest fan. It's definitely worth a shot, but I don't know much about social media. Could you help me with it?'

'Sure.' How could she refuse? She'd offered after all, but she wasn't particularly tech-savvy herself, and the idea of putting herself out there still squeezed her chest until she struggled to breathe. 'I'll do my best. I just don't... Well, I'm not sure people will read anything I post.'

'I'm sure they will, sweetheart.' Dotty looked at her with sad eyes. 'You need to stop thinking people automatically won't like you. I know you had a horrible time at school, but you've made good. You're one of the best riders around. Put the doubts away. I'm sure there are lots of people out there who know you and respect you and will be very interested in what you have to say.'

Dagmar nodded, hoping that was true. But putting the doubts away wasn't that simple. Maybe her lack of close friends was her own fault, but trusting people was something she found so difficult.

'Ok. Let's start with some photos of the café and the pastries.' Fancy write-ups had never been her thing, and she couldn't rely on herself to say anything clever or smart, so she'd just have to use plain words to tell it like it was.

'Thank you, sweetheart.' Dotty's smile returned, though it didn't wholly light her eyes. Her hair that had once been long and so blonde had lost its warmth and was like faded straw. Her skin, too, had lost its luminosity and was pale and lined with care. 'Let's have another pastry and then get started. I'll get us some fresh coffee to go with it.'

As her mother busied herself behind the counter, Dagmar pulled out her phone, an ancient, bashed thing with a cracked screen, took some photos, and started typing out a message.

This is a difficult post for me to write, but I hope you will take a moment to read it.

The Cosy Bean Café has been a beloved part of Glenbriar for as long as I can remember. My mother, Dotty, has poured her heart and soul into this place for nearly thirty years, creating a little bit of hygge from her native Denmark in the heart of Scotland. It's a place where friends can meet, families gather, and tourists can enjoy a bite to eat on a busy holiday. It's not just a café; it's a piece of our community's heart.

Unfortunately, we've faced some challenging times recently. Business has been slower than ever, and we're struggling to keep the doors open. The newer, more modern cafés in town have been drawing customers away, and while we understand the appeal of new and shiny, it's left us in a tough spot. The building is old and charming, but it requires repairs that we simply can't afford right now. Without your help, we might have to close our doors for good.

We know money is tight for everyone, but we're asking for your support. If you've ever enjoyed a cup of coffee, one of our famous Danish pastries, or eaten lunch in our little café, please consider visiting us again. Every purchase, every visit, helps more than you can imagine.

Please, if you can, come by for a coffee, tell your friends about us, or even just share this post to spread the word. Your support means everything to us, and together, we can keep the Cosy Bean Café open for many more years to come.

Thank you for reading and for your continued support.

After adding the pictures, her thumb hovered over the "post" button for a moment. She took a deep breath before she pressed it. There. Gone. She'd done it on one forum. She scrolled through a couple of other groups, posting it there too.

Now what? Watch and wait? Would customers start flocking through the door the second they opened it? Or would the post simply vanish into the social media ether and get lost among everything else that was on there?

The momentary buzz accompanying her post fizzled away. If that little plea didn't work, what else could she do?

Chapter Three

James

James rested back in his swivel chair at the head of the conference table in the Duchan Fayre boardroom, tapping his finger on the wood. His father was... Well, being his father. How anyone could muster this level of enthusiasm about a new range of cheese was beyond him. And yet Laurence kept going.

'It's not a local company, but they're very well known on the west coast.' Laurence glanced around the table at the nods of approval. He smiled and gave the greying hair at his temple a little flick. 'They won two categories at the Royal Highland Show last year and we're missing a trick not stocking them.'

'Sounds perfect,' Henry Dawson, the chief financial officer, said.

James nodded, his eyes straying back to his screen. He clicked open a browser window, half-glancing at it but looking like he was one hundred per cent present at the meeting. Since the weekend, his thoughts hadn't drifted far from the idea of riding lessons and he'd almost talked himself into it, but he wanted to do it on his own terms. If he told his parents about it, they'd want to micromanage the whole thing; they'd demand constant progress reports and probably tell everyone, so there would be no chance of pretending to Lady Victoria he knew how to ride already because she'd have heard on the grapevine that he was taking lessons, which would make the whole thing pointless.

He typed riding schools into the search bar and resized the window so it would be easy to hide. A couple of places came up. Someone called Ross McPherson who ran a stable yard and the Glenvorneth Estate. James held his breath as he read the name. That was where Ophelia lived – practically owned. He wasn't sure he ever wanted to go back there.

'So, James, your thoughts on this?' his father said.

'Hmm?' James looked up. 'Oh… I think it's solid.'

Laurence rubbed his hands together. 'Great. We'll approve that then.'

'Indeed.' What else could he say? It seemed like his lot in life to agree with people and not rock the boat too much. His choices usually consisted of "yes, probably" or "yes, definitely". Saying no wasn't something he'd mastered, especially when it came to his parents. He pulled a face at his screen, not overly delighted at that thought, but at a loss about how to escape the situation. His mum and dad held so much of his future in their hands and a lot of it he appreciated. He didn't want to upset or offend them. His father's health was a source of concern, but more than that, they'd built Duchan Fayre as a legacy for their family. James's sister Eloise was head of recruitment, though was currently on maternity leave after having her second child. This was where he belonged and for the most part he enjoyed it, though a little less time spent analysing cheese would suit him.

He narrowed his eyes as he reread the word *Glenvorneth*. A memory stirred. When he'd been at the Glenbriar Highland Games last year with Ophelia, they'd talked about her stable manager... Dagmar. James had recognised the name straight away. It was so unusual. He'd never heard it before or since Dagmar Ingenfeld. Surely it had to be the same girl he was at school with. She'd been horse mad then too. Ever since they were at Primary School, and she'd been obsessed with those plastic Schleich horses – his sister had been into them too. At High School, people had teased Dagmar about her love of horses, especially before she got braces, and her front teeth stuck out. She'd got some stick for that with people calling her horse face and other cruel names. It hadn't sat easily with James at the time, but she hadn't been in any of his classes, so he'd never had much opportunity to talk to her, though he'd often said to his friends to give her a break and leave her alone. Not that they'd listened. He didn't keep in touch with any of them now. He'd made his own friends, or his parents cultivated "better" friends for him. Some of them were ok, but others he kept at a distance. His parents' taste was so blighted by their desire to look "posh" that they now saw money and status as a better indicator of a good person than their personality.

James was sure they hadn't always been like that. If only he could shift their mindset back to how it had been before Duchan had got so successful. Wouldn't that make everyone happier? He just wasn't sure how to manage it.

Would Dagmar even remember him? Maybe he could pay for some private lessons on the QT. Would that work right under Ophelia's nose? Though by all accounts, she was busy with her builder boyfriend fixing up the estate properties. Maybe her eyes would be elsewhere. Ross McPherson was surely a safer option.

The meeting continued, with discussions about inventory, sales targets, and upcoming events. James needed to focus, but his mind kept drifting back to the stables and which course of action might be best. The sensible choice may be Ross McPherson, but something had sparked inside him at the memory of Dagmar. A burning curiosity that seemed to have come from nowhere, though it wasn't entirely new. He loosened his tie and rolled his neck a little. He'd had this sensation at school a few times, but he'd beaten it down. Dagmar had got so quiet and closed to the point of being icy at High School and even on occasions when he'd attempted to talk to her or offer an olive branch, she'd run away. It always seemed strange after they'd been primary school friends, but it wasn't unusual for people to drift apart, and he'd had so many friends. There had always been something about her. Something he could never quite put his finger on, but something that brought his mind back to her again and again... As it had done at school.

As Henry gave his report on the finances, James slipped his screen open again and typed Dagmar Ingenfeld into the search box. Unsurprisingly, every result was from horse shows she'd won. There were photos too of her in a smart jacket and jodhpurs. Christ. She wasn't an awkward buck-toothed schoolgirl anymore. Her stunning blue eyes caught him even from a photo that wasn't the best quality, and he frowned. There was something about her that kept him looking longer than he should. She had a pretty face, and it was interesting too – sharp eyes, a shapely nose, well-defined lips.

He glanced around and caught Henry's eyes. Not wanting to look like he wasn't paying attention, he leaned back, nodding.

'We've also expanded the pot for community outreach projects.' Henry put up a new slide on the whiteboard. 'It'll mean we can support more local causes and get our name out there.'

'That's great.' James said. Henry pulled up the next slide, and James flicked his eyes back to his own screen, ready to close the window when he saw a search result matching Dagmar to a post on a local business group on a social media site. He clicked it and the message opened.

Reading down, he frowned, running his fingers around his jaw.

Interesting. Yes.

He vaguely remembered her mother owned a café, but he hadn't recalled that it was in Glenbriar. Tapping his finger on the desk again, he refocused on Henry.

'Would this fund be something we could use to support other local businesses? Ones that are long established and well-known in the town, but maybe need some modernisation?'

'Absolutely,' Laurence cut in before Henry could reply. 'That's exactly the kind of thing we want to be seen doing. We want Duchan to be part of the community, working with other places. It gives us the family friendly image that we need.'

'Great.' James minimised the screen and looked out of the window. He was sitting here with the means to help Dagmar with the café. Should he suggest it or let it go? Maybe getting involved with her wasn't something he needed to stir up again.

Must be sensible.

Later he'd call Ross McPherson. His life had enough shit going on and while something about Dagmar still intrigued him, courting trouble was just plain stupid.

Ross McPherson sounded very pleasant, but unfortunately, he didn't have space available soon enough. Should James resort to Plan B? He definitely didn't want to ring Glenvorneth. His parting from Ophelia had been amicable enough, but that didn't mean he had a burning desire to talk to her again, and he definitely didn't want to explain what he was up to.

But now he knew his way around the estate, he was confident he could drive to the stables without drawing attention to himself. It was open for livery and lessons, so other people would be milling in and out.

Come the weekend, he'd talked himself into it and drove to the estate around the side of Loch Briar. He went in the main gate but turned off, so he didn't pass the big house. A small, gravelled car park was behind the old steading and a few cars were in it. None of them were Ophelia's crimson BMW, which was a good start. He craned his neck, scanning across the field. Some horses wandered about in the paddocks, but no one was with them.

A crow landed on the fence in front of him and sat on the post, glaring at him. Something about its unflinching eyes was unsettling.

The sound of voices caught his attention, and he snapped his gaze away from the crow to the yard in front of the stable. Two girls in riding hats came out chatting and James drew back. One of them was Ophelia's sister. Hopefully she wouldn't notice him – and even if she did, she might not remember him. He made to start the engine, when another person came out behind them. That hair was instantly recognisable. Who else had a plait that long? It ran the length of her back, falling straight down the middle of a green waxed jacket.

His hand hovered on the start button. Stay or go? Well, he'd made it this far. But really, this was insane. Time to go. A sharp knock on his window made him jump. His head snapped around and his eyes widened. Oh god. Ophelia. It couldn't get much worse, could it?

He opened the door and got out, standing to face her. Her height always made her even more intimidating alongside her model looks.

'James.' She half smiled and frowned. 'What are you doing here?'

'Oh, I... um.' He fiddled with his cuff. 'Just came to see how the building work went. The last time I saw the stables, they weren't complete.'

'Ah yes.' She smiled, and it was kind of disarming. He'd never fancied her in that way, but her attractiveness was never in any doubt. 'Jacinta mentioned something about it. You know, the way she rattles on. But I thought she must be joking.'

James furrowed his brow. What did she mean? Jacinta was her stepmother, a well-known gossip, but she couldn't have any clue why he was here. No one knew. Even himself.

'Mentioned what?'

'You're looking for a place to stable a horse, are you not?'

'Um...'

'Your mother told Jacinta you'd taken up riding again. I never knew you could ride.' She eyed him over and a small smirk played at the corner of her lips. 'You never mentioned it.'

His chest tightened. How ridiculous was this? He'd visited the stables with her before and probably shown himself to be the least horsey person imaginable. No wonder she looked suspicious. And she was related to the Earl of Dairvin. *Christ*. One word to Lady Victoria from Ophelia and this little charade would fail before it even started.

James cleared his throat. 'Oh, uh, yes. I'm not quite at the stabling stage yet. I need to... you know, refresh my riding skills. Haven't been in the saddle for a while.'

Ophelia raised an eyebrow, still watching him with steely eyes. 'Refreshing your riding skills? Right.'

She couldn't make it more obvious she didn't believe a word of it. And could he really blame her?

'So, would you like a lesson?'

He clenched his jaw. Not from her. Surely, she wasn't offering. 'Well, um...' He ran his hand through his hair.

'Because if you do, we have Dagmar Ingenfeld working here. She's the best instructor around. You know her already, don't you? Weren't you friends at school or something?'

'We knew each other. Not that well. She might not even remember me.' It might be best if she didn't. He may have tried to stop his friends teasing her, but how would she know that? She'd avoided him as much as the others and probably thought him equally culpable.

'Oh, I'm sure she does. I asked her once.'

Great. He let out a breath. 'She's probably too busy. I should have called first. I can still do that. Make an official appointment, you know?'

'Don't be silly.' Ophelia smiled. 'Come on, I'll take you to her. I'm sure she'll be happy to see you.'

He doubted it. Why had he ever thought this was a good idea? If Dagmar remembered him, it was unlikely to be for a good reason.

'She doesn't bite.' Ophelia raised an eyebrow, and her lip quirked like she was amused. And no wonder. She was undoubtedly trying to figure out what was going on. Good luck to her because James wasn't sure himself. All he knew was in a few seconds he would be face to face with someone he hadn't spoken to for over twelve years.

CHAPTER FOUR

Dagmar

Dagmar tugged her long plait out from under her jacket and flicked it over her shoulder. She'd got so used to being here alone that having Francesca and Caitlin helping her out still felt a little strange. But she couldn't knock it. Without their help, she'd be even more thinly spread, and she couldn't cope with that. Not when her heart was still tight with worries about the café and her mum. Her post on the socials had got a few likes and one or two comments, but not enough to make any difference.

'Francesca, can you check the feed and water in the lower paddocks?'

'Yeah, sure.'

'And Caitlin, you can start mucking out the stalls. We have a new arrival coming in later.'

'Ok.'

'Thanks.'

Francesca adjusted her gloves and headed towards the paddocks, while Caitlin grabbed a pitchfork and wheelbarrow and made her way to the stalls. Dagmar watched them for a moment.

Right, that was them sorted. While she appreciated everything they did here, she also liked to separate them at times, otherwise they wasted so much time gossiping. And these days they had loads to chat about. As Caitlin's dad, Brann, was the builder Ophelia was now living with, there was plenty for *everyone* to gossip about – Dagmar overheard lots of tittle-tattle, and she'd been as intrigued as anyone when she found out, but she wasn't as surprised as everyone else. Brann had been working here for months before he and Ophelia got together. He'd always been friendly and chatty, not to mention rugged and easy on the eye. Who wouldn't like him? It was only a scandal because Ophelia was supposed to marry someone with status and cash. Like James Charlton.

Dagmar turned back towards the stables and her eyes fell on two people walking towards her. *Seriously, what? Speak of the devil and he's sure to appear.* Her heart skipped a beat. She'd seen James and Ophelia here together last year, but only from a safe distance. But they were coming towards her. Why? What was he even doing here? He and Ophelia weren't together. He had no reason to be here, and why were they making a beeline for her?

Unwanted memories flooded back – school corridors, his face among the tormentors. That desperation to see him, but also the dread. What would he think of her? How ugly she must look next to her peers. Like now. There was no competing with Ophelia in a beauty contest. Give Dagmar a horse and she'd show her, but that wasn't really an option here.

'Good morning.' Ophelia smiled widely, almost like she was on the verge of laughing. 'Look who I found loitering in the car park.'

'I wasn't loitering,' James said.

Ophelia chuckled and winked at Dagmar like they had an inside joke going on, but Dagmar didn't know what it was and nothing about seeing James was making her smile.

'This is James Charlton. You know him, don't you? I can't recall if you met him here last year when we were—'

'Being thrown at each other?' he suggested.

'Well, yes, that. But you two knew each other at school, I believe.'

'Vaguely.' Dagmar didn't look at him but picked at her short nails.

'So, James is taking up riding again. You haven't done it for... How many years?'

'Oh... Several.' He covered his mouth like he was covering a cough, but there was no sound.

Dagmar narrowed her eyes. No way had he ever ridden before. She would bet her last penny on it. Whatever was going on, she was sure he wasn't here for that, which begged the question: why *was* he here?

'He's looking for some *refresher* lessons before he gets a horse.' Ophelia stressed the word "refresher" like she didn't believe him either. 'And really, there's no one better than you to teach him.'

Dagmar's mind raced. What? No way. She couldn't do that. The idea of spending time with him was the last thing she wanted. But how could she refuse? Ophelia was the boss.

'I, um, thanks, but we're really busy just now. I don't think I'll have time.'

Ophelia pulled a face. 'Yes, we are busy.' She rubbed her hands together. 'Though I'm sure you could make it worth our while.' She raised her eyebrow at James.

He put his hands in his pockets and looked away with a wry grin. 'Your family are still determined to get their hands on my cash, I see.'

'Unfortunate,' she said, 'but accurate.'

'I could definitely make it worth your while.' His eyes met Dagmar's and her insides flipped. *Oh no.* He couldn't. Nothing he could do would make her want to spend time with him.

'I need to get on,' she said. 'There's so much to do. But really, it'll be very difficult to fit in lessons anytime soon, no matter what he pays.'

'Hmm.' Ophelia rubbed her fingertips together. 'Well, you crack on. I'll show James about and have a look in the diary to see if we can juggle things around.'

'Right.' Dagmar stalked off, balling her fists. If Ophelia decided to change the plans so she could fit in lessons for James, what could she do about it? If she argued, she'd look like she was being belligerent just for the sake of it. How annoying. Especially when she knew he was up to something. He must be. Maybe he was trying to win back Ophelia.

'Hey! Dagmar.' Caitlin came out of the stables. 'I forgot to tell you my mum's coming up this morning to drop off some stuff I left at her house. She's just passed her driving test, and she's enjoying all the practice. Can I nip out and see her when she gets here?'

'Sure.' Dagmar nodded. Caitlin was just a volunteer. She could do as she pleased. 'But thanks for asking.'

'She might want to look around a bit too. Would that be ok?'

'Yeah, course it would.' Dagmar lifted a pile of rugs she'd meant to put away ages ago. 'I need to tidy up a bit in here.' Clearing out stuff would be cathartic, and she needed something to calm her nerves. Her insides burned. Seeing James had unsettled her.

She spent the morning clearing up stuff she should have done ages ago, but there was just so much to do. A car crunched into the car park, which was entirely normal, but today Dagmar was listening for comings and goings. The new people weren't due until the afternoon, but she hadn't seen James leave yet. Was he still here, hanging around with Ophelia? Something weird was going on.

Car doors bumped shut and Dagmar heard voices. She loitered by the window until she saw it was just Caitlin and her mum. Dagmar would leave them to it. Caitlin's mum scared her a bit. Not that she'd spoken to her much, but she dressed like a heavy metal rockstar and always looked intimidating.

'Come see this, Mum,' Caitlin said outside the door. What were they looking at? A tremor flickered through her that they'd burst in and one of them would laugh and say, 'Look, it's horse face.' But they seemed to be looking at something outside. Ten or so minutes passed quietly as Dagmar swept the floor before she heard the voices again. It sounded like Caitlin was saying goodbye to her mum. Dagmar propped the brush in the corner and pushed a couple of stray hairs from her face as she stepped outside.

Uh-oh. Caitlin's mum was still in the courtyard, her flowing floral dress ruffled in the breeze. This was one of the odd things about this woman. Her rather wild dress sense was mismatched – both soft and hard. She'd paired the dress with a leather jacket and studded boots. Her hair was flame red, and she ran her long black fingernails through it. She dipped her head as she spoke on a phone. Her ears, nose and eyebrow were pierced, and she had on several rings and a chunky crucifix necklace.

Dagmar might be able to slip by unnoticed while the woman chatted on her phone. She made an attempt, but Caitlin's mum glanced up and smiled.

'Hey.' She hit a button on the phone. 'How are you?'

'Fine.' Dagmar nodded. 'You?'

'Ah, not bad, thanks. Just the usual, trying to juggle everything, and then forgetting everything.' She pulled a face.

'Oh dear.'

'Yup. That was my sister reminding me I'd forgotten something.' She threw out her hands and smiled broadly. She had deep burgundy lips and very white teeth. Despite being so intimidatingly turned out, she was very striking and seemed nice. 'Naughty me.'

Dagmar smiled vaguely in spite of herself – a thing she rarely did for anyone other than her mum.

'I'm Caitlin's mum, by the way. In case you don't remember and think I'm just some weirdo talking to you.'

'I remember,' Dagmar said. She wasn't exactly someone anyone could forget.

'My name's Kristi... Well, that's what everyone calls me. Except Caitlin's dad. Brann still calls me by my full name. Kristalee. It's such a mouthful. My parents called us crazy names, but we all shorten them these days. It stops the weird looks.' She rolled her eyes around rather comically.

This woman was funny and a total chatterbox, but Dagmar couldn't help admiring her confidence in dressing like that and prattling on like they were old friends. Dagmar was certain she wouldn't have a personal conversation like this with someone she barely knew... Anyone for that matter.

'Is Caitlin behaving herself?' Kristi asked. 'I hope she's actually helping and not just getting under your feet.'

'No, I appreciate what she does.'

'Well, she loves it, and now that her dad's living up here, she's never away.'

Dagmar nodded. She was impressed by how Brann and Kristi seemed to still be friends. Caitlin had painted a fairly decent picture of their relationship, and it seemed to be accurate. But Dagmar couldn't imagine wanting to see an ex again if she'd split up with them. Not that it would ever happen. She didn't have any exes.

'Are you ok?' Kristi's heavily pencilled eyes gave her a don't-cross-me look but behind the make-up, her expression was soft. Was she actually interested? Dagmar always assumed people would dislike her or not give a shit. So far, a lot of her life had felt like that, but Kristi's expression was concerned more than anything else. 'You look exhausted.'

'It's tiring.' Dagmar let out a sigh. 'There's so much to do.'

Kristi looked around the stable yard. 'I can see that. It's tough for one person doing this. That's why I hope Caitlin is helping and not getting in the way.'

'Most of the time, it's fine, but Ophelia wants this place to make money. I understand that, of course I do.' Dagmar needed it too, otherwise they might stop paying her again. 'But some-times it means there's just too much.'

Kristi folded her arms. 'Yeah, she's ambitious and likes to get her own way. I can see that. But she's nice. I was surprised how kind she was. She helped Caitlin when she was having a tough time. I'm sure she'd listen to you if you let her know.'

'Maybe. But... Well, it's not that. I mean, that's ongoing. I just...' Should she say something? Trust this woman? It wasn't in her nature to do so, but she really wanted to tell someone and bizarrely, Kristi seemed like the right person. Possibly because she was partially a stranger, or maybe because she was a mum – someone caring.

'Tell me.' Kristi cocked her head. 'Is it something Caitlin's done?'

'No, not at all. It's just... this morning someone showed up and I've been asked to give him riding lessons. And, well, I don't trust him.'

Kristi's eyebrows lifted. 'Oh? Why? If he's someone who isn't safe to be here, I don't mind telling Ophelia myself.'

Dagmar shook her head. 'It's not that. It's someone I was at school with, and he wasn't exactly nice to me.'

'Ugh.' Kristi screwed up her nose. 'That must be really annoy-ing. And is Ophelia insisting you do it?'

'I'm not sure yet.'

'Well...' Kristi patted her arm. 'Hang in there and maybe it won't happen. I can sympathise with the whole school thing though. I hated it. Caitlin's had her share of nasty experiences too.'

Dagmar nodded. 'This probably sounds ridiculous, but I had a crush on him at school – I don't even know why. He never knew, so that's not an issue. But it brings back memories.' Now she was talking, she couldn't stop. Everything was pouring out.

'I don't want him treating me like shit. Of course, back then, he was too cool for someone like me. I was just an ugly girl with braces. And I don't need any more crap right now.'

'What?' Kristi cocked her head. 'Have you looked in a mirror recently? You're certainly not ugly. You're bloody beautiful.'

Heat stung Dagmar's cheeks. 'Um... Ok.'

'I mean it.' Kristi gave her a little pat on the back. 'And I totally get it. I still see people around town that I was at school with and god knows I don't want anything to do with them. But, best-case scenario, maybe this guy's changed. I know I've changed since school. So has Brann. Jesus, the way we carried on back then. But we grew up. Maybe this guy has too.'

'I'd like to think so, but I'm not sure. Something's not right. Last year, he was one of the guys Ophelia's father was trying to get her to marry, and I'm pretty sure he's never ridden a horse in his life before, but today he was here with her and he told her he wanted to "refresh" his skills. There's something strange about it.'

Kristi pulled a face. 'Weird, right enough.'

'Yeah, and I'm not sure what to do.'

'Sadly, I don't either. I'm still waiting for the day when I become a proper adult and have all the answers, but I'm thirty-seven, I've got two grown-up kids, and I still haven't got a clue.' Kristi reached out and put her hand on Dagmar's shoulder. 'Listen, if you need someone to talk to again, give me a shout, ok? It must be lonely up here by yourself.'

'It's fine.' Would Kristi guess that was a lie? Because she'd hit the nail on the head. But Dagmar didn't want to admit it. 'Thanks though.'

'No worries. And just remember, you're as smart and pretty as any of them. Don't let anyone tell you otherwise. I had years of people telling me how shit my life choices were, but you know what? I'm not changing just for them. You do you, let the other fuckers do what they want.'

Dagmar allowed a little laugh to escape. 'I need that on a t-shirt. Thanks... Really. You've cheered me up.'

'Anytime. See you about.'

Dagmar crossed the yard towards the paddock, unable to stop the smile from growing on her face. But it soon vanished when she saw James at the bottom of the field, leaning on the fence near her trailer. What the hell was he doing and why was he still here?

Chapter Five

James

James thrust his hands into his pockets as he strolled around the perimeter of the lower paddock. He scanned up towards the stable yard. He'd shaken off Ophelia with some excuse about wanting to get a feel for the place. Now, he just needed the right moment to approach Dagmar.

What a mess. He hadn't meant to lie about refreshing his riding skills, but he couldn't risk Ophelia going back to Lady Victoria and spilling the beans. Now he was stuck. He was pretty sure Ophelia saw right through him, so he needed to get Dagmar on her own and convince her to help him.

That would be no mean feat with their history. She couldn't have made it more obvious she hated him, and she possibly always had. His mind flashed back to their school days. He'd been so wrapped up in fitting in and not falling out with people that he'd lost the respect of the one person he'd really wanted to like him. How messed up was that? And had he really changed? His life revolved around making good connections, keeping people happy, and not causing rifts. But somehow, he'd never managed that with Dagmar. His attempts to stop his friends from making rude comments and to find opportunities to talk to her had never yielded anything. Maybe he just hadn't tried hard enough.

He kicked at the gravel beneath his feet. He couldn't change the past, but he could do something in the present – show her that he wasn't altogether bad.

Horses wandered in the distance, flicking their tails. Ophelia's sister and her friend chatted somewhere nearby. James needed to learn to ride, and fast. Dagmar was currently his best hope, but he had to guarantee she'd be discreet and play along, so Ophelia didn't discover the truth.

Must get this right. He had an idea, though it might not work.

The wind picked up slightly, rustling the leaves of the nearby trees. James pulled his jacket tighter around him. *Now or never.* His eyes darted back to the stables, where Dagmar had been a few moments ago with someone else. He had to time this perfectly. Approaching her in front of others would complicate things even more.

A horse ambled towards the fence, its curious eyes locking onto him. James reached out a hand, and the horse nudged it. He gave it a tentative stroke.

'Are you easy to ride?' he asked. It always looked effortless, but something told him it was far from it.

A door banged shut in the distance, and James thrust his hands deeper into his pockets, starting up the bridle path towards the stables. The air was heavier than earlier, like a storm was brewing, or at least rain was due.

He glanced up, catching a movement in his peripheral vision. Dagmar was marching in his direction, her expression hard, eyes fixed but not on him. She didn't look happy and seemed to be deliberately avoiding his gaze.

As she got closer, her pace quickened, clearly intending to walk past him without stopping. James poked his tongue into his cheek. Christ, this wasn't going to be easy, but he'd caught bigger fish than this in the corporate world. If he looked at this as business, he had a head start, just as his father had suggested he did with Victoria.

'Dagmar.' He stepped into her path.

She halted, not looking at him, her body rigid, jaw set, and her fists balled. For a moment, he thought she might just push past him, but she didn't move.

'Can we talk for a minute?' he asked.

'Not really,' she replied, her voice cold. She still didn't meet his eyes. 'I'm busy.'

'This won't take long. I need your help.'

'My help?' She finally met his eyes and glared. Her irises were a piercing shade of blue and cut through him like lasers. 'To "refresh" your riding skills?' She air-quoted, and her voice had a heavy, sardonic note.

He half smiled, half shrugged. 'Yes.'

'And what riding skills do you have already?' She folded her arms.

'I can't tell you that yet. If you agree to give me lessons and do it in the way I require, then I'll give you all the information you need on my current skills.'

Her lip curled, and she eyed him over like she thought him completely insane. And she had a point.

'I can pay,' he added. 'Whatever it takes. Enough to make Ophelia happy. And you. Just a few lessons...' Well, hopefully a few, enough to give Victoria the impression he'd done it before and knew his way around a horse. 'And then I'll disappear.'

Dagmar's jaw tightened, and she didn't respond immediately. 'If Ophelia says I have to do it, I won't have a choice anyway, so you'll get your way, but if it was up to me, I wouldn't do it.'

He watched her expression harden even more. He needed to convince her, and he needed to do it now because she looked ready to walk away.

'Listen.' He stepped closer. 'I know you don't trust me.'

She raised an eyebrow. 'Well, as you started off as a thief at the age of eight then progressed into a bully at high school, and now a liar at thirty, it's hardly surprising, is it?'

'I... What?' He frowned. What the hell did she mean? He hadn't stolen anything from her, had he? And he hadn't actually bullied her, even if he hadn't successfully stopped anyone else from doing it either. She was right about him lying though.

'You don't remember, do you? That doesn't surprise me either.'

'I don't know what I stole, and I didn't ever take part in bullying you. I'm sorry if you think I did. I often asked people not to tease you, but they didn't listen.'

She gave him a look as if to say "clearly".

He swallowed. 'Listen, I'm sorry about what happened in the past. I never wanted any of that for you. It's impossible for me to prove to you that I wasn't part of it and that I did what I could to stop it. With the value of hindsight, I probably should have done more, but I was a teenager... and an idiot.'

She didn't reply or look at him.

'Is it possible to leave the past behind for a moment?' he went on. 'Because I'm serious about needing these lessons. I'm willing to pay you privately. A lot more than I imagine you usually make.'

'Bribe me, you mean?'

'Sort of, but I see it more as a reward. I'm definitely willing to make it worth your while.'

She blinked slowly and deliberately, her arms still crossed. 'Oh really? And how do you propose to do that?'

'I can help save the Cosy Bean Café.'

'What?' Her eyes narrowed. 'How do you know about that?'

'I saw your post on social media,' he said. 'I know it's struggling, and I can help.'

Dagmar stared at him, shaking her head, her mouth slightly open. 'How can you do that?'

'Duchan Fayre has a community outreach fund, and the Cosy Bean Café is exactly the kind of place we want to help.' James inclined his head. 'But you have to agree with my terms.'

'Wait.' She held up a hand. 'You expect me to believe you'll step in and save the café just to get some riding lessons?'

'Yes. I'll write a contract if you want? You can read it before you agree. But you'll also have to sign an NDA if I tell you my conditions.'

'Seriously?' She folded her arms. 'What is this all about? It sounds like way too much hassle.' Her guarded stance reminded him of the awkward girl she used to be. Braces had corrected the teeth that had earned her some cruel nicknames. She looked so different now. A little sad, but very pretty in a cold kind of way, like an ice-queen. He'd always thought her attractive before but couldn't really explain why. He'd let it go as a schoolboy crush. And he had to keep on doing that.

'Ok, if I explain what it's about, can I trust you not to tell anyone? Or shall we sign papers first? I'll do whatever you prefer.'

'Just tell me what it is. Who exactly would I tell?'

'Ophelia for one, and she's someone I really don't want to know.'

'To know what?'

'That I can't ride at all.'

Dagmar glanced skyward with a little huff. 'Ophelia isn't stupid. I think she guessed that. It's pretty obvious.'

'Exactly. And that's the deal. I need you to make it not obvious. You're the best riding coach in the area. Help me look like someone who knows what to do around a horse. Someone who's been riding all their life and not someone who—'

'Worries about getting shit on their shiny shoes?'

He nodded. 'Yeah, that.'

'Why do you want that? I mean, who cares if you've never ridden before?'

'Lady Victoria Bruce, the daughter of the earl of Dairvin.'

Dagmar frowned and shook her head. 'I don't get it.'

'I need to find some common ground. Something she and I can do together. Something she enjoys.'

'Oh, right.' She looked like she was chewing her tongue as the penny dropped. Her face became an open book. Yes, this was who he was. A man who'd had a chance with Ophelia that hadn't worked out, so he'd moved on to the next big thing, the next person who could elevate him. Was it sad? Or was this just dating on a different level?

'So, will you do it?'

'I told you, if Ophelia says I have to, then I'll have to. And if you offer her money, then she'll insist.'

'I get that, but will you do it on my terms?'

She held her chin high. 'I suppose so, but only if you do this thing to save the café.'

'Scout's honour.' He raised two fingers to his brow.

Her expression told him she didn't trust him, but he'd prove otherwise. He was a man of his word, and he intended to keep it.

'I'll speak to the finance manager straight away, but I already mentioned it, and even my father said it was exactly the kind of project he wanted Duchan to get behind.'

'Fine. Then you better get used to getting up early. If I'm going to teach you without anyone else seeing, it'll have to be before people start arriving. Ophelia at the very least.'

'Suits me. Can we start straight away?'

'Tomorrow if you want.'

'Tomorrow it is.'

'Fine. See you then.' Dagmar nodded curtly and walked away, leaving him standing on the path.

Hopefully this would go to plan and not horribly pear-shaped as he suspected it might.

CHAPTER SIX

Dagmar

Birds chirping like crazy outside the trailer woke Dagmar before her alarm clock. Rubbing the sleep from her eyes, she groaned and sat up, blinking. It was still dark, but the glow of the approaching dawn was visible as she pulled back through the threadbare curtains. How did morning come around so quickly? It felt like she'd barely touched the pillow, and now it was time to get up. Early rises were part and parcel of life with horses, but some days were harder than others. At least winter had faded away and spring was well and truly on its way.

Dagmar had done this for years, rarely taking time off. Her whole life revolved around horses. So much so she'd never made time for relationships. What was the point? The only person she wholly trusted was her mum. Other people had come and gone in her life. She didn't stick around to make friends. Some pony club acquaintances she kept up with and they met up at shows and competitions. She very occasionally met them for lunches or coffee if they were arranging shows, and of course she stayed on good terms with the vet and the farrier, but outside of the horsey scene, she had no one. And there was Ophelia. She wasn't really a friend, but she was the only other person Dagmar had known for a long time and still had contact with. The interaction with Kristi the other day had been unexpected and quite nice. Could they be friends? She couldn't imagine anyone in that role, but Kristi was pleasant, and she'd been easy to talk to.

Dagmar swung her legs out of bed and slid into her worn-out slippers, pulling on a thick jumper against the morning chill. The trailer didn't have a toilet or shower area. Primitive, really. Often when she visited her mum, she used the opportunity to soak in the bath and use a shower with better water pressure than the ridiculous port-a-loo and matching shower cabin she was forced to use. The Chattan-Blythes had bought them second hand years ago, originally to be part of the riding school, but with Dagmar pretty much living in, she'd put her trailer next to them and rarely moved since, unless she was travelling to competitions.

Ophelia had once offered her one of the cottages on the estate when it was done up, but Dagmar wasn't sure when that would be, or if that offer was still even on the table. Would she be able to afford it?

She let the shower run for a while to heat up, but it was still little more than a trickle when she got in. Washing her hair took an age. These tresses hadn't been cut for years, and they trailed down her back to her hips. She was a natural blonde, but some days she fancied the idea of having the colour refreshed, maybe getting a trim and a more obvious style. She caked her head in conditioner and left it in for five minutes as she washed herself. It was the only way to keep her hair glossy, otherwise it went like straw and reminded her painfully of all the times she'd been dubbed horse girl. She wrapped herself in a towel and nipped back into the trailer. At this time of year, it was ok, but in the winter, this was a killer. It was a miracle she hadn't died of hypothermia.

As she combed her hair through and plaited it, her mind wandered back to James. Her thoughts had never been far from him all night. If she'd actually had time to dream, that was what she'd have dreamed of. His offer to save her mum's café had caught her completely off guard.

Could she trust him? The thought gnawed at her as she tied off her plait. James Charlton was not the kind of person she associated with charity. But a storm of butterflies burst into her chest when she allowed herself to believe his offer was genuine. Did she really want to be in his debt though? Would she be? Or would the lessons pay for it? The lessons and her silence. That shouldn't be too difficult. It wasn't like she and Ophelia were close. She wouldn't be beating a path to her door to spill the beans.

She had a quick drink of water, then grabbed her jacket and headed out of the trailer. Facing food this early was something she couldn't do. The early morning air was crisp against her cheeks. She zipped her jacket and headed towards the stables. The dawn light tinged the sky.

As she reached the stables, the horses shuffled in their stalls. Even if it was a pain getting up so early, these moments, when the world was still waking up, were her favourite. It was just her and the horses, a peaceful start to the day before the chaos began.

She started with the feed, hauling buckets of grain and hay. The horses shifted impatiently.

She scooped out the feed. 'It's just coming.'

As she filled the hay nets, her thoughts drifted back to James. He was due early. Would he show? The idea made her heart race, and she was pretty sure that wasn't a good thing.

She couldn't shake the images of him from school. Him all popular, always surrounded by friends. Her with braces and awkward ways, never with anyone. James was famously sociable, moving in the upper circles. Not only had he tried to win Ophelia, but he'd dated Genevieve Harrington, a well-known influencer. He was that kind of guy and attracted women with beauty, style, and wealth.

And she'd never even had a boyfriend. Was it obvious to everyone, or did it seem far too ridiculous? She remembered overhearing some girls talking at a horse show once about a book they'd read where the heroin was a virgin at twenty-five. They'd moaned about how utterly unrealistic it was and that everyone had "had a fumble" by the time they left school. Dagmar hadn't enlightened them that they were completely wrong, and she was a living example. It wasn't exactly something she wanted to draw attention to. She often read online that it was nothing to be ashamed of, but it still played on her mind. What she didn't want to do was have some random hookup just to rid herself of the "V-card". She'd waited this long. And really it would have to be someone pretty damn understanding. Otherwise they'd think her a right weirdo. Wasn't that the story of her life?

While she continued waiting for something she was sure wouldn't happen anytime soon – if ever – James would be chasing Lady Victoria Bruce. Yet another posh young woman with money and looks. Dagmar knew her from the riding scene and could see her being right up James's street. No doubt there would be wedding bells before long. She could easily imagine it even without the riding lessons.

She'd started mucking out the stalls when she heard footsteps. Her heart lurched. She straightened up, gripping the pitchfork tightly.

'Hi.'

She turned to see Caitlin approaching. 'Oh, it's you. Morning.'

'Yeah. I'm on study leave, so I don't have to rush out, and I don't want to hang about in the house. Dad and Ophelia are so lovey-dovey.' She pulled a grossed-out face.

Dagmar gave her a little smirk. She could well believe it. Ophelia and Brann had been all over each other from the moment they met; even when they apparently hated each other, they'd made eyes at each other.

'Well, if you can look at the livery book and see who needs to come in this morning and start bringing them in, that would be great.' Dagmar checked her phone. 'I'm supposed to be doing a lesson this morning, but he hasn't showed.' Surprise, surprise.

'That's early.'

'I'm fitting him in because he's paying big money.'

'Ah, right.'

'I'll get Conker in just in case he arrives. He's a good horse, and I'm sure Ophelia won't mind.' He was Ophelia's own horse, but she let other people ride him, and he was probably the most easy-going of all the horses they had.

Dagmar went outside and spotted a pile of feedbags. She'd meant to move them yesterday. This was why her muscles ached every night – from lifting stuff like this. She picked up the first one and dumped it in her wheelbarrow. As she loaded the next one, she heard a car door bang. Seconds later, James strolled around the side of the stable, hands in his pockets. He stopped when he saw her and gave her a little smile. His jaw was dusted with early morning stubble, and he wore cargo trousers and a casual sweater. Dagmar's tummy flipped. Oh Christ, he was handsome. But she really didn't want to think about that or notice.

She lifted another bag of feed and deposited it in the barrow.

'Hey.' James approached her.

'Morning.' She lifted the barrow and began to wheel it.

'Here, let me help with that.'

'I can do it. I do it all the time myself.'

'I know you do, but let me give you a hand. Put me to use while I'm here.'

'I'll give you another job.' She glanced at him as she set the barrow down. 'A more suitable one.'

'Does it involve shovelling shit, by any chance?'

'It may do.' She brushed off her hands and couldn't stop a smile creeping onto her face.

'I don't think I've ever seen you smile before.' James tilted his head as he looked at her, his gaze soft but powerful.

She blinked and sucked on her lower lip. *Shit*. What was she meant to say to that? Their eyes met, and for a moment, the world paused. His focus was steady, and an intense warmth spread through her chest.

'Well.' She cleared her throat, breaking the moment. 'You can help me load the other bags, then I'll introduce you to Conker.'

'Conker? Isn't that Ophelia's horse?'

'Yes, but she lets other people ride him for lessons. He'll be good for you. He's very patient and has lots of experience in carrying new riders.'

James glanced around and put his finger to his lips. 'Riders needing a refresher.' He tipped her a quick wink, nudging his head in Caitlin's direction, though she was at the far end of the block and was unlikely to have heard, as she had her earbuds in.

'Yeah, that too,' she said. 'And luckily he doesn't speak English, so your secrets and lies are safe with him.'

He gave her a discreet thumbs up and a cheeky little smile. Her tummy felt like someone was using it as a trampoline and it flipped over again. This was not good... Really not good.

'I normally spend the whole first lesson teaching you how to groom and tack up, but I'll show you today and then you can have a go the next time. I know how keen you are to get started.'

'Yeah, great.'

She fetched Conker and led him out of the stable, across the courtyard and into a barn behind the stable block. Dagmar flicked on a light and the arena lit up.

'There's so much to learn about horse-care before you even start, but with the limited time, you'll have to learn as we go along. I like students to learn grooming, basic horse anatomy, equine needs and behaviours. It would be good to study body language and learn how to recognise a horse's signals, postures and facial expressions.'

'Really? Horses have facial expressions?'

'Of course. Oh, and you also need to know what to do if you fall off.'

'Is that likely?'

'Better safe than sorry. If it happens, don't clutch the reins. We all want to do it as a reflex but it's better not to as it allows the horse to avoid us on the way down, if we clutch, the horse is more likely to hit us with their head or hooves as they're stuck with the reins in our hands.'

'Right. That's the way to scare me before I even get on.'

'Well, this is what you signed up for.'

'True.'

'Now, if you take the leadrope, I'll show you how to lead him safely, stop, and reverse. Once you've mastered that, we'll tack him up and get you on top... Of him.' She swallowed. Her mind had taken a leap in a completely different direction. One she really didn't want to think about... But it was hard not to, as it always had been with James.

CHAPTER SEVEN

James

J ames stood next to Conker in the arena, eyeing the chestnut-coloured giant all tacked up. How was he ever going to remember all this stuff? There were years of learning just to get all the tack on the horse, never mind actually riding him. *Just stay calm.* Animals could sense fear, right? His dad had always insisted businesspeople could too and had brought him up to project an aura of control and collectedness in the boardroom, whether he felt it or not. So far, he'd succeeded in business. Hopefully he could do the same with the horses.

'Right.' Dagmar frowned at him, and he raised his eyebrows, already sensing he'd done something wrong, but then he remembered how bizarre he must look in the riding hat. 'First things first. Let's get you up on him.'

'Ok.' James glanced at the saddle, recalling the countless movies where people just hopped on effortlessly. Surely if all these actors could do it, he could too.

Dagmar led Conker alongside the mounting block, climbed the step, and placed her foot in the stirrup. 'Just put your foot in there, hold on to the saddle, and swing your other leg over.'

James took a deep breath, sure there was comedy value in what she'd just said, but he was no joker, and his mind was too caught up in trying to get himself on top of the beast before him.

She jumped down.

'Ok.' James climbed the step, took hold of the saddle, put his foot in the stirrup, and lifted his leg. He went to the gym and ran to keep fit, but Christ, this was awkward. Dagmar suppressed a smile as she steadied Conker.

He swung his leg over and landed on the saddle but felt like he was listing to one side. He attempted to adjust his position without actually moving too much. This elevated position didn't feel at all safe, and rocking about seemed like a foolhardy move.

'That's fine.' Dagmar adjusted the stirrups, moving his boot, so it was at a different angle. 'Now, keep your heels down and sit up straight.'

James gripped the reins tightly. Conker shifted, and James's heart jumped. 'Holy shit, how do I stop him?' He was used to having brakes.

Dagmar's lips twitched. 'Don't worry. He's not going any-where yet, so open those hands a little, they're too tight. To stop him, you close your fingers around the reins gently and say "whoa". But for now, just try to relax. It's best to sit centred, with as much weight on either side. Your shoulders should be lined up with your hips and ideally your heels, in what feels like a stable posture. It looks ok from here. How does it feel?'

'Ok, I think.' James took a deep breath. Conker's muscles moved beneath him, and the power was evident. This was a living, breathing creature, not something mechanical that he could control. They would have to work together.

'Let's start with the basics. We'll do a lunging lesson first. I'll lunge Conker at a walk and trot and all you have to do is find your seat and keep your posture.'

'Um, ok. What does that mean exactly?'

'I'll hold the rope in the middle and Conker will go around the arena. He's well voice trained, and I'll be here as backup. If anything goes wrong, just relax and let me handle it. Your job is to keep your posture centrally aligned.' Dagmar looked up at him, and he sent up a silent prayer. *Thank god she's here.* At least she knew what she was doing. 'Now, to move forward, you gently squeeze with your legs and say, "walk on". Try it.'

'But what if he starts running?'

'He won't until you tell him to,' she assured him. 'Just stay calm. You're doing fine.'

James squeezed his legs lightly. 'Walk on.'

Conker began to walk. The motion was unfamiliar and bizarre. Dagmar stood in the middle, holding the rope as Conker and James went around the arena. 'That's it.'

Conker carried on steadily, and James started to feel a little more confident.

'How does it feel?' she asked.

'Different.' He adjusted his balance, trying to keep his weight even as she'd told him.

'The more practice you have, the more you'll get used to it. Conker's very gentle, but it takes time to get to know about horses and to understand their triggers and cues. The only way to learn that is to keep doing it. Keeping calm is important, as is being clear with your signals. You might want to get some books and read up on horse care. I can tell you some good ones.'

James nodded. 'Right, ok.' Actually, it wasn't too bad at all. The initial panic was giving way to something close to enjoyment. He might actually have found something he liked doing.

'Do you feel like you're able to go a little faster?'

'Yeah, ok.' He took a deep breath. 'You just tell me how and I'll do my best.'

He glanced at Dagmar; her face was calm and focused. She always had a serene expression, earnest and a little sad. At school, her features had seemed a little out of proportion, but not anymore. She'd grown into her face and was really very pretty with that cute little nose, her sweet pink lips and those piercing blue eyes.

Why was he even noticing stuff like this? This was what happened when he went through a dry spell. But he hated sleeping around. The thought of frequently changing partners made his skin crawl, but he wasn't doing well in finding one who would last. A few years back, when he'd dated Genevieve Harrington, they'd done it more as an arrangement for them both rather than as a mutual attraction. It had helped get their parents off their backs, but he didn't want that again. He was ready for the real thing. Hopefully Lady Victoria Bruce would be that person. Which meant he really should stop looking at Dagmar.

She explained how to trot, and James went for it, amazed at himself. Suddenly the balance he thought he had found was going, as Conker moved, and his muscles shifted. James tightened his legs to grip the saddle.

'Relax,' Dagmar said. 'Don't tighten your grip too much, just try to keep your balance.'

He wasn't entirely sure how, but he tried not to grip anything too tightly.

Even though they were still in the arena and Dagmar was holding on to the rope, the feeling of freedom and power was incredible.

'You can change the pace,' Dagmar said. 'Give it a try. Use the voice commands and the body gestures.'

James did as she said. 'Easy,' he told Conker, who slowed to a walk straight away. Dagmar was right, he was a good horse and was listening for his cues. Eventually, Dagmar stopped him and nodded. Her hair trailed down her back in her trademark long plait. Even when they'd been little kids at primary school, she'd had that. Occasionally two, one on either side. James had probably been the boy who pulled them. He couldn't really remember, but it was more than likely.

'I think that's enough for today,' she said. 'Time is ticking on.'

'Ok.' James frowned slightly. Memories of their primary school days jumped into his mind. 'Do you remember Mrs Taylor?' His recollections threw up the image of a seriously grumpy teacher they'd had in primary five.

Dagmar huffed and nodded. 'Yeah. The one who never got anyone's name right?'

'The very one,' James laughed. 'She always called us by our surnames, but not the actual name. Like she used to call me Charlottetown instead of Charlton. Drove me mad, and I think she did it on purpose.'

'I'm sure she did.' Dagmar smiled. 'I've heard some weird pronunciations of Ingenfeld over the years, but she called me "Inkenstein" more times than I can count.'

'Inkenstein?' James grinned. 'I remember that.'

'I suppose she thought any foreign-sounding name would do.'

'Where is the name from?'

'It's Danish. That's where my mum comes from. Her family came here when she was fifteen and she stayed.'

He assumed she had a father, but she'd never mentioned him, and he didn't recall ever seeing him, even as a child. It didn't seem his place to ask.

'She must have liked it here,' he said.

'I suppose.' Dagmar glanced up at him and an almost sneaky smile crept over her face. 'Well, Charlottetown, that's your lesson over for the day.'

He pulled a face. 'Very funny, Inkenstein.'

She smiled, and it lit up her face, sprinkling colour into her cheeks and making her eyes shine. The sight struck James in a way he didn't expect. She was pretty before, but with that smile…

What had happened to his resolve not to notice her?

She gently led him towards the mounting block. 'Did you enjoy that?'

'Yeah.' He adjusted his position in the saddle. 'How do you turn him from up here?'

'I can show you that before we stop for the day.'

He sat tall, trying to imagine how this would feel if she weren't beside him.

'So, to turn him, it's all about looking where you want to go, then moving your shoulders, your hips, closing the outside leg – so to turn right you close the left leg – and finally opening one rein towards where you want to go if that's not enough.'

'Ok, that sounds complicated.' James gripped the reins a bit tighter. First no brakes, now no steering wheel. Cars were a lot easier.

'Don't grip the reins.' Dagmar edged closer. She placed her hand over his, guiding his grip. 'Here, like you're holding a little bird, or a rose with thorns on. You want to suggest and guide him, not hurt him.'

A shiver ran through him at the unexpected contact. Her hand was warm and steady, her presence suddenly close. 'Like this?' he asked.

'Yes.' Dagmar adjusted the reins slightly. 'Now, if you want to turn right, look right, turn your shoulders that way, good; now your hips, good; now bring your left leg closer to him – as if you wanted to hug his ribcage. See him begin to turn? Now you can confirm it with your right hand. Move it in an arc out this way, like you're opening the path for him.'

She demonstrated, her hand guiding his. Conker responded slowly, turning his head and body in the direction indicated.

'I think I've got the idea.' James's voice was huskier than he intended. Her closeness was making it hard to concentrate, and that couldn't be good.

'Now try the other way.'

James followed her instructions, and Conker turned smoothly. 'This is great,' he said.

Dagmar's eyes met his briefly. 'Just take it slow and once he's understood your idea, let him finish the move. Don't carry him through it all. You might get it wrong a few times before getting it right consistently.'

'I've got a good teacher.' He gave her a wink.

Her cheeks coloured, but her lips quirked up like she was pleased. 'Ok, try walking him across the arena and turning him to come back. I'll wait here, but I can come over if you need me. Focus on asking, then letting him follow through... and enjoy.'

James did it. So far, so good. Conker seemed to respond to his cues without a fuss.

'How's this?' He returned to Dagmar.

'You're doing really well.'

'Thanks. That was a different start to my day. Guess I better get back to the boardroom now.'

Dagmar raised an eyebrow. 'Guess you should, though you might want to get changed first.'

'What time is it?' he asked. 'I need a shower too.'

She checked her phone. 'Quarter to eight.'

'Yeah. I better go.'

'Ok. If you take your right leg out of the stirrup.'

His dismount was as ungraceful as his mounting. 'Ouch.' He turned away from Dagmar and adjusted his trousers. 'That feels very strange.'

'It takes a while to adapt. Once you've done it a few times, your muscles will get used to it too.'

'I hope so.' He unclipped the riding hat and took it off. 'You're a very patient horse.' He gave Conker a brief nose rub.

'He's a good jumper too.'

'I'm not sure I'm quite there yet. In fact, I don't think I'll ever be.'

'It could take a long time to get to that stage.'

'Well, thank you. I'll be back tomorrow.'

'Ok.' She sucked on her bottom lip as she watched him. 'Tomorrow you'll be wishing you could spend the day in bed, and the day after that will be way worse.'

He snort-laughed. 'Ha. Thanks for the warning. Should I help take the saddle off him or anything?'

'I'll do that after. If you could just hang up the hat in the tack room. I think I'll give Conker a quick run before I turn him out.'

James left the arena with a brief glance over his shoulder. Dagmar was still next to Conker. James paused at the door, still watching as Dagmar mounted Conker with such ease she might just have gone up a step.

She took Conker out on a few spirals and circles at a walk, looking like the horse was doing everything of his own accord, except for his ears flicking to her now and then. Suddenly, they moved into a floating trot, and again she looked effortless, like an elegant passenger on the horse. He should be going, but he couldn't take his eyes off the spectacle unfolding. When they moved into a canter, her body remained in perfect sync with Conker's motions, and then they popped over a few jumps with ease and grace, landing with soft thuds after each one, Conker's muscles rippling under his skin. Dagmar looked so serene and at ease on this athlete.

Wow. This was strangely hot.

Dagmar circled back, slowing Conker to a trot and then a walk. She scratched the horse's neck, her face flushed with the exhilaration of the ride. James sensed a twitch in his groin. This was making him all kinds of turned on, which was completely bizarre. But Dagmar's confidence was inspiring. So much for the shy and quiet woman he associated with her.

He closed the door and continued towards the tack room, glancing back to see Dagmar leading Conker towards the barn, probably to untack him. Hopefully Lady Victoria Bruce would have the same effect on him, but he had a sinking suspicion she wouldn't.

CHAPTER EIGHT

Dagmar

Dagmar lifted a saddle from the hook. She routinely had to inspect the tack, and as there were no lessons until later, this was the best opportunity. She wasn't expecting anyone, so when she heard voices approaching, she stopped to listen. Caitlin had gone home to study, but it was probably just some horse owners dropping by to check on their animals. As they had full, part and a couple of DIY liveries, it was entirely likely, but she liked to make sure. She peered into the courtyard to see Ophelia and Brann.

Could she slip back in again unnoticed? These two were very demonstrative and didn't mind public displays of affection. Dagmar wasn't surprised Caitlin left the house to avoid them. This wouldn't be the first time Dagmar had walked in on them mid-kiss. Maybe if she was as beautiful as Ophelia and had a boyfriend as sexy as Brann, she might want to do the same, but she wasn't and she didn't, and she wasn't that thrilled about watching them either. Thankfully they seemed to be talking and nothing else – for now. She should make her presence known in case they were thinking of nipping in here... to do whatever they fancied.

'Hi,' she said.

Ophelia spun around and Brann put his hands in his pockets, grinning.

'Hello,' Ophelia said. 'I was just looking for you.'

'Were you?'

'Indeed.' Ophelia's eyes were sharp. 'I've just seen the bank account, and James has paid for a block of lessons. And I saw an email saying he was starting today. When is he due in?'

Dagmar kept her face impassive. 'He's already been. He wants most of them to be early in the morning or in the evening.'

'I see. I suppose that's to fit around his work.' She narrowed her eyes. 'I wish I knew what he was up to.'

Brann gave a little shrug. 'He definitely didn't look like he'd ever been riding in his life. When I saw him here before, he looked like he'd never even been on a farm.'

'Did he say anything to you?' Ophelia looked at Dagmar.

Dagmar shrugged. 'Not really.'

Ophelia studied Dagmar's face. 'Well, it seems very strange to me.'

'I just teach the lessons.' Dagmar held out her hands. 'Doesn't really matter to me why he's taking them.'

'True.' Ophelia gave her a half-smile. 'I've been thinking. With the extra lessons and everything, we could employ some more staff. It's long overdue.'

Dagmar's stomach tightened. 'Maybe,' she said, and while she knew it was true, she could also see problems.

'Caitlin says it's a lot of work,' Brann added. 'She can be a lazy so-and-so like all teenagers, but I believe her. You did a great job teaching her to ride when she was in a bad place, and that's what you should be able to focus on; not all the livery stuff too.'

'I manage.' Dagmar gave him a brief smile, shifting her weight from one foot to the other. She always found it hard to believe he was Caitlin's dad, and even stranger that he had a son who was twenty. He just didn't look old enough – and neither did Kristi. They must have been very young parents.

'I know you manage,' Ophelia said. 'But managing isn't thriving. We want you to have a bit more breathing room. I'll start looking into it.'

Dagmar ground her teeth. The idea of someone new filled her with dread. It meant getting to know another person, meeting someone different and hopefully liking them. She coped with Caitlin and Francesca because they were young and not officially staff. What if Ophelia employed someone much more "out there" than Dagmar, someone who would take over? Dagmar's insides roiled. She didn't see herself coping well with that.

She forced a smile. 'Ok. Thanks.'

Brann nodded. 'If Caitlin was a bit older, she'd probably want to do it, but I'd like her to at least sit her exams first, though if she's anything like me and her mum, she'll find a more practical job than an academic one.'

'Of course.' It made sense, though Dagmar had never done well with exams. Her calling had always been horses, and she'd been happy to take an Open College course on equine studies alongside the job here. But it wasn't up to her to make that decision for Caitlin, and she didn't even feel she could mention it to Brann without seeming too pushy.

'We'll keep you updated,' Ophelia said.

'Thanks.' Dagmar backed into the tack room, her gaze darting to Brann and Ophelia as they crossed the yard. Brann put his arm around her shoulder, and she tucked her hand into the back pocket of his jeans. Honestly, they should get a room. *Or maybe I should look for some romance for myself.* It might make her less uptight about it. But how she'd go about that now, she really wasn't sure. Sometimes she felt like a regency spinster transported to modern times. She didn't really fit anywhere except with horses.

When she finished inspecting the tack, she tidied up a bit, then went outside. Everything was quieter now, and the lessons weren't until later. She could use this time to do some shopping and nip in to see her mum. But the conversation with Ophelia and Brann lingered, unsettling her. The idea of new staff gnawed at her, making her tense and a little twitchy.

She grabbed her keys and headed for the truck. The drive to Glenbriar was always pleasant, and a brief change of scenery would do her good.

As she drove, the landscape rolled by, lush green fields and trees around the lochside blurring together. She usually enjoyed these sights, but her thoughts kept circling back to new staff.

Just what I need.

The idea of having to interact with someone new, to explain her routines and preferences, was daunting. She barely managed with the people she already knew. Gripping the steering wheel, she thought of some stranger coming in, disrupting her carefully constructed world.

And then there was James and the lessons. Another worry to add to the list. What if she accidentally blurted out something to Ophelia?

The truck rumbled along the country road towards Glenbriar. When she arrived, she parked in the car park of the small super-market, unclipped her seatbelt, and got out. She only needed a few things. She didn't eat a lot, and she had to be frugal. Her wage didn't go far. As soon as she had what she needed, she'd nip down to the Cosy Bean Café for a chat with her mum. Boy, did she need it. If anyone could help her clear her head, it was her mum.

When she pushed open the door to the Cosy Bean Café, the familiar bell jingling overhead. Sadly, there were no customers, but the smell of fresh coffee and baked goods was like a com-forting embrace. Her lovely mum stood behind the counter, scribbling something on a notepad. She looked up and smiled as Dagmar approached.

'Hi, darling. Good to see you, love. What can I get you?'

'Just a coffee, please.' Dagmar leaned on the counter.

Dotty nodded and started making the coffee. 'How's your day been?'

'Busy. And complicated.'

Dotty set the coffee in front of her. 'What's happened?'

Dagmar took a sip of the coffee. 'I'm not sure if you remember someone I was at primary school with called James Charlton.'

Dotty raised an eyebrow. 'Of course I do. He stole your Schleich horse and upset you so much.'

'Exactly.' Dagmar knew she'd remember. 'Don't tell anyone this...' She knew it went without saying, but she'd promised not to say anything. 'But he came to the stables the other day asking for lessons.' She recounted the story to her mum and how he'd said they were to be "refresher" lessons.

'But he was lying?'

'Yes. He's never ridden a horse in his life. Ophelia's desperate to know why he's doing it, and I can't tell her the real reason.'

Dotty's expression turned concerned. 'Why not?'

'He's doing it to impress someone rich – I better not say who – with a view to marrying her. But he doesn't want anyone to know, especially Ophelia, so don't tell anyone else. I probably shouldn't be telling you, but it's all so confusing.'

Dotty nodded slowly. 'I won't tell a soul.'

'It's stressing me out. I hate keeping things from Ophelia. She's my boss. I didn't want to teach him at all, but he made me an offer I can't refuse.'

'Oh?' Dotty frowned. 'Nothing bad, I hope.'

'He said he'll save the café.'

'What?' Dotty gaped at her.

'Yup. He read my social media post, and he said he'll use some community fund at Duchan Fayre to save the café if I get him riding well enough to fool this person into thinking he's been doing it all his life.'

'Dear, dear. Are you sure you can trust him?'

Dagmar let out a wry laugh. 'No, I'm not sure I can trust him at all. But then, I never trust anyone.'

'Oh darling, you get that from me. After your father, I found it so hard to trust. It's easier to have many acquaintances but few close friends.'

'But you're outgoing and sociable. I'm not.'

'You were always a quiet and thoughtful girl.'

'Ophelia's also talking about hiring new staff, which means more people, more complications.'

Dotty reached across the counter and patted Dagmar's hand. 'I know you've always liked horses better than people, love. But sometimes, you've got to let them in a bit, even if it's hard.'

Dagmar sighed, her shoulders slumping. 'I know. It's just... new staff means new routines, new dynamics. I'm not good with change.'

'You're stronger than you think,' Dotty said. 'And as for James, just do the lessons. I'm not sure I believe he'll do anything for us in return.'

'Well, he's promised, so he better.' Dagmar took another sip of her coffee. The worst thing was, she wanted to believe him. Her heart ached for him to be telling the truth and to save this place. It would help so much. But her mum was right. She just had to keep her head down, do the lessons and not let anything complicate matters further.

The following morning, Dagmar plaited her hair again, as she did every day. James was due, and he was going to try tacking up Conker himself. Once he'd got the hang of that, she would teach him more about body language and how to use rewards. Whether he remembered it all was another matter. If he failed in front of Lady Victoria, would he blame Dagmar and refuse to honour his promise?

Trusting him wouldn't come easy. Not with his history.

When she arrived at the upper paddock, she saw a figure leaning on the fence, silhouetted against the rising sun. Was that James already? She marched towards him. As she approached, his shape got clearer. He had on a greyish blue sweater with the sleeves rolled up, and he rested his forearms on the fence. His clothes always looked expensive, even the casual ones, but they'd get wrecked. Horses were messy. A fact a lot of people overlooked. Ophelia always looked immaculate somehow, but it was a mystery to Dagmar how she did it.

'Morning.' He straightened up and faced her.

'You're early.'

'I thought I'd come and have a chat with Conker. He's going to have to put up with me tacking him up this morning, so I'm doing a bit of bonding.'

'Oh.' Why did that surprise her? Maybe it shouldn't, but she hadn't thought of him as someone who would actually care about the horses – just his chances with Lady Victoria.

Dagmar gave him a nod, trying to keep her expression neutral. 'Well, let's get started then. You can lead Conker into the stables.'

'Ok.'

'But you'll need to fetch a head collar first.'

He pulled a face. 'You want me to go into the tack room just to come back out again?'

'Yeah... Why?'

He groaned. 'I can hardly walk. I feel like I've been run over by a bus.'

She gave him a little smirk, then pulled the key from the chain on her belt, made her way to the tack room door, and opened it. 'Well, you better get used to it. Lady Victoria won't be very impressed if she sees you walking like that.'

'Nice.' He raised an eyebrow and shook his head.

'This is Conker's tack here.' She led him to the far corner of the room that was neatly laid out with stations for each horse. The whole thing had been built by Brann and still smelled of new wood, as well as the leather of the saddles and the overriding smell of horses that was everywhere.

'This one?' James lifted a collar from the hook.

She nodded.

He gave a small smile and went back outside. 'You see, I was paying attention.'

She opened the gate to the paddock, and James approached Conker, speaking to him in a low, soothing voice. 'Hey, remember me? I'm back. Hopefully, I don't cause you too much trouble. And maybe you'll do the same for me. Just be a good lad and hold still. That's it.'

Dagmar watched, her arms crossed over her chest. This was better than she'd expected.

James reached out his hand and let Conker sniff it. 'Are we good?'

Conker nudged James's hand. James slipped the halter over Conker's head.

'That's it, now walk on.' He led him out of the paddock. Dagmar followed, raising an eyebrow at the way he held the rope, just like she'd showed him. His grip was a lot looser on the reins than yesterday. Not bad for a first go.

Once they were in the stables, Dagmar helped him get Conker into his stall. 'Start with a good brush down.' Dagmar handed him the grooming kit. 'Get him used to your touch before we put the tack on.'

James took the currycomb she explained was for his muscly areas. 'Sounds sensible. It's like buttering him up for the main event.'

Dagmar felt the heat in her cheeks. Was he making a euphemism? Was that what he was like in bed? Did he take things slow? One thing was certain, she'd never find out. Maybe she'd die an old maid and never discover if she liked being buttered up before 'the main event'.

He ran the brush over Conker's neck and shoulders. 'You like that? Then let's have some more, huh? That's a good lad.'

Dagmar swallowed. This was a really bad moment for her to be thinking stupid thoughts, like did he say that kind of thing to his dates? Did anyone? Who knew what people said to each other in intimate moments? She suspected Brann and Ophelia would have no qualms about talking dirty to each other during sex. Their eyes said it even in public.

Dagmar had him move onto the dandy brush and then the body brush, trying to rein in her straying thoughts as James listened to her instructions and groomed Conker while talking to him in that low, soothing voice.

'That should be enough,' Dagmar said after a few minutes. She fetched the saddle and saddle pad, placing them on a nearby stand. 'Remember, saddle pad first.'

James took the saddle pad and approached Conker. 'You ok for me to put this on?' He held it out before draping it over his back. 'Like this?' He frowned at Dagmar. 'I think it looked neater when you did it.'

'A bit more forward,' Dagmar said. 'You want it to cover his withers properly.'

James adjusted the saddle pad, then picked up the saddle. He hefted it onto Conker's back, struggling to get it in the right position. The saddle slid off to the side. 'Ok, this is not as easy as it looks.'

'Yeah. Try swinging to lift it higher and placing it more gently.' She mimed what she meant from outside the stall.

James tried again, this time getting the saddle in place. He looked over at Dagmar and raised his eyebrow. 'What's my rating so far?'

'I don't give out ratings. Now check the girth.'

'Yes, ma'am.' He fumbled with the girth straps, not looking as confident as he had with the brush. Conker shifted slightly.

'Take your time,' Dagmar said. 'Make sure it's snug, but not too tight.'

James nodded. He secured the girth, then stepped back, wiping his forehead with the back of his hand. 'How's that?'

Dagmar inspected his work, tugging the saddle pad up over the withers for better clearance. 'Not bad. A bit more practice and you'll have it down.' Then she had Conker stretch his front legs forward to make sure there was no pinching under the girth, under James's watchful eyes.

He grinned when she finished. 'Great. I'm not sure I'll have to do my own tacking up if I go riding with Victoria. Won't she have grooms?'

'No doubt, but she might like doing it herself.'

'I haven't even met her yet.'

'I have,' Dagmar said.

'Have you?' He met her eyes and stared as if trying to extract the story from her wordlessly.

'Well, yes. At horse shows and events.'

'What's she like?'

Dagmar gave a little shrug. 'She seems ok.' It wasn't like they were great friends and Dagmar so rarely warmed to people. She assumed somebody like Lady Victoria Bruce wouldn't give her the time of day unless she wanted her as part of a riding team. That was the only time Dagmar became popular.

'That's hardly a glowing review.'

'Well, I don't know her well. Ask Ophelia about her. They're second cousins or something.'

'That might be a little awkward.' He straightened up and put his hands on his hips. The pose opened his chest wide, and he looked a lot broader and muscly than she'd noticed before. Again, she must stop noticing this kind of thing, but old habits died hard, and she'd crushed on James forever.

'I guess. Now, do you want to lead Conker out?'

'Sure.' As he passed her, he gave her a little smile. Was this ever going to get easier? She doubted it. But what could she do? Nothing. She just had to let these moments exist, because in a few months' time, James wouldn't need her anymore and the next time she saw Lady Victoria at a horse show, she may well have a new boyfriend on the scene. A boyfriend Dagmar was grooming especially for her.

CHAPTER NINE

James

James gripped his golf club, staring down the fairway. Saturday mornings on the golf course were something of a ritual. Usually, he enjoyed it, but his insides were antsy, plus his muscles ached from all the riding. Even with that though, he'd much rather be at the stables, continuing his lessons. Dropping golf, however, might look suspicious. And keeping up appearances was important.

He lined up his shot, then took a swing, sending the ball arcing through the air. It wasn't exactly his best shot. These movements were so different compared to the ones he'd been practising on Conker, and his body was protesting.

His friend Matthew clapped him on the back as he stepped off the tee, and James winced involuntarily. 'You ok?'

'Yeah. All good.' James stepped aside to let Matthew take his shot. He couldn't exactly confess to why he was walking like John Wayne and barely able to pick up a club, let alone swing it. 'How's everything at home? Still chaotic with the baby?'

Matthew smiled as he took his stance. 'That's an understatement. But it's great. I love watching her grow and learning new things. She's walking now.'

'Already?'

'Yeah, she had her first birthday a couple of weeks ago.'

'You're kidding? That's gone so fast.'

'Yeah, tell me about it.'

James had met Matthew a few years back when they'd been paired together in a fourballs competition for the club championship. Matthew was older, but his life seemed so settled – and normal. James felt the usual pang of inadequacy.

He watched Matthew's ball soar. 'Nice one.'

'Thanks.' Matthew stifled a yawn.

'Is the little one keeping you up all night?'

'She's not too bad at going down and she only wakes occasionally, but she likes her early rises.'

'Oh dear.' James could relate. He might not have a baby, but his alarm going off at five thirty was bad enough. Still, it was the best way to cram in the riding lessons.

'Yeah. But it's worth it. She's a sweetheart, and so like Nina. Peas in a pod, those two.'

'Nice.' He couldn't imagine feeling that way about someone. So far, he'd failed miserably in making a deep connection with anyone. Instead, he was fixated on riding lessons to impress a woman he'd never met. What if all this effort was for nothing?

Well, at least the experience itself was enjoyable – mostly. He could do without the muscle ache.

They reached their golf balls, and James lined up his next shot. It landed just short of the green. 'Didn't Nina want to play today too?' he asked, remembering she was a very good golfer.

'She didn't mind, but I'm sure she'll come another day.' Matthew stepped up to his ball and placed the club behind it. 'She's taking Maeve to a party today, which will be right up her street. She likes all the gossip. And she's such a great mum, so patient and loving. I'm always in awe of her.' He cracked his ball onto the green.

'Sounds like you hit the jackpot.' *Unlike me.*

'Yeah, I did.' Matthew shoved his club into his bag. 'But enough about me. What's new with you?'

'Not much.' James shook his head, keeping his face boardroom straight. 'Just... you know, the usual. Work and stuff.'

Matthew gave him a searching look. 'Is everything ok?'

'Yeah, just busy.' James waved his hand airily and smiled. 'Got a lot on my plate.'

'Duchan Fayre must be quite a place to manage.'

'It really is.' Though it was a shitload easier than his private life.

They reached the green, and James focused on his putt, trying to stop his mind from wandering onto uncertain routes, especially ones that looked like the bridle path near Glenvorneth. But as he lined up his shot, Dagmar trotted to the forefront of his mind on Zephyra. What the hell was it with her? Why couldn't he rid her from his brain?

Golf with Matthew took James until lunchtime. He didn't have time to hang about afterwards as he was dining with his parents. Living in a wing of their house meant he could dine with them every day if he wanted, but he preferred not to, and his mum made such a big fuss about meals when he joined them. He knew better than to turn up in his golf clothes, so he went back and changed into a shirt and jeans before making his way into the main part of the house.

Their mansion had been custom-built in the same style as Duchan Fayre, smoothly rendered and painted white on the outside with a sandstone trim. On one side was a large round tower that housed the main living area on the ground floor and his parents' bedroom on the first. The gardens were all neatly landscaped and kept very tidy, with rolling green lawns and well-tended flower beds. The view across the loch was exceptional, and Sherri liked to host corporate parties on the lawn with a marquee.

'Hello darling.' She greeted him with a kiss on both cheeks. 'I've set up lunch on the terrace today as it's so warm. Come on out. Dad's already waiting.'

James followed his mother out to the terrace. The scent of freshly cut grass filled his nostrils, reminding him of simpler days when they lived in a normal house on the edge of Perth. His parents were ambitious though and had built themselves a mini empire that had been more successful than either of them could have imagined when they started it up.

Laurence was already seated at the table, sipping on a glass of iced tea.

'Afternoon, Dad.' James took his seat.

'James,' Laurence nodded. 'Good game?'

'Not bad.'

Sherri fussed around, making sure everything was perfect. She finally sat down and beamed at him. 'I've got some news, James. You'll love it.'

'Do tell.'

'Guess who I met the other day?'

His mum knew so many people it could literally be anyone. 'I wouldn't know where to start.'

'The countess of Dairvin.'

James raised an eyebrow. 'Oh?'

'Yes, and we had a lovely chat. All about Lady Victoria.' She pulled a wide-eyed smile. 'I let her know that you love riding.' She winked.

James's stomach dropped, and he gaped at her. 'You did what?'

'Don't worry.' Sherri took a sip of wine. 'It did the trick. Wouldn't you know, the countess went back and told her daughter, Lady Victoria? Apparently, she is very keen to meet you for a ride.'

'Right.' James chewed his tongue.

Laurence looked at him over the rim of his glass. 'What's the matter, son? You look like you've swallowed a wasp.'

'You do know I can't actually ride yet.' James looked between the two of them.

'Aren't you taking lessons?' Laurence frowned, then glanced at his wife.

'Yes, but I've only had a few. I'm hardly a skilled rider.'

'I know what you're like.' Sherri waved her hand dismissively. 'Once you get the bit between your teeth – excuse my bad pun – there's no stopping you. By the time you meet Victoria, you'll look like a natural, and I just know she'll be charmed by you.'

James clenched his jaw, biting back everything that was going through his mind. 'When is this meeting supposed to happen?'

'Oh, soon, I'd imagine.' Sherri nibbled her cucumber sandwich. 'The countess is very eager. She thinks you and Lady Victoria would get along famously and I quite agree.'

James forced a smile, though his insides were burning. He wasn't even close to being ready for a ride with Lady Victoria. The basics were hard enough, and he had no idea how he'd manage to fake his way through anything more advanced than jogging up and down a field.

'Let's hope.' He lifted a sandwich.

'Isn't this exciting?' Sherri clapped, her eyes sparkling.

Laurence leaned back in his chair, studying his son. 'You'll manage,' he said. 'You're a quick learner and I have every faith in you.'

'Thanks.' Shame James didn't share their sentiments. Neither of them had any idea just how difficult riding a horse actually was. He might have to increase his lessons. That or hope for a miracle. One thing was certain, he couldn't afford to make a fool of himself in front of Lady Victoria. It wasn't just the connection to her that mattered, but his family wanted the connection with the Earl and Countess of Dairvin. Messing that up would put them all in an awkward place going forward.

Sherri continued chatting about the countess and her daughter, but James could barely focus. He nodded and smiled at the right moments, his mind a hive of worry. As soon as lunch was done, he was going back to the stables. Maybe he should just go live there for a while, at least until he looked vaguely competent on horseback.

As the meal wound down, James excused himself. 'Thanks for this, Mum.' He stood up and kissed his mother on the cheek. 'I need to go make some calls.'

'Alright, darling.' She patted his hand.

'Bye, Dad.'

Laurence gave him a wave as James headed back inside. Once he was out of sight, he let out a deep breath. He had his work cut out for him, and he didn't want to waste a moment.

He drove back to the stables, his mind racing almost as fast as the car. He should probably slow down, but this was an emergency. Putting his foot down, he whizzed along the lochside until he reached the main gates of the Glenvorneth Estate. He pulled in and took the track to the stables. The car park was full of cars. Riders were out on the bridle path and a few people were in the outdoor arena. Brann's daughter, the volunteer girl, was leading a horse across the yard, followed by a woman with bright red hair. James had seen that woman talking to Dagmar the first day he came here. Was she the girl's mum? Brann must have eclectic taste if he'd gone from her to Ophelia. James couldn't imagine two more different people. But who was he to judge?

He made his way through people and horses, scanning the area, hoping to spot Dagmar, but she was nowhere to be seen.

'Excuse me.' He caught up with Brann's daughter. 'Have you seen Dagmar?'

'Yeah, she went back to her trailer to have a shower. One of the horses had a bit of a dodgy tum and she kind of got covered.'

'Oh.' James covered his mouth, not wanting to imagine. Every vision he'd had of riding being an elegant pastime was being busted one by one.

'Poor girl,' the red-haired woman said. 'She could do with a break.'

'You're not wrong, and thanks.' James started walking around the top paddock towards the bridle path. Sadly, she wasn't going to get a break from him. The opposite, unfortunately. He needed her. His gaze wandered across the paddocks to the trailer at the bottom of the hill. Did she live there permanently? He'd assumed she either lived with her mum or had a house and only used the trailer to move the horses about and live in when she was travelling to shows, but come to think on it, he'd only ever seen her coming from there and it looked almost like a permanent fixture.

Making his way to the path, he opened the gate and continued down the hill. Finally, he reached the trailer. He'd never gone right up to it before. Should he knock or call out? He paused outside the door, then knocked, but there was no answer. He knocked again, louder this time.

'Dagmar? Are you in there?' Nothing. He ran a hand through his hair. Brann's daughter had said she'd gone to take a shower. Did this thing have a shower? It looked spacious, but wait, was this a door for horses? Maybe it had a different section for people. He marched around and found another door on the side. Close to it were two little cubicles like portaloos. Was one of them a shower? Surely to god she didn't use that day in, day out? No one should have to do that. Did Ophelia think that was ok? Or maybe it was Dagmar's choice, though he wasn't sure why anyone would choose that.

Before he could ponder any more, one of the cubicle doors opened and Dagmar emerged in nothing but a towel and a pair of flipflops. The hair she usually had plaited hung wet over her shoulders, dripping onto the grass.

'What the hell?' She gaped at James, clinging to the towel around her.

Being in front of the door, he was clearly blocking her way, but he'd temporarily frozen. 'Um... Hey.'

'What are you doing?' Her eyebrows knitted together. 'And can you let me in to get dressed?'

'Oh, sure.' He stepped aside, but he couldn't take his eyes from her. As she got closer, he caught the scent of strawberry shampoo and something else delicate and floral. Like a fresh garden in spring. 'I need to talk to you though.'

'It'll have to wait.' She reached up to open the door.

'Well, yeah. Obviously.'

The towel wasn't really big enough and, as she stretched, it opened, revealing her tight tummy. He briefly glanced at it, then lower, to a place he knew he shouldn't be looking, and he quickly averted his eyes.

Dagmar seemed to be having trouble with the door.

'Can I help?' he asked.

'I doubt it. It's just this door.' She rattled the handle. 'It jams at the worst possible times.'

'Here. Let me.' He reached up and his hand caught hers before he captured the handle. His insides ignited at the contact, not to mention the proximity of her bare body. A primal urge to wrap her in his own clothes and pull her close roared through him. His groin twitched at the thought and he steadied his breath, clutching the handle and turning it firmly. 'There you go.'

'Thanks,' she muttered.

'Oh... You've got...'

She glared at him.

'A ladybird on your shoulder.' He put his thumb out and gently flicked it away. Dagmar froze like she'd turned to stone. Was she feeling the same way he was? He'd often tried to kid himself he didn't find her attractive, but he wasn't fooling anyone now.

She shivered a little, then climbed into the trailer and closed the door, leaving James alone with his messed up, completely wild thoughts.

Chapter Ten

Dagmar

Dagmar closed the door behind her, leaning against it for a moment to catch her breath. Her heart pounded. She glanced at her shoulder where James had swept the ladybird from her. Was it more humiliating to admit that was the first time a man had touched her naked body or to face up to her stupid reaction? Why was she letting it affect her like this? But the lingering warmth from his touch was like a burn. She tightened her grip on the towel.

Oh god. Had he been looking at her? Her towels were ancient and didn't properly cover her. But no one came down here normally. She never had visitors. Plus, there wasn't room enough to change in the shower cubicle and she was so used to just nipping over from it to dress in here. Who'd have predicted him turning up like that? Could it get more embarrassing?

She crossed the small living space to the cupboard, pulling out clothes with quick, jerky movements. Her pulse and her mind raced each other. Was James still out there? She pretty much always kept the curtains closed in here, but she checked there were no gaps just in case.

She pulled on her knickers and a plain white bra. Jeez, did everything have to look so virginal? She really should buy some black ones, or maybe red. Not that it mattered. Who would ever see them? She tugged on a pair of jeans and a plain pink T-shirt. At least now, if he decided to come in, she was decent. But fuck no. She didn't want him in here. He lived in a mansion and this place was cramped and barely had room to move. The threadbare furniture, the old, worn curtains, and the tiny, cluttered kitchenette all seemed glaringly inadequate.

He must think I'm a hermit. She dragged a brush through the ends of her wet hair. Maybe he was right. She had a perfectly lovely room in her mum's cottage, though the whole thing suffered from damp. Living on site was so much easier when she had early starts and late finishes, plus needing to be constantly on call in case there were sick or injured horses.

She moved to the small mirror above the sink. Her reflection showed flushed cheeks and wide eyes. She rarely wore make-up, but she kind of wished she had time to put some on to hide behind. Splitting the curtains with her fingers, she peeked out. James was still outside, hands in his pockets, grinding his foot into the ground.

She took a deep breath and opened the door. 'What is it you want?' She leaned her head to the side and split her hair into three sections, ready to plait it.

'I'm in trouble.'

'What's happened?' And why was he telling her?

'My mother met the countess of Dairvin and told her I was looking forward to riding with Victoria soon. Now, she's desperate to meet me, apparently. I need to up my game. How can I do this?'

Dagmar worked her hair into a plait. James cocked his head, watching with a slight frown. Her nerve ends tingled at the stupid idea that he was going to say something about her looking nice with her hair down. But why would he? That was some kind of fantasy she was playing inside her head. All he cared about was impressing Lady Victoria. 'I suppose I could take you out on a hack this afternoon.'

'Really? As in out of the arena?'

'Yes. I think Conker is free. I'll ring Ophelia and check she doesn't want to use him.'

'But there are loads of people here. They'll see me.'

'Then act like you know what you're doing.' Sheesh, he was one of the most confident guys she'd ever met. If anyone could blag their way through something like this, it was him.

'Yeah, ok. I think I can do that.'

'I *know* you can. But stay humble with Conker. Horses can smell right through bullshit projectors.'

He laughed, flashing her his very white teeth, and she felt a little weak at the knees. 'But you'll come with me, yeah?'

'Obviously. Ophelia would kill me if I let you loose with Conker on the bridle path after only a few lessons.'

'Good point.'

'Just act like you're out riding for fun though and not like you're on a lesson. Then no one will suspect a thing.'

His smile grew, and he nodded. 'I like it. You're smart.'

She scoffed and tied off her plait, but his words gave her a little bubble of pleasure that she wasn't used to.

'But I'm not exactly dressed for riding.'

'You'll pass in that.' She scanned his grey polo shirt and dark trousers. 'As long as you don't mind the possibility of getting messy.'

He held up his hands. 'Nope. Everything is replaceable.'

'Then you'll do fine.' She gave him a quick nod. 'Let me just call Ophelia.' After a brief chat, she confirmed Conker was free for the afternoon. 'Let's get the horses ready.'

'Good stuff.' He rubbed his hands together.

Dagmar marched towards the stables, not sure if she wanted to make small talk with James. But she'd have to during the ride. Hopefully he wouldn't mention anything about earlier. What did she expect him to say? "Oh, by the way, I happened to see your lady bits and realised they were untouched by a man." A giggle escaped her, and she covered her mouth. She liked regency novels and really, that was worthy of one.

'What are you laughing at?' James eyed her.

'Nothing.'

He raised a brow, but she didn't elaborate.

'Are you happy to saddle up Conker on your own? And I'll get Zephyra ready.'

'I'll give it my best shot.'

'We'll do them next to each other, so I'll be there if you need help.'

'A very strong possibility.'

They retrieved everything they needed from the tack room, and Dagmar watched for a moment as James entered Conker's stall and started to groom him. She moved to Zephyra's stall and began brushing her down. If she was on her own, she would talk more, maybe confide in Zephyra, knowing she would listen, but no way would she say anything with James so close by.

When she finished tacking up, she checked on James. He'd done surprisingly well. It seemed he really was a fast learner. They led the horses into the yard.

James had a bit of his swagger about him, flashing a smile at people as he passed. If he pulled out this kind of charm for Lady Victoria, she'd be all over him, whether he could ride or not.

Dagmar bit her lip, suppressing a smile as he made a bit of a business mounting Conker. His foot slipped once, and he clung to the saddle for a moment before finally swinging his leg over.

'Nice and smooth.' She smirked.

'It's my middle name.'

'Just remember to keep your heels down and relax. We're not in a rush.'

He nodded, settling into the saddle faster than during his last lesson. They rode out of the yard together. Dagmar glanced at James, noting his stiff posture and the slight tension in his hands, but he maintained his smile, making him look almost at ease. Certainly, passersby wouldn't think anything was amiss.

They reached the gate to the bridle path, and Dagmar leant over to pull a lever, then proceeded through the gate and pivoted Zephyra.

'Through you go,' she told James.

'Are you sure?' He eyed the narrow passage suspiciously while Conker shook his head, obviously wondering why he hadn't been let through yet.

'Yes. Just let him walk through and stop when you're clear of us so we can shut it and catch up.'

'Catch up? What if he doesn't stop?' James kept his voice low, but his posture stiffened.

'You've practised stop and go enough, and Conker's a good boy. Take a deep breath, let it out, and go.'

Still looking doubtful, James finally released the tension on the reins, and Conker stepped through, stopping a couple of strides ahead to wait for Zephyra. Dagmar shut the gate, rubbed her mare's neck and caught up with James, sensing the nerves he was trying so hard to hide. No matter how confident he was on his feet, in the saddle you couldn't lie. He was doing better than he knew for a total beginner.

'I have to admit, I'm freaking out a bit.' He kept his voice low.

'Are you?'

'Well yeah,' he said, clearly not catching the sarcasm. 'I don't really feel in control. It's like I'm at his mercy.'

'You are. So respect him. Just breathe and keep calm – you know he's trustworthy, and this is supposed to be enjoyable.'

'Easier said than done,' he muttered. 'I keep thinking about Lady Victoria and all the ways I could mess this up.'

'You're doing better than you think.'

'Well, that's something, at least.' They walked on, the path winding through the trees, the quiet rustling of leaves and the horses' hooves the only sounds. In another world, this could be quite pleasant and companionable.

Dagmar glanced over at James as they continued along the bridle path. His initial tension seemed to be easing. He sat taller yet more fluid, and his hold on the reins had softened. Conker ambled along contentedly, clearly picking up on James's growing confidence.

'You're looking better already,' she said.

James chuckled. 'Thanks. I still feel like I'm about to fall off any second, but at least I don't look it.'

'Some say fake it till you make it.'

He gave her a sideways look. 'Won't be the first time.'

'What do you mean?'

He let out a little huff. 'Don't judge me for what I'm about to tell you.'

'Um... ok.'

'So, I had a relationship a few years ago that was basically fake. To be honest, I don't see myself ever having one that's genuine. All the expectations and stipulations mean I'll most likely have to manufacture feelings.'

'Really? And you're ok with that?'

'I'm not sure I have a choice. I suppose if a relationship is built on mutual respect, it can still work.'

'Yeah.' She frowned. With no experience to draw on, she wasn't exactly in a place to comment, but it sounded the opposite of what she wanted. If she found someone, she wanted a profound connection, not something "manufactured". Then again, maybe there was nothing wrong with that. Who was to say that two lonely people couldn't meet and rub along happily? Maybe with work, it could become more. Wasn't that how she worked with horses? She met them and learned what made them tick. It took effort. If she wanted to have a relationship, maybe that was the way forward. But even that was a huge ask. How would she meet people to start with? The thought of online dating terrified her. And she didn't exactly have a big friend circle. It always felt so hopeless.

'What about you?' James smiled at her.

'What about me?'

'Are you just you, or is there a significant other?'

'Oh... Just me.'

'What's the deal with the trailer? That's not your permanent home, is it?'

'Yup.'

He cast her a sideways look. 'Do you like it?'

She urged Zephyra to lengthen her stride with her seat. This conversation was weird. She'd never really considered whether she liked it or not. 'I don't know. It's not a question of if I like it. It's just what I have to do. That's the easiest place for me to live while I do this job.'

'I get that, but are you happy in this job? I don't want to overstep, but you seem awfully overworked. You might be doing something you love, but if you live here too, then you're never away from work.'

She gave a little shrug. What else was there? This was the job she'd done since she left school. It allowed her to be with horses. She could ride and compete in shows. That was her life. She didn't need to "be away". In the back of her mind, a little thought chipped away at her. One that had been there for some time, but she'd ignored it. One that said she should take more time for herself, live a little, do something outside of the horses. She loved to feel needed by the horses. It made such a change to the bullying or indifference humans have given her, but the horses didn't need her – not constantly. They just needed safety, forage, water, friends, and space. Technically, anyone could give them that.

They rode on, the trees providing dappled shade. Dagmar's thoughts tapped away like someone sending her morse code messages. And they made about as much sense. Her brain was jumbled, and she knew she wouldn't be able to straighten her-self out until she was alone. Except she didn't really want that either. She wanted this moment with James to go on. Being with him like this was strangely pleasant. This was the "me-time" she needed, and it was with someone else. Granted, it was someone she'd crushed on, but even so, he was an easy guy to get on with, even if he had stolen her Schleich horse all those years ago and seen her half-naked and flustered just a short time ago.

'This is actually so nice.' James glanced over at her like he'd read her mind. 'Beautiful really.' His eyes were still on her and heat rushed into her neck and cheeks. Seriously? Obviously, he meant the ride, not her.

'Yeah... It's a nice path,' Dagmar agreed.

'I always used to think a bridle path was something to do with weddings.' James smiled. 'Took me years to discover it was spelt differently.'

'Hmm, yeah. Maybe this will be the path to your wedding.'

'You think?'

'With Lady Victoria.' The words rushed out because she didn't want him to think she meant with her... And why would he? Oh god. She was so ridiculous.

James looked thoughtful. 'Let's hope. My life has always been about business and impressing people. This is just an extension of that, I suppose.'

'The opposite from me.' She'd never impressed anyone, unless she included dressage judges.

'How do you mean?'

She cast him a dark look. 'You were at school with me. You know everyone hated me.'

He tipped his head to the side. 'It must have felt like that.'

'It didn't just feel like that. That's how it was.'

'I'm sorry.' His look was sincere, but no doubt practised from his experience of winning people over in the office. 'For any part I played in that. I truly never meant to hurt you. If I'd had more guts, I'd have been more active in stopping other people. My words fell on deaf ears, I'm afraid, and I was too self-obsessed, too caught up in my own image.'

'I guess I'm just not very likeable.'

'You're just very quiet and we had a particularly vocal year group who didn't properly take time to get to know you. Our loss. As I'm discovering. You're smart. You literally know every-thing about horses.'

'I'm not sure that's a compliment.'

'It is. And you have very high expectations and standards for your students. I appreciate that. I'm exactly the same at work.'

She gave him a little smile. 'Something in common then.'

He nodded, and his strong eye contact made her a little shaky. That smile was very disarming. She urged Zephyra forward be-cause she couldn't keep looking at James like this. It wasn't good for her. Plus, he was doing this to win some other woman, so all these smiles and pleasantries were nothing more than friendly gestures.

The path went through the woods around the estate and emerged on the other side, close to a row of workers' cottages that were being renovated.

'You should move into one of them,' James said. 'Ophelia shouldn't expect you to live in a trailer onsite. Why on earth does she allow it?'

'Because it's not up to her. It's what I want.'

'Is it?'

Dagmar huffed. 'It was my idea. Ophelia offered me one of the cottages when they're done, but I couldn't afford the rent on one of those houses with my wages. That trailer cost a fortune. I'm still paying it off, plus I have the pickup truck. I can't afford that and a house.'

James nodded. 'Sorry. I shouldn't have said anything.'

Maybe he shouldn't have, but the fact was, he *had*. And his words had woken thoughts in Dagmar that she knew she'd struggle to put to bed.

CHAPTER ELEVEN

James

James straightened his collar for the third time, standing in the grand hallway of Dairvin Castle, and checked himself for the umpteenth time in the giant, ornate mirror. This was it. The moment had arrived. Somewhere in this building was Lady Victoria Bruce. Was he about to meet his destiny? As the youngest daughter, she was in no position ever to inherit this place, but the connection was good enough – for his parents anyway. James smoothed his hair, not entirely convinced this was the path he wanted to follow. Did he really want to be rubbing shoulders with the aristocracy for the rest of his life?

His mum certainly did.

The man who'd let him in reappeared. He was dressed in a smart suit. Was he a butler? Seriously, did people still have them in this day and age?

'If you'll follow me.' He led James into an expansive drawing room where the Earl and Countess of Dairvin awaited. The earl, a short, balding, rather portly man with a stern countenance, stood by the fireplace, while the countess, elegantly dressed, sat on a chaise longue. A young woman with dark, glossy hair stood near the window.

'Ah, James,' the earl said. 'Good to see you again and welcome to Dairvin Castle.'

'Thank you. It's an honour to be here.' James inclined his head slightly.

The countess smiled warmly. 'I seem to run into your mother all over the place. She's told me all about your love of riding. I had no idea. When we met at the Highland Games last year, you didn't mention it and Ophelia didn't either.'

'Oh, well... One doesn't,' James said with a nervous chuckle, glancing at the woman.

'Indeed.' The countess raised an eyebrow, then turned to the window. 'Victoria, come and meet James Charlton.'

The woman at the window smiled and came forward. 'Hello. I've been looking forward to meeting you.'

'Likewise, Lady Victoria.' He moved towards her and took her outstretched hand. Her grip was very firm, almost crushing. Was she trying to make a point? She may be small, but she was fierce, perhaps?

'Please, call me Victoria.'

'Thank you, Victoria.'

'Shall we sit?' The earl gestured to the seating area.

They all took their places, James feeling like a show dog on display. Victoria sat next to him, rather closer than he'd expected.

She smiled at him again, her lips wide and red. The earl and countess took the opposite sofa.

'So, are you looking forward to riding?' Victoria leaned closer.

'Yeah, of course.' James drew back a little. He'd met some fast women before, but he didn't expect her to be quite so in his face, especially when her parents were in the room with them.

The countess rubbed her fingertips together, watching James closely. 'Victoria is quite the equestrian herself. She's won several competitions, you know?'

'Mother, you're embarrassing me.' Victoria flapped her hands about, though from her broad smile she obviously wasn't bothered.

'I'm sure you're very talented,' James said.

'We'll have to see if you can keep up with me.' She gave him a playful nudge. James forced a smile, but his insides twisted. He wasn't sure he liked this familiarity.

'I probably won't. My mother loves to exaggerate my skills.'

'We mothers do that.' The countess clasped her hands in her lap. 'Tell us more about yourself, James. What do you do when you're not riding?'

'Work, mainly.' He sensed all eyes on him. 'Duchan Fayre keeps me busy, but I try to find time for other pursuits.'

'Such as?' Victoria's gaze was intense.

'I enjoy golf and reading. Crime novels and the like.'

'Father enjoys golf,' Victoria said. 'You should play together sometime.'

'Absolutely.'

The earl nodded. 'I'm not particularly good, but it is quite an enjoyable pastime.'

James imagined them playing a round together and having to lose on purpose to make sure he didn't fall out of favour.

'Let me ring for tea,' the countess said.

James kept his smile in place. When he'd had hopes of a relationship with Ophelia, he'd called at her at father's home a few times and each time he'd thought her father's dress sense ludicrous: he was a fan of plus fours and looked like a character from Downton Abbey. This was even worse. These people had servants and rang for tea. Unreal. His parents had a housekeeper, but she didn't wait on them. She cleaned the house, did the washing and ironing, and prepped meals. This was a whole new level.

'We'll ride after.' Victoria raised an eyebrow at him. Was that a deliberate innuendo? He rather suspected it was, and it put him even more on edge.

'Er, yes.'

A woman brought in a silver tea tray laden with fine china, delicate sandwiches, and an assortment of pastries. James watched as the countess poured the tea, holding the lid on the pot with a dainty finger. This was straight off a film set. He took a cup gingerly, willing himself not to spill any of the contents.

Victoria moved even closer, her eyes bright. 'Have you been to the Royal Atholl Horse Show? It's one of my favourites.'

'Oh, um, no,' James said. He'd never been to any horse shows. 'I've heard it's quite an event.'

'Oh, it is. You must go sometime.' Victoria beamed. 'Last year, I competed in the show jumping. Came in second. The competition was fierce.'

James took a sip of his tea. 'Impressive. You must be really good.' And that wasn't the best news for him.

'I just enjoy it.' Her coy smile was ruined when a laugh burst through. 'And what about the Horse Trials we hold here? Did you attend last year?'

'I think I was abroad.' James took another sip of tea. 'On business.'

'Well, you simply must come this year.'

The countess watched him over the rim of her cup, her gaze sharp. Was she evaluating him? Measuring his responses? He forced himself to meet her eyes, hoping she couldn't see through his façade.

'It's not long now.' Victoria looked at a gold wristwatch as though she was checking the date on it. 'Just a few weeks. I'm sure you'll love it.'

'I'm sure,' James replied, though the prospect filled him with dread. 'Though I'm nowhere near good enough to compete. I only ride for fun, you know. I'll leave the competition to the accomplished riders.' His mind strayed to Dagmar. Did she take part in it? It was on the tip of his tongue to ask Victoria if she knew, but he thought better of it.

'Excellent.' The earl set his cup down. 'It'll be good for you two to spend some time together.'

'Indeed.' The countess's eyes never left James. 'We're delighted you're so enthusiastic about riding, James. It's a passion of ours, as you can see.'

James smiled, trying his utmost to appear genuine, but this was worse than any business meeting he'd ever attended. 'I'm looking forward to it.'

Victoria's hand brushed his knee as she reached for another sandwich. 'We'll have so much fun. I can show you all my favourite trails.'

He froze for a moment. Why did she keep touching him? Did she have no boundaries? Or was he just particularly sensitive to it because he couldn't warm to her yet? 'Sounds great.'

The earl launched into a story about his favourite hunting trip, and James did his best to listen attentively, occasionally glancing at the countess. Her expression remained serene. He didn't have a clue about any of this stuff. Not only would he have to keep learning to ride better, but he'd need to study all the different riding disciplines and various shows and events. But was there really any point? He'd promised to try his best with Victoria, but was it worth it if he felt nothing for her?

Keep trying.

Like anything else, relationships could succeed with hard work and practise – or so his father kept telling him. Maybe he just hadn't put the work in previously.

As they finished their tea, Victoria chattered on about various horse shows and events. James kept nodding and smiling but couldn't bring anything else to the party. She might as well have been talking Greek. When he and Dagmar talked about the horses, it was interesting. He liked discovering their personalities and learning how to work with them. But all this horse show stuff wasn't something he had any interest in. But he had to keep trying.

'You must have some wonderful stories yourself.' Victoria turned the conversation back to him.

'Oh, well.' He searched his mind for something plausible. 'I've had my share of interesting rides recently. My life has been rather taken up with business. But I enjoy meeting new horses and getting to know them.'

'Oh, really?' She pulled a surprised face. 'That's so cute.'

'Is it?' He downed some more tea.

The countess set down her cup. 'Perhaps you should prepare for your ride?'

'Yes, let's.' Victoria leapt to her feet. 'I can't wait to get you in the saddle.'

James rose, giving her a brief smile. Was she attempting more innuendo? He didn't really want to know. His insides were knotted. What if he made a total balls-up of this? Conker was such a good horse. What if the one Victoria gave him to ride wasn't as easy or didn't like him?

He made his way back through the grand hallway, his footsteps echoing off the polished wood floors. As he stepped outside, the fresh air hit him like a splash of cold water. He took a deep breath. Dairvin Castle was impressive, but completely overwhelming, not to mention over the top. He reached his car and popped open the boot to retrieve his riding boots.

As he changed his shoes, he gathered himself. *Just keep plugging away.* Victoria was attractive and seemed genuinely interested in him. This was a significant opportunity, and he owed it to himself and his family to at least try. Just because the attraction wasn't there yet, didn't mean it wouldn't ever be there.

'I got this,' he muttered under his breath.

Once he was in his brand-new riding boots, courtesy of Duchan Fayre's equestrian section, he closed the boot, straightened up and took another deep breath. This was just another challenge. He could handle it.

Walking back towards the stables, he spotted Victoria waiting for him. She was dressed in riding gear now, with tight jodhpurs, a tweed jacket and long boots. The look reminded him of Ophelia, except Victoria didn't have the height or the presence to carry it off in the same way. She smiled as he approached.

'Ready for the ride of your life?' She waggled her eyebrows.

Was this her flirting? Would he normally find this ok? *Maybe.* So why then was it making him bristle? 'Absolutely. Let's do this.'

They walked together towards the stables.

'So, how long have you been riding?' he asked.

'Since I could walk, really.' Victoria's eyes lit up. 'I was on a pony when I was tiny. It's been a part of my life forever.'

'The best way, I guess.'

'Was it the same for you?'

'Oh... no. I was later.'

As they reached the stables, the scent of hay and horses hit him and brought with it an image of Dagmar. He'd much rather be at Glenvorneth talking to her than here. A young woman was waiting with the horses already tacked up.

'Morning,' she said. 'I have Dizzi ready for you, and Caspar for Mr Charlton.'

James clipped on his riding hat and admired the two horses.

'Great. You'll love Caspar.' Victoria indicated a large white horse. He looked about the same size as Conker but had a somewhat snooty expression. Maybe he sensed a fake. James remembered everything Dagmar had taught him about being respectful to the horses and trying to build a rapport with them. He approached Caspar slowly, talking in a low voice. When the horse responded, James moved closer and gently patted Caspar's neck.

'You're very good with him.' Victoria mounted Dizzi like a pro from the mounting block the groom had led them to.

James followed suit, getting into the saddle with barely a hitch. That was better than expected. The familiar pang of uncertainty hit him and intensified as he realised he was on his own up here. Dagmar wasn't close by to help if anything went wrong. And he couldn't very well confess to Victoria that he was little more than a novice. Forcing calm, he took up the reins and gave Caspar a gentle squeeze to move him forward.

They started off down the path and James reminded himself to breathe. Caspar seemed gentle and good-natured, though he wasn't quite as responsive as Conker and James felt like he was working harder to control their direction. But maybe it was partly because he wasn't sure where they were going. He glanced at Victoria, who looked quite serene. She had good posture but still appeared natural. What did he look like? He was possibly too straight or too slouched and probably looked petrified.

'Let's take the trail through the woods.' Victoria pointed ahead. 'It's lovely this time of year.'

'Lead the way.' James forced another smile, and pressed Casper to follow Victoria onto the woodland path, then caught up with her.

They rode side by side. The path wound through lush greenery surrounding the estate. It reminded him a little of Glenvorneth, but the surrounding hills were higher, more dramatic, and even a little threatening.

'So, what do you think of the estate?' Victoria asked.

'It's stunning. A gorgeous place to live.'

'We don't live here all the time. When the castle is open in the summer and the tourists are in, it can get quite annoying. The gates open at eleven, so by the time we're heading back, you'll see for yourself. This path will be crawling with people.'

'Hmm.' James didn't mind the idea in terms of bringing people to the area. Visitors here were often enticed to travel a few miles more to Duchan Fayre and enjoy the country shopping experience. But purely on a selfish level today, he wasn't sure he wanted to be dodging people here and there, jostling for a place on a path when he was up here, and they were down there.

The path opened up to a wide field. Victoria's eyes lit up. 'Let's have a gallop, shall we?' She shortened her reins a fraction.

James's stomach flipped. No freaking way. That would be a dick move. He needed to keep it slow. 'Actually, I was thinking we could take it slow. Walking gives us more time to talk and enjoy the scenery.'

Victoria frowned slightly, but then her expression softened. 'Ok, if you insist. Though I do love a good gallop.'

'Another time, perhaps. I don't feel as confident on a new horse and I don't want our time together to be over too quickly.'

She laughed and pulled her coy face. 'You're quite the charmer, aren't you?'

Was he? Sometimes maybe, but so far, that charm hadn't yielded the results his family wanted for him. But maybe this time it would.

'So, what's your favourite route to ride?' He'd said he wanted more time to talk, so he'd better use it.

'Oh, that's a tough one.' Victoria pulled a pout. 'This one is great, but there's a lovely hill trail through the Dairvin woods if you go back into the village. It's across the bridge. There are some quite fantastic views from up there.'

'Sounds amazing.' James shifted his position. His backside was chaffing from being so often in a saddle this week. 'I don't actually know this area as well as I should. I grew up in Perth and my family moved here after I left school. Duchan Fayre was only built twelve years ago. The design was deliberate to make it look old.'

'Oh, it's wonderful. Mother adores it.'

'Happy to hear it.'

Victoria eyed him over with a smile and he forced himself to return it.

They continued along the trail at a leisurely pace. James grew easier as the time passed. Birds chirped in the trees and an occasional wood pigeon shattered the quiet with a loud flappy landing.

'You know,' Victoria said after a while, 'it's kind of nice to slow down and take everything in.'

'I'm glad you think so. There's something to be said for enjoying the moment.'

They reached the edge of the field, where the path re-entered the woods. The canopy of trees provided a cool shade. They continued at a walk, passing a few people on foot, as Victoria had predicted. James held his breath every time he stopped to let them by, praying Caspar would stay still and not bolt or get spooked.

As they neared the stables, Victoria looked over at James. 'I had a good time today. Even at a walk.'

'Me too. We should do this again sometime.' That was the plan, after all.

'I'd like that.'

James dismounted, feeling every ache and protest from his body. He wasn't used to this. He grimaced slightly as his feet touched the ground and he felt like he had a wedgie. Was there any way of adjusting it without looking totally uncouth? Victoria slid off her horse effortlessly, landing lightly beside him.

'I really enjoyed spending time with you.' Victoria stepped closer. 'I think this could be the start of something.' She gave him a little wink.

'Indeed. Let's see how it goes,' he kept his tone light. 'And we should definitely arrange another ride soon.'

Victoria's smile widened, and before James could react, she pushed onto tiptoes and kissed him on the cheek. It was quick, but it left him stunned. Ok... What the hell? He hadn't expected that.

'I'll sort the horses.' Her eyes lingered on him for a moment. 'Unless you want to stay a bit longer.'

'I should probably get back now. Will you say thank you to your parents for me?' He'd already done so before they set off, but it seemed only proper to do it again.

'Of course.' She raised her hand in a little wave, and he had a funny feeling she might try to kiss him again, so he backed away. 'Goodbye, Victoria.'

As he returned to his car, he let out a long breath. What had just happened? He started the engine. Everything had gone better than expected, but he just wasn't feeling it, and he wasn't sure how to change that.

He drove home, showered and changed, but his mind was restless. Memories of the day kept jumping up and slapping him. He cringed as he replayed the conversations about horse shows and events, and how he'd fudged his way through them.

One thing kept coming back to him. *You need more practice.* How else could he get better? By early evening, he'd wound himself up so much, he knew the only thing to do was to go to Glenvorneth and train. This was like prepping for a business takeover.

He arrived in the stable car park, not entirely sure how he'd got there. The drive was a blur. What had been a fairly decent day earlier was cloudy and a little grey. The horses were in the field, looking settled. Was this a sensible time to ride Conker? He needed to find Dagmar and ask her. Even if he couldn't ride right now, maybe she would spare him some time, so he could pick her brains about events and shows.

He checked the stables. Nothing. He sighed and turned. Maybe she was in her trailer. The evening air was cool and a little breezy.

As he neared the trailer, he spotted her sitting by a small fire pit. Her hair was loose, cascading over her shoulder. He'd rarely seen her hair out of a plait. The crimped waves still bore the markings of it. The firelight danced on her face, highlighting her features and her lithe figure in a way that made his breath catch. For a moment, he just watched her. She had on a thin white t-shirt and the ridge of her bra strap was visible on her back.

She shifted slightly, smoothing her hands over her hair, her gaze fixed on the flames. James cleared his throat, stepping closer. 'Hey.'

She looked up, and her hand leapt to her chest. 'You gave me a fright. What are you doing here?'

'I... uh, need to ask you something. Do you mind if I join you?'

'Ok.' She gave a little shrug.

He took a seat, feeling the warmth of the fire. Possibly he'd misjudged the weather and put on too many layers, but at this time of year, in late spring, it was hard to judge what to wear. He glanced at her, and for a moment he couldn't remember why he was here. Their lingering eye contact sent blood rushing to his groin. Every hot-blooded sensation he'd hoped for with Victoria had decided now was a better time to show up. 'I had a rough day.'

'Did you fall off or something?' Her eyebrows raised in the middle.

'No. The ride itself actually went pretty well, except when she wanted to gallop.'

Dagmar straightened up. 'You didn't, did you?'

'No. I managed to fob her off for now. But I'm going to have to learn. And that's not all.'

'What?'

'I need to know about events and gymkhanas and all that jazz. Most of the time, I didn't know what she was talking about.'

'What do you want to know?'

James held out his hands. 'Everything.'

Dagmar smirked and poked the fire with a stick, sending a shower of sparks into the evening air. 'Well, we haven't got time for that, but I can tell you a few of the main things she's likely to talk about. I know which events she likes. There are several disciplines. You've got dressage, which is all about precision and elegance – horse and rider performing a series of movements from memory. Then there's show jumping, where the aim is to complete a course of jumps, without knocking any down or refusing any, in the fastest time. Cross-country is jumping but over natural terrain and obstacles.'

'I've heard of them, but I've never really thought about the differences.'

'There's also eventing, which is a bit like an equestrian triathlon – it includes dressage, cross-country, and show jumping. She's into all of them. I've seen her take part in several events.'

'Like something she came second in last year. A Royal something.'

A little smile grew on Dagmar's face. 'The Royal Atholl Horse Show?'

'The very same.'

'Do you know who came first?'

'Should I?' He cocked his head.

'You're looking at her.'

James dipped his head and rubbed his brow. 'Christ, I'm slow off the mark today. Sorry. I didn't click. You must be really good.'

She gave a little shrug. A cool breeze swept over them and Dagmar wrapped her hands around herself, rubbing her arms.

'Here.' James shrugged off his sweater and handed it to her. 'Take this. I'm too hot and you look cold.'

Dagmar hesitated for a moment, then reached out and took it. 'There's no need. I've got stuff in the trailer.'

'It was to save you getting up, but it's no big deal if you don't want it.'

She draped the sweater across her shoulders with a brief nod of thanks.

'So, do you do eventing?' James leaned back on his hands.

'I do.'

'I remember Ophelia saying you were really good.' He smiled. 'I think she was jealous.'

'Ophelia is a good rider, but she doesn't put in the practise. She admits it herself.'

'Fair enough.' His eyes lingered on her. The firelight highlighted the contours of her cheeks and chin. Her face had a strong shape, but she still looked delicate, with her slender neck and round shoulders. Her thin shirt hugged her svelte shape and small perky breasts, which were really rather cute. *Fuck*. Why was he looking at them? He'd forgotten about Lady Victoria, and why he was actually here. And his mind didn't want to go anywhere else.

Chapter Twelve

Dagmar

Dagmar adjusted James's sweater around her shoulders. It smelled of his expensive cologne and she imagined falling asleep with this on. Where might her dreams take her? But dreams were the only place she could go with James. He wasn't going anywhere with her in the physical world. Nope. His path was with Lady Victoria, and every word he said cemented that thought.

'It wasn't all bad then,' she said quietly.

'It was actually ok. The riding part anyway. I mean, I didn't fall off.' James gave her a small smile. 'Though I think she liked me more than I liked her.'

'Don't you know how hard it is to find a partner if you're into horses and shows? Victoria will want someone who'll understand and support the hours, days, weeks and money that goes into horse shows. I'm lucky I can practise as part of my job. But look at what I sacrifice to make the money.' She indicated the trailer. This was how she existed to afford to live her dream.

'Victoria won't want that. She wants someone who can keep her in the style she's used to and fund her hobby.'

James nodded. 'That makes sense then. I wondered what was in it for her. But I can work with that.'

'I'm sure you can. Aren't all the ladies around here after your bank details?'

He smirked and shook his head, staring into the flames. 'It seems so, but I still haven't bribed any of them hard enough, it appears.'

'Maybe once they meet you, they decide it's not worth it.'

'Ouch.'

Dagmar gave a little snort. 'Yeah, sorry. That was uncalled for.'

'But very possibly true.' He gave her a look that told her he found this conversation amusing rather than insulting, which was good because she'd meant it more as banter than as something to upset him. It was an alien concept to her as she rarely bantered with anyone, except maybe Brann or the farrier – both of them usually instigated it and invited it.

'What about you?' he asked. 'Who can we find for you? Someone who knows their stuff about horses.'

'I'm too busy just now.' She fiddled with her hair.

James rolled up his sleeves, exposing his forearms, then unbuttoned his shirt. 'This fire is actually really warm.'

Dagmar's eyes were drawn to him. The muscles in his arms flexed as he moved. She became fixated on the rise and fall of his chest, the open collar giving her a glimpse of the skin beneath, covered in a light dusting of hair.

'You should make time for yourself.' He locked his eyes on her. 'You can't always be a slave to the horses. You're allowed some time for you.'

'Um, yeah, but I...' She avoided his gaze. She didn't want to delve into her personal life, especially not with him. 'I'm happy on my own.'

'Fair enough. I can definitely see the benefits of being single.' He gazed into the fire. 'I just... Well, miss company.'

Dagmar nodded, her eyes still on his forearms. They were well-toned and looked strong. Her focus wandered upwards. The firelight played on his skin, accentuating his sharp jaw. He'd always been a good-looking guy, even as a teenager, but as a man, he was gorgeous. What would it feel like to touch him, to feel the warmth of his skin under her fingers?

'This may sound shallow, but I miss... you know.' He gave a little shrug. 'Physical stuff as well as emotional stuff. But I don't like sleeping around. Hookups aren't my thing.'

Dagmar swallowed. Why the hell was he talking about stuff like this?

'Well, maybe Victoria will be the one to scratch that itch.' She'd heard rumours that Victoria liked to put it about a bit, but as these stories came from jealous people at horse shows, Dagmar wasn't sure she believed them, and she definitely didn't want to sully Victoria's name to James without proof or at least giving her the chance to defend herself.

He huffed out a laugh. 'Yeah, maybe. I just don't feel it. I wish I did. It was exactly the same with Ophelia. I tried. I really did.'

'If it's any consolation, I don't think she liked you either.'

James chuckled and shook his head. 'Thanks for the reminder.' He leaned back, stretching out his legs and sighing. 'How the hell did we get talking about this?'

'You started it.' She gave a little shrug.

'I wish you and I had got on better at school.'

'I didn't *not* get on with you. Or anyone. People just didn't like me.'

'I know. And I hate that. Because I missed a good friend in you. You're a good listener and you've really helped me with the lessons, even though I know you didn't want to initially. Not that I blame you. I must have been such a dick at school.'

'You were.'

'Thanks.' He cast her a wry smile. 'I occasionally tried to talk to you, but you were having none of it. And quite rightly. My friends were such twats. I can't apologise enough, but I'd like to think we could be friends now. Or maybe you still think I'm a total dick.'

'Only a partial one.'

He gave a low chuckle. 'An improvement then. I'll take it.'

She sighed, throwing him a little grin.

'Friends then?' He raised an eyebrow in her direction.

'Sure.'

Friends. Wow. She'd never really had friends, but the idea of having James as a friend was better than the alternative... Nothing. She'd never managed a romantic relationship, but maybe she could do a platonic one.

She glanced up at the sky. The clouds were thickening, and a chill crept into the air. She shivered slightly and pulled James's sweater tighter around her shoulders. The warmth from the expensive, very soft wool, combined with his lingering scent, made her a little lightheaded.

'It's getting cold.' She glanced at James. 'Maybe you should head home before it gets worse.'

He nodded, rubbing his hands together. 'Yeah, I guess. I'm sorry to have bothered you. I feel like I've wasted your time.'

'It's fine. Maybe you should do some further reading on eventing.'

He flashed her his most beautiful smile. Even without his money, it was no wonder Victoria was charmed by him. Who wouldn't be? 'I'll do that, Miss Inkenstein.'

Dagmar relaxed and allowed herself to return his smile briefly. 'Make sure you do, Charlottetown.' Why did she always feel if she gave in, she'd lost? Lost what? Her dignity? Her determination to hate him for what had happened at school? She wasn't sure, but dropping her guard and letting him in even a little bit made her heart quicken and her chest tighten, until she wasn't sure she could breathe. Maybe it had not so much to do with the actual letting him in and more to do with the aftermath. Where would things go? Or where would she like them to? Just as well he wasn't interested in her because if he was, everything she was feeling would explode.

How could she bear him finding out she'd never been with anyone all her life? Most men would either run a mile at the thought or consider themselves something special. Far easier just to keep him at arm's length and try not to let these thoughts enter her head.

Perhaps a more experienced woman would ask him to come inside and take things from there. After all, he wasn't actually dating Victoria. Not yet. But even the thought of inviting him into her cramped trailer made her uneasy. She didn't want her life laid bare before him when he already thought her mad for living like this.

'I'll see you tomorrow, then. If you want to ride, that is.' She stood up and brushed off her jeans.

James got to his feet and stretched, giving her a warm smile. 'Sure, I do. And sorry I bothered you.'

'It's fine.' Part of her didn't want him to go anywhere. How much nicer would it be if he were to stay? She didn't really do hugs. Only with her mum, but she kind of wanted one right now. From him. Wouldn't it feel good sitting here, cosied up in his arms? But that wasn't for her.

'Take care, Dagmar. And thanks.' He gave her a little pat on the arm, holding his hand there for a moment. She glanced at the spot, frowning. A desire to seize him tore through her, but she didn't dare. He raised his hand into a little wave, and she watched him walking back up the path beside the paddock. He stopped there and chatted with the horses. Conker moseyed over to see him. Sweet. They had a nice little bond going on.

Once he was out of sight, Dagmar went to the loo and brushed her teeth before heading into the trailer. As soon as she closed the door, she slumped onto the little couch and put her head in her hands. Living like this wasn't normal. It was like camping every single day. She should have a house with a proper kitchen and bathroom. A bedroom that wasn't just an extension of the seating area.

Tears pricked at the corners of her eyes. She was stuck in a rut and had no idea how to get out. If it got really bad, she could go back to living with her mum, but she liked her independence and didn't want to be a burden on her mum, who already had so many things to worry about. It was also so much further away. And she'd already discovered that she needed to be onsite all the time, or something was bound to happen when she wasn't there.

The wind rattled past the trailer, and Dagmar shivered. Cold was seeping into her bones. She needed to change into her jammies, pull out the bed and get under the covers with a hot water bottle. Once she was warm and curled up with a good book, she'd be fine. Her hand brushed something soft. James's sweater. She still had it around her shoulders. She placed it on the table and changed for bed, then set the kettle to boil. As she waited, she lifted the sweater and hugged it close for a moment, then she slipped it on over her pyjamas. It was too big, but it was warm, and it smelled like him.

She filled her hot water bottle, climbed into bed, and pulled the covers up to her chin. The sweater was a small piece of James keeping her safe. She closed her eyes and breathed it in, imagining he was lying beside her, holding her tight. His warm hands soothed over her skin and he kissed her tears away. Later, he might kiss her some more. On her lips, her neck, her shoulders, her breasts, her belly button, an even more intimate place. She moaned at the thought, her mind supplying images and partial sensations of what it might feel like. Would she ever find out for real?

The new day brought new energy. Dagmar couldn't believe she'd been such a mope the previous night. She mustn't let herself get too taken with James. Shaking off the thoughts of him, she quickly dressed and headed out to get things sorted at the stables.

The morning air was crisp and cool, the sky a clear blue promising a bright day ahead. She started with feeding the horses, each one nuzzling her for treats and attention. As she was filling the hay nets, the sound of a car pulling up caught her attention. Lots of people rode on Sunday mornings, so it was nothing unusual for cars to arrive, but her starved heart woke a fraction at the idea that it might be James. Would he arrive early, even on a Sunday? Or was he making the most of the weekend and having a lie in? She wouldn't blame him. When was the last time she'd had one of them?

'Morning, Dagmar.' Ophelia strolled into the stables, looking like a million dollars, as always.

'Hi.' Dagmar frowned. What on earth brought her here this early on a Sunday? Wasn't she enjoying a lazy morning with Brann?

'I'm really sorry to do this now, but I've been so busy I haven't had a chance to talk to you.'

Dagmar's stomach tightened. 'What about?'

'The new staff.'

'Oh,' Dagmar said. She'd temporarily forgotten about that. Maybe a little on purpose. 'I see.'

Ophelia reached out and touched her arm lightly. 'Listen, I get it. I've known you for a long time. You do a great job, and I know you like autonomy and doing things by yourself, but that really isn't an option anymore. It's too much for one person, especially with all the horses we have. I'm expecting a new arrival for the last space later today.' She let out a sigh. 'From what I've heard through the grapevine, it's a tricky horse with even trickier owners. I need to set out the ground rules firmly. But that's by the by. The important thing is to make sure we're properly staffed here. You can't do all this by yourself. I'll get pulled up by employment law if I allow it.'

Dagmar nodded, her mind racing. How could she counter that?

'Also, your trailer.'

'What about it? Do you want me to move it?' Maybe it was a bit of an eyesore.

'No, but I can offer you one of the worker's cottages now. Brann says they're all ready. I hate the thought of you living like that. I know how dedicated you are and believe me, I appreciate it. If it hadn't been for you, this place would have died a slow and painful death in the years I was away.'

'I'm not sure I can afford a cottage, and they're too far from the field. I won't be able to see everything.'

'But that's ok. You don't have to be here all the time. If we have another member of staff, you can work proper shifts, take time off. If there's an emergency when you're not here, I'll be around, and so will Barbara. She's in the estate office most days, and I'm here most evenings. There will always be people around, and Brann is going to arrange for CCTV to be installed. It's different from how it was before I came back. We've got the estate working again. You've been a big part of that, but I don't want you to feel the burden of being solely responsible for the horses.'

Dagmar glanced away and bit her lip. Sometimes it was a burden. She couldn't deny it, but it had been her life for so long.

'And as for paying for a cottage, I wouldn't expect it. I never did,' Ophelia said. 'It would all be part of the deal; I thought I'd said that before.'

Dagmar wasn't sure that she had, or maybe Dagmar just hadn't listened – or simply heard what she wanted to hear.

'We need to negotiate and find something that works for both of us,' Ophelia went on. 'When I interview new staff, you'll be with me, and we won't hire anyone unless it's someone you agree on. We'll find someone who respects your methods and works under your guidance. You'll still be in control.'

Dagmar sighed, blinking away errant tears. Why was she so emotional these past few days? 'Ok.' What else could she say? But everything was changing, and it felt like a landslide ready to wash her away.

'Hey.' Ophelia put her hand on Dagmar's arm. 'Why don't we grab a coffee or something? We can chat, not about work, unless that's what you want. I feel like we never get a moment to speak properly.'

Dagmar finally met Ophelia's eyes. 'Ok.'

'Great.' Ophelia led the way into the little office and put on the kettle. 'Let me know about the cottage. There's no rush, but I think you'll like it. It'll be a lot more comfortable than the trailer.'

No doubt it would, and wasn't that exactly what she'd wished for last night?

'How's James getting on with his riding?' Ophelia poured boiling water into two mugs.

'Oh... He's pretty good actually.'

'Amazing.' Ophelia handed Dagmar a mug. 'I heard an interesting rumour about him.'

'Did you?'

'Yes. Apparently, he and Lady Victoria Bruce are an item.' She sipped on her coffee. 'Honestly, James is a nice guy. I like him, though I never wanted there to be anything between us. I tried to make that scenario work, but he just wasn't for me. But now I hear about him chasing Victoria, it makes me wonder about him. And his family. They're chasing status, even though they have more money than the earl.'

'I imagine Victoria would like someone with a lot of money.'

'You're not wrong. But get this, I've heard he's not the only man she's got her sights on. I heard she's keeping her options open and that she's got her eye on some banker from London.'

That didn't surprise Dagmar in the least. But was James aware?

'Not sure if James knows he has competition.' Ophelia's words echoed Dagmar's thoughts.

'I'm sure he'll find someone else.' Dagmar sipped her coffee. With his money and charm, he'd have no trouble. 'He attracts people like that.'

'Yeah, people who have families like me – and Victoria. For long enough, I thought I'd have to marry someone for their money. A sad thought in this day and age.'

'What changed your mind?'

'Brann.' She let out a little laugh. 'He was the one that...' She looked away and her cheeks glowed pink. 'It sounds clichéd, but he was the one who set my world on fire. Every time he came near me, I wanted to murder him. Until I realised that wasn't what I wanted to do at all. I hated the fact I couldn't have him, not *him*. Once I sorted that out, I knew I had to find a way, because I didn't want to live without him.'

'That's so nice.' Dagmar cradled her mug. She'd never had anyone set her world on fire. Maybe she wasn't flammable. Her mind wandered back to James – unsurprisingly. He definitely affected her, but was that just because he was, as Ophelia had observed, a nice man? And Dagmar was so unused to men paying her any attention that when one did, she read more into it. But when she'd had his sweater on last night, she'd felt more – on her part at least. An awakening desire.

What to do about it?

Ophelia looked out the window at the sound of voices in the yard. 'It's Kristi and Caitlin. I should go out and see them. Brann's got some stuff he wants Caitlin to look at. If she's got a minute, I'll run her up to the house to have a look.'

Dagmar followed her out, as it seemed silly staying in the office on her own when she had other jobs to be doing. She watched Ophelia greet Kristi and Caitlin and laugh with them. The dynamics of this relationship intrigued Dagmar so much. Neither Kristi nor Ophelia seemed to dislike the other, despite the fact that Ophelia was now with Kristi's ex. They were so unlike how exes and new girlfriends were portrayed in books and on TV.

Ophelia and Caitlin hurried off towards the car park and Kristi ambled over to Dagmar, who was still clutching her mug.

'Hey.' Kristi ran her nails through her long red hair. 'How are you getting on?'

'Not bad.'

'Well, whatever you do with Caitlin, it's working. She loves coming here. She talks about it all the time. If she was just a little older, I'd love her to go for the job. I know Ophelia wants someone with experience, but she'd learn, and she's enthusiastic.'

'She'd actually be ideal.' Dagmar drained her coffee, more for something to do than because she actually wanted it. 'I'd prefer someone I can train over someone who has their own ways. I wouldn't want to clash with someone.'

'Makes sense,' Kristi said. 'But she's only sixteen, though she'll be seventeen later in the year.'

Dagmar raised an eyebrow. 'About the same age I was when I first started working here.'

'Really?'

'Yup.'

Kristi frowned and shook her head. 'And who trained you? Or did you learn all this yourself?'

Dagmar let out a sigh. 'I had lessons when I was young, and latterly I taught myself. I also did an Open University course, but there was a stable manager here before me who knew loads and I learned a lot from her. She couldn't stand Jacinta though – you know, Ophelia's stepmother – so she left.'

'Oh her. I get that. She's an odd one.'

'Yeah, she can be a strange lady sometimes, though she doesn't come up here anything like as much as she used to.'

'Probably scared of Ophelia.' Kristi grinned. 'She's a lovely person, but she can be a bit terrifying.'

Dagmar smiled, and it almost came out as a laugh. Coming from a woman who looked like a goth rockstar it was quite amusing to think she found Ophelia terrifying, though Dagmar knew exactly what she meant.

'How's it going with the man you didn't want to give lessons to? Did you ever sort that out?' Kristi asked.

'Yeah. He's getting the lessons.'

Kristi folded her arms and raised her very dark eyebrow over her heavily pencilled eyes. She had a proper don't-cross-me look that made Dagmar draw back – just as well Kristi and Ophelia got on well; they could both be intimidating in their own way. 'I hope he's treating you nicely. I remember you saying he'd been a dick at school.'

'He seems a bit better, thanks.'

'I'm glad to hear it. Just don't take any shit from him. And did you find out why he wanted lessons?'

She gave a little shrug. 'Just interested in improving, I think.'

'Well, I'm glad it's worked out.' Kristi gave her a pat on the arm. 'You looked a bit sad the last time I saw you.'

Dagmar bobbed her head a little. 'Yeah.' Even now, her heart ached. She ignored it for the most part, but it was always there, and recently that pain had escalated from dull ache to sharp twinges. And it all seemed to coincide with James Charlton returning to her life.

CHAPTER THIRTEEN

James

James pulled into the stable car park and narrowed his eyes. Something was off. Instead of the usual Sunday afternoon calm, people were rushing about, shouting to one another and talking in hurried voices.

He closed the window, got out of his car and searched around for someone he recognised. A woman with bright red-hair, heavy eye make-up, and an array of piercings caught his gaze. He'd seen her here before, though this time she looked a little worried. She held a hand to her forehead, scanning around.

'Excuse me.' James approached her. 'Has something happened? Why is everyone—'

'A new horse arrived, but it bolted before they could even get it in the field. People have gone out looking for it and things have got crazy.'

James frowned. 'Is it dangerous?'

'I hope not. I'm not sure how they're going to catch it though.'

'Are they planning on ambushing it or something?'

'No idea. Dagmar went with Francesca and Caitlin to the bridle path, and Ophelia and Brann took the car to the far end of the woods, thinking they might head it off. It ran that way. But it could be anywhere really. The owners panicked and ran after it, but I think that made it worse. Then other people went off to help and everyone up here isn't sure what to do for best.'

'I'll walk towards the woods and see if I can see him,' James said. 'What colour is it?'

'Dark brown. He's called Stroman. I wouldn't approach him on your own.'

'I won't. If I see him, I'll call Ophelia.'

He headed around the field to the bridle path where a few other groups of chattering people were also striding down. At the bottom, instead of turning towards Dagmar's trailer, he took the path into the woods.

The trees loomed ahead, and it wasn't quiet or still today. Voices ahead sounded eager. Someone was shouting. 'Stroman!'

Even a horse novice like him knew that was the worst thing to do. If the horse wanted to be found that easily, its owners would already have tried that.

Surely the horse wouldn't be on the path. And with this many people, it was more likely to be miles away, seeking peace. A smaller path cut off deeper into the woods. It probably wasn't even a path, more like a deer track. James veered onto it, venturing deeper into the woods. He wasn't into this kind of outdoor thing, never had been, but he'd feel crap not at least trying to help.

The horse wasn't likely to be anywhere here, but he kept his eyes peeled anyway. How would he know if it had been found? He wasn't sure he had Dagmar's number. Last year, he'd had Ophelia's, and he was pretty certain he hadn't deleted it. Pulling out his phone, he went to check as he waded through the undergrowth. The track was slowly being engulfed by thick bracken.

A sudden rustling to his left made him freeze. Then he felt a sharp tug on his back. Someone had grabbed hold of him. Before he could speak, a hand slapped over his mouth. *What the fuck?* Was he being abducted?

He turned his head as much as he could within the grip hold to see Dagmar. She yanked him in behind a tree, mouthing, 'Be quiet.'

When she let him go, he frowned. 'What was that for?'

She put her hand to her lips and pointed through the tree branches. James moved closer behind her to follow her sightline. He peered through the branches. Stroman was just ahead, standing in a small clearing. The horse's ears flicked back and forth, muscles tense and ready to bolt. His owner, a tall man with a weathered face, approached cautiously, speaking softly.

'Easy, boy. Easy.' The owner inched closer.

James held his breath, unconsciously drawing closer to Dagmar, so he was right behind her, his nose level with her sweet-smelling hair. The owner reached Stroman and put out his hand, but Stroman's head shot up, eyes wide. With a snort, he turned and bolted straight towards James and Dagmar.

'Move!' James grabbed her arm, pulling her to the side. They stumbled as Stroman came straight for them. Dagmar let out a little gasp, lost her balance, and tripped backwards over a fallen branch. James, still holding her arm, was dragged down with her. They tumbled into the bushes.

Stroman veered off, galloping away into the woods. His owners yelled, bolting after him.

James landed on top of Dagmar in a bed of bracken. *Shit*. This was not where he needed to be.

'Are you ok?' he struggled to move himself off her, ending up on his knees before he pushed himself to his feet.

Dagmar was now sitting on the ground, brushing leaves from her jacket. 'Fine, you?'

'I think so. Sorry, I didn't mean to—'

'It's ok.' She didn't meet his eyes. 'We should go after them.'

'Yeah, sure.'

'What are you doing here anyway?' She looked up, frowning at him.

'I heard what was going on and I came out to help.'

She sighed and put her head in her hands. 'This is such a shitshow. There are too many people out shouting and moving around. It's just going to freak him even more.'

'Yeah... I did wonder.'

'I'm not sure Glenvorneth is the right place for him. He needs a lot of work. If he doesn't get on with other horses, then a busy livery like this will be a living hell for him.'

'Is there nowhere else he can go? A solitary field or something?'

'We were planning to fence him off from the others, but if he's this bad, he'll be constantly stressed and that can affect the other horses. I don't ever want to exclude a horse for any reason, but I can see this one being a whole lot of trouble. He needs intensive training and therapy. I just don't have the time.'

James crouched on the ground beside her. 'It isn't your job to do that though.'

'No, but I'll want to. It feels like my responsibility to make sure all the horses are safe and happy. And if he escapes again, I'll be called out to help.'

'Assuming they catch him.'

'Yeah.' She shook her head, flicking some stray strands of hair. Bits of bracken and twigs were still tangled in it.

One twig at the back was stuck, and she struggled to get it out.

'Watch,' he said. 'You'll pull half your hair out doing that. Let me. I can see it.'

With a brief hesitation, she turned the back of her head to him.

He reached out and untangled the stick, then tossed it away. She faced him again, running her fingers through the strands that had escaped her plait. His eyes met hers and she looked like the proverbial rabbit in the headlights. Was she just worried about the situation, or was it him? Maybe she'd always be wary of him after their school days. Did she think he'd hurt her now? He'd never do that. At school, he hadn't meant to either. Sure, he'd never succeeded in stopping people from saying things, but he hadn't taken part or condoned the behaviour. When he'd tried to talk to her, she'd always run off in the other direction. It looked like she wanted to do that now.

'I'm sorry,' he said.

'What for?'

'Just everything. I see the look on your face whenever I'm nearby.'

She blinked and frowned, shaking her head a little like she didn't really understand him.

'I know how much I hurt you at school. I swear I never wanted to be part of it, but I know I didn't do enough.'

'It isn't that. I mean, obviously I hated those days, but you weren't the worst by a long stretch. And... Well, you seem ok now.'

He let out a half laugh and ruffed up his hair. 'Thanks. I think. But if it's not that, then what? I didn't mean to land on top of you, and if that seemed inappropriate, I'm truly sorry. It definitely wasn't intentional.'

'Really. It's fine. I'm just worried about Stroman. We should go and help.'

'Sure.' He got to his feet and instinctively made to help Dagmar, but he stopped himself. She was managing fine and no matter what she may say, her eyes told a different story. Something was off – like a brick wall between them. And although he'd maybe chipped a few bricks around the edges, he couldn't get any closer. Did that matter? It wasn't like he should want to get close to her – but he did. And more than just friends. Something about her attracted him and he couldn't stop the pull.

'I'm really worried,' she said as they trudged through the undergrowth. 'I wish I could have stopped them from bringing Stroman here. He's obviously had some trauma in his past that makes him dislike the company of other horses, so he needs to be eased in gradually. Like with one or two sociable horses to start off with. This is too busy a place for him to start in. But they arranged it all with Ophelia and I only found out when it was too late.'

'I never realised horses could be so complicated.'

'Of course they are. Just like dogs, cats, people. They have their own personalities.'

James side-eyed her. Maybe Dagmar was a little like Stroman. She needed to be eased into things gradually. After all, she'd had a lot of trauma in her life.

'So, will it be possible to catch him?'

'I hope so, but we really need a plan and for everyone to work together, but the owners are in such a state. Now we don't even know where he is. If we see him, a couple of us should stand on either side, one deterring him from going forward and the other from going back, but we need to stay far enough away not to increase his stress. If treats are part of his training tools, that can help. But I don't know if he's been trained that way.'

'I think whatever happens here, you've got a strong case, either to have Stroman moved somewhere more suitable or to make sure he gets better trained.'

'I can help the owners with that, but I won't have time to carry out the training myself.'

'Isn't there someone who can help you?'

'Ophelia wants to hire someone else, but—' Dagmar threw out her arm to stop James. She pointed, and through the branches, James saw Stroman again, standing in a small clearing. Ophelia and Brann were approaching cautiously from opposite sides, trying to herd the horse back towards his owners, who were hovering at the edge of the clearing, out of breath and red-faced.

'Ophelia knows what to do,' Dagmar whispered. 'We worked with a tricky horse years ago.'

'What should we do?' James asked.

'We need to move closer but stay low and out of Stroman's immediate line of sight.'

Ophelia and Brann were positioned towards Stroman's rear, gently moving him forward.

'His flight zone is large, so if we can form a kind of circle around him.'

'Ok. Let's do it.'

Every step closer made Stroman twitch and take a few steps back. James didn't like to say how twisted his insides felt. He wasn't just stepping out of his comfort zone; he was whizzing like a baseball, getting knocked out of the park.

'Let's get on either side to guide him,' Dagmar hissed, waving him forward.

They split, James inching to the right while Dagmar went to the left. Ophelia and Brann noticed them, and Ophelia gave a slight nod before turning her attention back to Stroman. The horse lowered his head. Was that a good sign?

'Easy, boy. Easy.' The owner stepped forward with the head collar in hand.

James watched as Dagmar shifted her weight, gently influencing Stroman's movement. Ophelia mirrored her on the other side, creating a soft barrier that guided Stroman forward without making him feel trapped. Brann held his position at the back, ensuring Stroman didn't bolt in that direction. James inched in, mimicking the others' slow movements, painfully aware he had no clue what he was actually doing.

He held his breath as Stroman's owner finally got close enough to slip the head collar over his nose. 'Good boy.' He secured the strap with a shaky hand.

'Back off a bit,' Dagmar said. 'Let them lead him back but stay close enough in case he spooks again.'

James followed her lead, retreating a few steps and giving Stroman the space he needed. Ophelia and Brann did the same on the other side. James saw Brann hooking his arm over her shoulder, and Ophelia sagging with relief. James would have done the same to Dagmar, but she'd likely throw him off – much like Stroman. She needed gentle handling and a slow approach.

But he shouldn't be thinking about that. His job was to find a way to Lady Victoria's heart – not Dagmar's.

The horse's ears flicked back and forth, but he seemed calmer now that his owner had control. Slowly, they all began to move, guiding Stroman towards the field. The owner led, whispering soothing words to the nervous horse.

Brann had stayed behind and was talking to the other owner, who looked like she was crying. *Rather him than me.*

'We should keep to the sides,' Dagmar told James quietly. 'That way, if he tries to bolt, we can attempt to steer him back.'

They continued through the woods, James staying on Stroman's right and Dagmar on his left, keeping a careful eye on the horse's movements. Ophelia was closer, on the other side from the owner.

Dagmar was on her phone and when the field came into sight, he saw one of the stable girls holding the gate open. The owner led Stroman into the paddock with the jumps. He assumed that wasn't where they were planning on keeping him, but it was the closest option. When the girl shut the gate and bolted it, James let out his breath and made his way over to Dagmar.

'Wow, that was something.'

Dagmar exhaled long and slow. 'I need to speak to Ophelia and see what she wants to do.'

'Listen.' James took her wrist and held her back, letting go immediately at the look on her face. 'I guess this isn't an appropriate time for a lesson now, and it's probably an even worse time to talk, but... I need to ask you something.'

'What?' She narrowed her eyes.

'We agreed to be friends, but...' He ran his hands through his hair. The midges were awful. 'Well, apart from what happened at school, are you angry with me about something else?'

She shook her head. 'No.'

'Good. And listen, I'm sorry if I haven't made enough progress with helping your mum with the café. I haven't forgotten. I've spoken to Henry, the finance manager, and he's all for the idea. But I need to meet with your mum, so we can chat about the road forward and I can find out exactly what she needs and give her some timelines.' Christ, he always sounded like such a dull businessman.

'That would be good.' Dagmar gave him a small smile, then pulled out her phone. 'How about I give you my number and you can call me?'

'Great.'

She sucked on her lip as she opened her phone, and it looked like she was oddly pleased about something.

'I'll call you if you know your number,' she said.

James recited it, and she called it. He took out his phone and silenced the call. 'There. We're connected.' He caught her eye, and her cheeks reddened a little. It was very cute. 'Do you need any more help with Stroman?'

'Not unless you've become a horse expert in the last five minutes.'

Shaking his head, he winked. 'Definitely not compared to you.' He gave her a little pat on the upper arm. 'I leave him with the pros. And I'll message you.' For a moment, he kept eye contact and a powerful urge to lean in and kiss her surged up in him, but he pushed it away and made his way back to his car.

Once inside, he didn't start the engine, but sat for a moment, refocusing his breathing, mulling over the day's events. All very dramatic. And yet, the only thing he could really keep in his mind was the image of Dagmar's smile and the swooping sensation it caused in his gut every time he recalled it.

CHAPTER FOURTEEN

Dagmar

Stroman was still skittish, his ears flicking, but he wasn't running. Dagmar approached Ophelia, who was at the fence by the paddock, talking to Caitlin.

'Hey,' Dagmar said to announce her arrival. She always hated butting in, but Ophelia turned and smiled.

'Oh god.' She let out a sigh and patted Dagmar on the upper arm. 'I'm so glad you turned up when you did. I wasn't sure I was doing the right thing, and Brann doesn't have a clue about horses. He was just doing what he could. Thank goodness he's sensible.'

'Dad? Sensible?' Caitlin sniggered and Ophelia nudged her.

'Most of the time,' Ophelia added. 'And definitely in situations like that. What do you think we should do now?' She turned her attention back to Stroman.

'We need to give him some time to calm down. After that, maybe his owners can try leading him around the paddock, get him used to the space before they try to get him inside.'

Ophelia nodded. 'Makes sense. He's been through a lot today.'

'But I'm not sure what's best in the long run. We don't want to risk this happening again. We should probably try to find out more about him from the owners and come up with a plan, because this is going to take time and work. It's not something that can be left to us. The owners will need to be involved. They should be the ones doing most of the work, as they're the ones who need the relationship with him.'

'Yeah, all good points.' Ophelia let out a sigh. 'He seems ok with Maurice just now, so there's clearly a bond of some sort.'

'If he's easily stressed, this whole move was probably tricky for him.'

Ophelia rubbed her hands together. 'Ok. When Brann comes back with Avril, we should have a word with her and Maurice. We'll see where that goes. I still need to get together with you so we can discuss advertising the post here.'

Dagmar's insides lurched; she'd been deliberately putting that off as long as possible.

'But now's not the time.' Ophelia glanced at her. 'I saw James helping too. Has he gone?'

'Yes. He left.'

'How's he getting on with his refresher lessons?'

Dagmar's heart skipped a beat. 'Um... good.'

'Great.' Ophelia smiled and raised an eyebrow. 'Has he said anything else about why he really wants to learn to ride?'

'Erm... No.'

'Oh, well.' Ophelia brushed a lock of hair behind her ear. 'I guess if he is doing it to impress Victoria, we'll see for ourselves at the horse trials.'

'I guess.' Dagmar's cheeks heated. Of course, Victoria would want him there. Dagmar would be there too, as would Ophelia. It might turn into quite a spectacle. But even so, the thought of seeing James again brought that warming sensation to her chest. She could still feel the tingle on her skin from where he'd placed a hand on her arm, see his intense gaze, and the way he looked at her. Why *did* he look at her like that?

Her phone buzzed in her pocket. She withdrew it and saw a new message from James. Her insides danced, but she had to keep it hidden. Ophelia didn't need to see her fangirling over him.

'We should suggest to Stroman's owners that we keep him separate for now, maybe try some desensitisation techniques. Gradual exposure to the other horses, starting with the calmest ones.'

'Yes, let's do that,' Ophelia said. 'They might need to bring in a specialist trainer. Maybe if they're up for discussing it just now, you and I could sit down with them and make a long-term plan.'

'Sure. We should do it as soon as possible.'

Ophelia put a hand on her shoulder. 'Thank you. You're so great with the horses. I really appreciate having you here.'

'Thanks.' Dagmar was always surprised when Ophelia was so nice to her, even though she'd never been anything but. Dagmar just expected Ophelia not to like her, but maybe she'd missed a friend here all these years.

'Let's see what they say. Here's Brann and Avril. Let me see if she's ok.' Ophelia headed off. Caitlin was watching her.

'Do you think I could do the job here?' she asked. 'I want to, but it would mean leaving school. Dad thinks I should stay on and do exams, but this is what I want to do.'

'I think you'd be really good, but it's not up to me. And if your dad's against it, Ophelia won't employ you. She won't want to upset him.'

'I dunno.' Caitlin watched her dad and Ophelia talking to Avril. 'She's not exactly a pushover, is she? And she likes her own way. I think if I could convince her to take me on, she might talk dad into it.'

'Well, you could try. I started here when I was young, and I learned as I went along. You could definitely do that, but you'd be best to sit your exams first. You've already learned a lot in a short time, but it would be best for you to do vocational training in equine husbandry and horse care. I did that while I worked here.'

'I'll speak to mum and dad and see what they think.'

'No matter what you decide, you should do your exams first. They'll be starting soon, won't they?'

'Yeah, next week.' Caitlin pulled a face.

'Well, concentrate on doing your best in them. You'll be in a better position for the job if you at least have some qualifications.'

Dagmar watched Stroman as he started to nibble at the grass near the fence. Her eyes returned to her phone, and she opened James's message, her heart beating just a bit faster. He'd put a list of times and dates he was available to visit the café. A date with James Charlton? She smirked. Ok, so it wasn't really a date, but it felt a bit like one. Her teenage self had craved a moment like this and now it was here... Except nothing that happened on it was likely to fulfil her fantasies – either past or present.

Dagmar wiped down the counter for the third time, her nerves making her hands fidgety. She'd never worked in a café, but she could see herself getting obsessed with getting every last mark off the tables. These old wooden things were so scratched and worn however, that she was possibly just removing the varnish.

The café was closed, the chairs neatly stacked on the tables, and Dagmar checked the clock for the hundredth time. Four thirty. Friday had come around like lightning after the drama with Stroman at the weekend. His owners had agreed to the plan for his integration and were taking it in turns to work with him. That was a relief. This meeting wasn't.

Dotty was in the back, making a new batch of pastries. The smell was delicious, but Dagmar could sense her mum's anxiety, and it was doing nothing to quell her own. Why should her mum trust James? She remembered him as a cheeky little boy who once stole Dagmar's Schleich horse. How could Dagmar convince her he'd changed? Did she believe it herself? He'd apologised, and his actions seemed to indicate that he had. But trusting him wasn't coming easily.

'Mum, do you need any help?' Dagmar asked.

Dotty poked her head out from the kitchen. 'No, love, I've got it. Is there any sign of the lad yet?'

Dagmar forced a smile. 'Not yet.'

'I'm not going to deny I'm nervous about meeting him. Are you sure he's trustworthy?'

'He's been a lot nicer than he used to be.'

'I don't understand what he's getting out of this. Why is he bothering to help us?'

'Because I'm giving him riding lessons.'

'But he's paying for them, isn't he?'

'Yes, but he knew I wouldn't want to do it. I suppose this is his goodwill gesture, and it's part of some community drive that Duchan Fayre is doing.'

'Hmm. So, it's a publicity stunt for him really.'

'Possibly. But if it helps, does that matter?' Dagmar moved around the counter and hugged her mum. 'If you get a bad vibe or don't trust him, we don't have to agree to anything.'

'Ok, darling. That's sensible.'

A thud on the glass pane on the door made them both start. Dagmar's heart skipped a beat as she turned to see James waving through the glass.

'Oh lord.' Dotty fiddled with the collar of her shirt. 'He's grown up handsome.'

'Shh,' Dagmar hissed, rushing to the door and opening it. 'Hi.'

'Hey.' James smiled, and for a moment, the tension in her chest eased. He looked around the café. 'This place is cute.'

'Thanks.' She sucked on her lower lip. Her mum had a point. James was very easy on the eye. He'd obviously come from work, and, in his shirt and suit, he looked smoking hot. 'Come in.'

He made his way in, and Dotty came around the counter. 'Well, James,' she said. 'It's been a long time. I haven't seen you since the two of you were at primary school together. You won't remember me.'

James shook her hand. 'Of course I do. You haven't changed a bit. Hopefully, I've grown a little since you last saw me.'

'Oh dear,' Dotty replied with a chuckle. 'I'm sure my hair is a hundred per cent greyer than it was back then. Now, why don't you two sit down and have a chat? I'll bring out some pastries.'

Dagmar watched her mum bustle off. So much for being nervous. Her mum had given into the Charlton charm without any resistance. James took a seat at a table near the window. Before Dagmar could sit down, Dotty called her and handed her some cutlery.

'He seems very nice,' she whispered. 'I can usually tell.' She made her way over to where James was sitting without letting Dagmar reply, then she sat in the outside seat on the opposite side to James, which meant the only seat Dagmar could get into was the one right next to him as her mum was blocking the one opposite. Why did she get the feeling her mum was doing it on purpose?

Feeling stupidly awkward, Dagmar took the seat next to James. He was leaning his elbow on the back of the chair, his chest open to her. His top two buttons were undone, and a wedge of bare skin was visible beneath. Dagmar tried not to look at him as she sat, but his expensive fragrance threatened to overpower her. The warmth of his presence beside her made her both comforted and anxious at the same time and she didn't know where to focus.

Dotty got up almost as soon as Dagmar sat. 'I'll just grab a tray of pastries and some coffee.'

Dagmar slowly turned her gaze to James. He was smiling at her and her insides wobbled so much it was like they'd rearranged themselves.

'Have you had a good day?' he asked.

'Yes, it was ok.'

'How's Stroman getting on?'

'Slightly better. Every day he seems a little more confident.'

'That's great. Little steps.' His smile was wide, and he very subtly dropped his focus from her eyes to her lips. Dagmar froze. What the hell?

'Here you go.' Dotty placed a tray in front of them, then took her seat. 'Now, tell me, James. Why are you offering to help us? It's bothering me. Why us?'

James took a bite of a pastry and smiled. 'These are delicious, Mrs Ingenfeld.'

'Call me Dotty.' She waved her hand. 'I'm not a Mrs as I never had a husband. Dagmar's father was, well, not a nice man. And we were never married. I never wanted to be married after that.'

Dagmar sipped her coffee, hoping her mum wouldn't say anything else. She'd never met the man who'd got her mum pregnant. Dagmar couldn't even think of him as her father. Her mum wouldn't tell her the whole story, but from what she had said, it sounded like the man had pressured her into unprotected sex, and then left her when she got pregnant. Maybe that was a factor in Dagmar clinging to her celibate life. She'd grown up believing men were never trustworthy, and even now, she wasn't sure she trusted James. She wanted to, but it was difficult. And James hadn't answered her mother's question, which set her on edge.

'Why do I want to help you?' He placed his remaining pastry on the plate and dusted the corner of his lip.

So, he was going to answer it, was he?

'Well, there are a few reasons. I really need the riding lessons. And I know Dagmar didn't want to teach me, because of things that happened at school.'

'Like you stealing her Schleich horse?' Dotty raised an eyebrow.

'What?' He frowned at her, then glanced at Dagmar. 'Um...
ok, that. And, well, I needed to make it up to her somehow. I read
the post you put on social media and instantly thought it was
exactly the type of project that would qualify for our community fund. It seemed like the perfect opportunity and something
that could be mutually beneficial. You're looking for an investor.
Here I am.'

'Well, that really is very kind, and it'll definitely make up for
that horse. But I'll feel we're always in your debt.'

'Not at all. Once the riding lessons are done, then we're quits.
You might be asked to do a couple of photoshoots and articles for
Duchan's publicity campaigns, but it won't be taxing or detrimental. In fact, it'll be something that gives as much exposure to
you as it does for us.'

'And what exactly can you do? The landlord wants me out of
here.'

'We have a few options. If you can negotiate an extension
on the lease, the fund could be used to upgrade the equipment
and redecorate. Depending on the asking price for the building,
the fund might stretch to purchasing it. Or we could look into
finding a different location for the café.'

'I see.' Dotty glanced at Dagmar, who guessed what her mum
was thinking.

The way he spoke about business was always so casual, like it
was just a little thing. Maybe to him it was. He could fork out a
hundred thousand pounds for a building, just like that.

'I need to clear it with finance and my parents first, but I don't see there being a problem. They already provisionally said it was fine, and this is what the fund is for.'

Dotty smiled. 'It sounds almost too good to be true.'

James lifted his pastry again and Dagmar took another sip of coffee.

'Might I get a picture of the two of you?' Dotty said. 'Not to post it anywhere. Just for my own memory. This is something I want to remember.'

'Sure,' James said.

Dagmar looked up from her coffee. She hated having her picture taken. Beside her, James had on his kilowatt smile and looked like he could be on the front cover of a business magazine.

'Come on, Dagmar.' Her mum held up her phone. 'Give me a little smile.'

Dagmar tried.

'James, lean in a bit so I can get the two of you.'

Heat flared in Dagmar's cheeks. 'Mum, that's not necessary...'

James put his arm along the back of the seat, close to Dagmar's shoulders. The heat of him and the strength of his arm sent a shiver down her spine. She tried to relax, hyperaware of his proximity. His cheek was almost touching hers. And he smelt divine. An overpowering urge to kiss him slammed through her at a hundred miles an hour. She'd never felt anything like it.

'Perfect.' Dotty snapped the picture and looked at it. 'Oh, you both look so gorgeous.'

James sat back, still smiling.

'Gorgeous?' Dagmar scoffed. 'Not me. Look at me next to Ophelia and you won't think that.'

'Of course I will.' Dotty got to her feet, lifting the empty cups and plates. 'You're my daughter. To me, you are the most beautiful person in the world.'

'And you don't need to be beautiful like Ophelia,' James added as Dotty disappeared through the kitchen door. 'You're beautiful as you.'

The heat in her face could now rival molten lava. Did he mean that? Or was he just being nice... And if so, why? *Christ*. Talk about confusing. She couldn't look at him. 'Thanks.'

He gave her a little pat on the arm and said quietly, 'I'm not sure what you see when you look in the mirror, but I don't think it's the same as what everyone else sees.'

Dotty returned to the table and took up her seat. 'This building has been a curse. Honestly, there has been so much wrong with it. My house is the same, though it has a lovely location.'

'Location is important, though it doesn't always work out.' James pulled a face. 'I bought a plot at the end of Loch Briar, some time ago. Thought it would be perfect, but I kind of regret it now. It's too close to town for the kind of house I want. The views are stunning, but I'm not sure if that's enough to make me build the house.'

'Ah, shame,' Dotty said. 'I'm sure you'll find the right place eventually.'

James smiled. 'Yes, I'm sure I will.' He checked the time on his phone. 'Ladies, I should go. I'm dining with my parents tonight. They want to go over the campaign.'

Dagmar frowned at him. 'Campaign?'

'On what we're going to say to you-know-who at the horse trials to move things along.' He pulled a face and sighed.

Dotty shook her head, and Dagmar shot her a look, warning her not to say anything, as she wasn't supposed to have told her about Victoria in the first place.

James pushed his chair back, and Dagmar stood up to let him out. 'I'll see you there.' He smiled at Dagmar. 'Wish me luck.'

'Good luck.' She held her breath as he passed her, sensing that he might kiss her cheek or something, but he didn't. Her mind wanted to retract the good luck she'd just wished him and replace it with a hope that Victoria would find someone else – maybe the rich banker Ophelia had spoken about. Dagmar hated the thought of James being with Victoria. Could she avoid seeing them together as she'd be there too? The way she'd avoided seeing him with Ophelia at the Highland Games last year?

'Bye-bye and thank you,' Dotty said.

James gave them a final smile and left. Dagmar watched him go, then turned to her mum and realised she was peering at her with a curious expression.

'Do you think he and Victoria will be a good match?' Dotty pulled a face.

Dagmar nodded. 'No doubt.' But her heart crumbled and fell apart like flaky pastry. *Why can't it be me?*

Chapter Fifteen

James

James adjusted his tie, trying to steady his nerves as he and his parents walked through the grounds of Dairvin Castle. Hundreds of spectators, riders, horses, and food trailers had converged on the sedate gardens he'd seen a few weeks ago. This event was a lot bigger than he'd made it in his head. By the side of one of the large fields were small grandstands and marquees.

'Looking sharp, son.' Laurence clapped him on the shoulder. 'What woman could resist?'

James restrained his eye roll. Plenty had so far, but the first meeting with Victoria had gone well and hopefully he could build on that. Or so he kept telling himself, because his heart seemed to have other ideas. It ached away constantly in his chest and the only times it seemed to feel ok was when he was with Dagmar. He'd developed a fixation with her. Maybe it was the forbidden nature of it that drew him, because whichever way he swung it, he couldn't be with her. His destiny lay along a different path; he'd promised his father he'd do whatever he could to marry into a family with a name and a legacy. Victoria might be the best chance he ever got. And, really, did Dagmar even want him anyway? The way she recoiled every time he got close told him she would never forgive him for his childhood sins.

'This is wonderfully laid out.' Sherri looked around. 'We should sponsor it next time. I'd love to see Duchan Fayre banners around the arena.'

'Cool, great idea, Mum.' James patted her on the back. Just a quick glance around showed several people who would love Duchan's country clothing range and probably spend a packet in the restaurant while they decided which pieces to buy.

James and his parents made their way through the crowd, James fidgeting with his cuffs. May was a warm month in Scotland and the sun was beating down, which made his suit feel too hot and stifling. The grandstand loomed ahead; it was nothing like the size of the ones at the Open Golf Championship – which he often attended with his golf club friends – but was still quite something. Alongside it was a smaller stand, covered over and decorated with flowers, bunting and drapes. So ostentatious. That must be the earl's box. It was like something from Royal Ascot or Wimbledon.

'Do we just go up?' Sherri tugged at the neckline of her bright pink top.

'I think so.' Laurence headed for the steps. 'They invited us, and we have tickets. I see someone at the gate.' He marched forward and a woman in a hi-vis vest checked his tickets, then opened the gate to the steps.

Laurence went first, almost running. Was he that eager? James wasn't. He followed with his mum. Now he was here, he wasn't sure he really wanted to be. This would be another tedious afternoon of questions, his parents trying to big him up in the eyes of the earl and countess, and him attempting to make small talk with Victoria. Somehow that small talk was supposed to lead to more, but the steps in between weren't clear. It was hard when he wasn't feeling it. This was what had happened with Genevieve, his ex. They'd felt nothing for each other, but they'd both been in the same predicament, so faking it for a while had worked well. Faking anything with Victoria, however, was not going to work – because he needed this for the long term.

The earl and the countess sat leaning forward, watching a rider. Victoria, dressed in her riding jacket, stood at the railing staring at the field. James followed her sightline, and his eyes landed on the horse and rider in the arena. Dagmar. She'd rolled up her long plait, and it was coiled into a hairnet, but it was still so obviously her. She flew over jumps like the pro she clearly was. He'd seen people do this kind of thing on TV, but seeing it live was different. His heart stopped. Jesus Christ, she could ride. Of course, he knew that, but with her perfect poise and control, she looked incredible. His father stopped to watch too and for a few moments, everyone's eyes were pinned on her as she completed a flawless round. *Wow.*

Spectators clapped as she left the arena, and James joined in – though slower and less enthusiastically than he should have

– because his eyes were still on the now-empty arena, and his mind was struggling to process what an incredible sight he'd just witnessed.

'Ah, hello. You made it.' The countess got to her feet and James flicked his focus to her. 'Wonderful to see you. You came just at the right time. That was Dagmar Ingenfeld. She's a brilliant rider, and she's Victoria's main rival this year, but I think she's had her day.' With a little frown, the countess seemed to weigh her own words. 'Then again, that ride was pretty special, so Victoria will have to do very well indeed.'

Victoria smiled coyly at James, apparently not paying any attention to her mother. 'Nice to see you all.'

James returned her smile, though his jaw was working very hard to do so. 'Hi.'

'When are you riding?' Sherri asked. 'I'm glad we didn't miss it.'

'Oh, there are several people before me.' Victoria waved an airy hand. 'I probably should go and start warming up though.'

'Do that,' the countess said with a pointed look. 'We'll entertain our guests until you get back. And make sure you do your best.'

'Of course.' She left the box with a little wave.

'Sit, please,' the earl commanded.

'I can't wait to see Victoria riding.' Sherri sat herself down next to the countess. 'She must be fantastic. I'm sure she's better than the other girl.'

'I don't know.' The countess let out a sigh. 'Dagmar has been doing this a long time. Too long, if you ask me. It's time she stepped aside and let other people have a chance. She turns up at these events every year and goes home with all the prizes.' She leaned in. 'Between you and me, she's a bit of an oddity. Rather obsessed with the horses. To the point where it's got ridiculous. She must be about thirty now. I'm sure she's around the same age as Ophelia Chattan-Blythe. You'd think she'd have moved on, had a family, that kind of thing, instead of obsessing over competitions she's already won several times.'

James balled his fists. This woman was a piece of work. He'd never warmed to her, despite the way his mother idolised her. Who was she to criticise Dagmar like that? And what jealousy! The only reason she wanted Dagmar to step aside was so that Victoria would win. Well, sure, James had to support Victoria in public, but inside he was rooting for Dagmar every step of the way.

'Some people are very dedicated to what they do. Age shouldn't be a barrier.' James forced a smile at the countess. 'If she's still fit and healthy, why shouldn't she keep riding as much as she likes? If she wins everything, then kudos to her.'

The countess raised an eyebrow, and a little smirk played at the corner of her lips. 'Quite right, I'm sure.'

His parents gaped at him, but he didn't make eye contact.

'The weather is perfect for the trials today,' the earl remarked. 'Such a glorious day, not even a hint of rain.'

'Ideal,' Laurence agreed.

'How is everything at Duchan Fayre?' the countess asked Sherri. 'I so adore a visit.'

'Very good, thank you so much.' Sherri beamed, looking relieved that the countess hadn't taken offence at James's words, but the woman shouldn't be badmouthing anyone like that – especially Dagmar. Not in front of him. 'We're thinking of sponsoring next year's event. James can talk to you about it at another time.'

'That would be splendid.' The countess's focus remained on the arena. 'Sounds like a partnership made in heaven.'

James winced. Was that meant to be symbolic of something else?

When Victoria and her horse finally entered the arena after what seemed like hours of small talk, the countess leaned forward, clenching her fists. 'Go on, dear. Show them what you can do.'

The crowd fell silent, all eyes on Victoria. She started her course, looking every bit as good as Dagmar. James's pulse increased. *Don't let her win.*

'She's quite something,' Laurence whispered to James. 'We're lucky to be here.'

James nodded, his eyes on Victoria but his mind with Dagmar. *Just make a mistake. Clip a fence, nothing too serious. Just something to keep Dagmar ahead.*

But Victoria's ride was flawless. She moved over the obstacles with ease, her horse responding perfectly to her commands, each jump executed with precision. The crowd began to cheer.

'Come on, Victoria!' Sherri called out, clapping enthusiastically.

A knot formed in James's stomach. As Victoria approached the final jump, his heart pounded. She cleared it effortlessly, and the crowd erupted in applause.

'Brilliant, simply brilliant.' The earl got to his feet, clapping.

James ground his teeth. The timing was close. Too close. But Dagmar was still ahead. Just. It was by a fraction of a second, but still a win.

The countess's smile faltered, a flicker of irritation flashing in her eyes. 'Well, it seems Dagmar still has her edge.'

'That was very close.' Sherri shook her head. 'Victoria was amazing. I'm sure she'll win next time.'

'Of course.' The countess pinched her lips together. 'There's always next time.'

James exhaled, attempting to look gutted on Victoria's behalf, but his insides were bouncing up and down, cheering for Dagmar.

The earl left the box to present the rosettes. Sherri and the countess leaned forward, eyes sparkling, putting their heads together and chatting like old friends.

The announcer called third place, and the earl handed a rosette to a freckly young girl with ginger hair.

'And in second place,' the announcer's voice rang out, 'we have Lady Victoria Bruce.'

The countess and Sherri erupted in cheers, their applause louder than anyone else's. Victoria gave a small wave, her eyes fell on James and, although she looked disappointed, she gave him a broad smile. He reached his hands forward and clapped her... Well, it wouldn't do to not look like he was supporting her, even if his heart wasn't in it. He watched as the earl moved to the first-place podium.

'And our winner,' the announcer said, 'with a remarkable performance, is Dagmar Ingenfeld.'

The countess and Sherri's applause slowed to a deliberate, tepid clap. James frowned at them; their lack of enthusiasm was so blatantly rude. He glanced back at the arena and rolled his eyes, suddenly aware Dagmar was looking at him. Hopefully she didn't think he was rolling his eyes at her. He clapped as she stepped forward to accept the rosette from the earl, but she wasn't looking anymore. Her smile was vague, her eyes a little watery. James saw the sadness behind her polite expression. Poor Dagmar. She wasn't stupid. How obvious was it that the majority of the support was for Victoria?

He swallowed hard, wishing he could reach out to her, but that wasn't possible. He'd be stuck here for the rest of the day with Victoria. Possibly for the rest of his life.

Victoria returned to the box, her head dropping a little.

'Oh, darling, you were brilliant!' the countess exclaimed, jumping up and patting Victoria's shoulder.

'Absolutely,' Sherri agreed. 'Second place is fantastic. You were so close!'

Victoria nodded, her eyes flitting to James. 'Thanks, everyone. It's just frustrating to come so close.' She threw her hands up and waggled her fingers dramatically. 'That Dagmar is just so... so damn good. Which is truly irritating.'

'You did wonderfully,' Laurence said. 'The other woman just has more experience from what your mother tells us.'

'Oh god, yes. She's got experience because she's devoted her life to this and nothing else. If I had the time, I'm sure I'd love to do that. She literally lives and breathes horses. I'm not quite so obsessive.' She slid into the seat next to James.

'Maybe, but you can't have it both ways.' He raised an eyebrow and gave her his most charming smile. 'If obsessing over horses and getting better isn't worth the sacrifice, that's a choice. But you can't dis someone else winning if it's theirs and they've made it work for them.'

Victoria nodded, apparently chewing her tongue, but she looked almost impressed that he'd disagreed with her.

'Oh, totally. And maybe I'm guilty for not putting in enough hours, but I've got interests outside of horses, thank goodness.' She rested a hand on his arm, her fingers lightly brushing his sleeve. 'Just as well, huh?' She gave him a cheeky little smirk.

What meaning did she want him to take from that? He couldn't be certain, but he interpreted it as her suggesting she enjoyed fooling around with guys, whereas Dagmar didn't. Was that her point? That Dagmar was so focused on horses she'd given up on relationships? She was a closed-off person, but surely someone had penetrated those walls at some point. Or was she celibate, fully devoted to her work?

Her choice, of course.

He shifted slightly. Victoria still had her hand on his arm. 'You did well. It was a tough competition, and the timings were very close.' The words came out with practised monotony but were a reminder of how lucky things had turned out – for Dagmar. She'd won by such a fine line. He hated to think how Victoria would crow if she'd been that fraction of a second quicker. Jesus, if he wanted a relationship with this woman, he'd have to learn to hope for just that. But all he could think about was Dagmar. As always.

The countess and Sherri exchanged a smile, and James tried to mirror it.

'Let's take some tea,' the countess said. 'That'll cheer us up.'

'Yes, absolutely,' Sherri added. 'Next year will be the year. I'm hoping for many exciting events next year.'

Victoria giggled and gave James a little wink. 'They're funny, aren't they?'

'Oh... Very.'

After they'd had tea and a selection of mini cakes, James, Victoria, Sherri, and the countess left the box for a stroll around the grounds. The countess pointed out various sites to Sherri, while Victoria took James's arm. James kept his smile in place, trying to ignore the way his stomach curdled at the touch.

'Such a lovely day.' Sherri glanced around.

'Indeed,' the countess agreed. 'And there's Ophelia. Let me speak to her. She's a lovely girl.'

James pulled in a slow, steady breath. Great, just what he needed.

Ophelia looked as immaculate as ever, smiling and laughing with Brann, who always looked like some kind of warrior tugged into modern times. He was dressed in his kilt and a tight t-shirt that showed off his muscly frame. His arm was looped over Ophelia's shoulder, and while they were a couple you probably wouldn't put together, they were clearly perfect for each other. James didn't feel jealous of Brann, but he was envious of his and Ophelia's situation. They'd found the all-consuming love James couldn't even come close to.

'Ophelia!' the countess called. Ophelia's head whipped around, and she waved, then flicked her long golden hair over her shoulder. 'And I see we have the notorious builder who stole you away.' The countess winked at Brann.

'Yup, that's me.' He threw out his hand and pulled a sorry-not-sorry face.

James caught his eye. *Yeah. It was me you stole her away from.* Not that he was complaining. He'd never been right for Ophelia and once Brann had arrived on the scene, she couldn't look at anyone else. Something tugged at his insides, an unsettled feeling that the same thing was happening to him.

Ophelia's circumstances were different however... Weren't they?

Brann extended his hand to James. 'Good to see you.'

James shook his hand. 'You too.'

Victoria leaned in closer, clearly staking her claim. 'Nice to meet you, Brann,' she said. 'I've heard a lot about you.'

'All good, I hope.' Brann grinned.

'Absolutely not. You're completely scandalous from what I hear,' Victoria replied, and everyone laughed.

'Well, he much prefers being a bad boy.' Ophelia patted his arm. 'Even though he isn't at all.' She raised her eyebrow at him, and he winked.

'Aren't you competing?' James asked her.

'Not this time. I very rarely do these days. I'm simply not good enough.'

'You competed at the highland games last year.'

'I thought it would be moderately more amusing than... Well, other options.'

James guessed she probably meant more amusing than spending the day with her father and her stepmother, though he couldn't shake the feeling that she maybe meant him.

'But I was terrible,' she went on. 'So, I'm not bothering this time.'

'You weren't terrible.' Brann leaned in and kissed her forehead. 'You just set yourself ridiculously high standards.'

Victoria pressed her lips together as she watched them, then glanced at James. If she thought he was going to kiss her like that out here, she had another think coming.

'Don't mention Dagmar.' The countess held up her hand. 'She's already done Victoria out of first place in the showjumping.'

'She is a very good rider,' Ophelia said. 'She always has been. I think she's wasted with us. She could have done this internationally.'

'Not everyone has that kind of ambition,' James said. 'But she is very good.'

'Oh totally.' Ophelia glanced at him, and he remembered with a stab that Ophelia knew he and Dagmar were doing lessons together. *Please god, do not mention that.*

'Well, she's left it too late to do that,' the countess said. 'And her time winning the local competitions is coming to an end too. I feel rather sorry for her, because without the competitions, what does she really have in her life?'

'A very good job at Glenvorneth.' Ophelia eyed the countess, and James felt a rush of respect for her. Ophelia could be snooty and headstrong at times, but she didn't take shit from anyone, even the countess of Dairvin.

'Of course.' The countess gave her a condescending smile.

'Mother.' Victoria gave her a sharp look, then made a funny movement with her head, as if indicating something.

James followed her sightline. Dagmar was walking by, absently fiddling with the lapel on her riding jacket, not looking their way.

'Hey,' Brann said, catching her attention. 'That was some ride this morning. Well done.'

The countess looked livid, but Ophelia seemed to be barely holding back a smile. She briefly caught James's eye, and he glanced away in case he started laughing.

'Thank you.' Dagmar's focus travelled from Brann around the group, and her cheeks reddened.

'Yes, you were so lucky to pip Victoria again,' the countess said in an icy tone.

'Sorry.' Her eyes flicked to Victoria.

'You don't need to apologise,' James said. 'All's fair and all that.'

Victoria stared at him.

'Yes, you were the better rider on the day,' Ophelia said, then added to Victoria, 'No offence.'

Victoria looked like she was barely mastering an urge to slap her... And possibly James too.

'I should introduce you to Sherri Charlton and her son James.' The countess lazily flicked her finger between the two of them. 'This is Dagmar Ingenfeld, winner of everything every year.'

Should he say they'd already met? That might throw up some unwelcome questions, though Ophelia could burst the bubble at any second if she chose to. 'Good to meet you.' James smiled. 'And congratulations on earning a title like that.'

Ophelia barely disguised a laugh, but Dagmar didn't react.

'Indeed,' Sherri said.

Dagmar gave Sherri the briefest flicker of a glance.

Ophelia patted her on the back. 'You have such an amazing record in this event. We're lucky to have you at Glenvorneth.' Her eyes travelled to James, and her puzzled look didn't escape him. Yes, she knew too well he and Dagmar had met countless times at Glenvorneth. No doubt she was wondering what the hell was going on. He couldn't tell her – definitely not here and now. His thoughts had locked in combat inside his head, making it ache, and he felt like he should say something else, though he wasn't sure what.

Sherri eyed Dagmar like she was nothing more than dirt on her shoe. 'Yes, huge congratulations. Quite an achievement.'

'Thank you.' Dagmar shuffled her feet and blinked. Poor thing. She so obviously wanted to be miles from here, and who could blame her?

'Well, I'm coming for you next time,' Victoria said. 'Though I can't guarantee I'll be able to dedicate as much time to the horses. Definitely not as much as you. Because well...' She glanced up at James. 'I might be engaged elsewhere.'

His insides froze. Engaged? *Fuck's sake.* His parents would be over the moon. This was exactly what they'd dreamed of. Exactly what he should be dreaming of, but it didn't give him one second of pleasure.

Dagmar's cheeks reddened. 'Um... Yeah.'

'Ah well,' Brann said. 'Sounds like good, healthy competition.'

Ophelia gave Victoria a pointed look. She and the countess were both sharp as needles, though Ophelia had more compassion. But James kept his face impassive. He wouldn't put it past either of them to stab a guess at what was going through his head, and he couldn't allow that.

Dagmar's gaze flickered between the group. 'I'll let you all get on.' Her eyes only briefly found his, and he was quite certain she was trying to avoid meeting them.

'Indeed,' the countess said, her tone dismissive, 'we mustn't keep you from the horses.'

Dagmar gave a little nod. 'Well, excuse me.' She turned to leave, her posture stiff, her expression controlled.

As she walked away, her shoulders seemed to slump, and James's heart ached to see her like that. He clenched his fists, fighting the urge to go after her. It would only make things worse. But she didn't deserve this.

'Poor girl,' Victoria said with a loud sigh. 'She really needs to get a life, doesn't she?'

'She has a perfectly good life,' Ophelia said. 'She just chooses to spend it in a different way from you. We should all respect that.'

James could have kissed her. 'Agreed. We can't all be the same. It would make for a very boring world.' He took in a deep breath, his insides in knots. His parents would be casting this event up as one of the most successful in recent months, but all he could think about was what an utter shitshow it had been. And how the hell could he make it up to Dagmar?

Chapter Sixteen

Dagmar

Dagmar gripped the steering wheel of her trailer as she drove back to Glenvorneth, her knuckles white. Her wins today should have thrilled her. The rosettes neatly pinned on the dashboard would make anyone smile, no? She'd defended her titles, remained unbeaten, but she may as well have come last. Who cared? Who actually cared about her wins? Her mum would, but she couldn't take a Saturday off during the summer season, so no one that would cheer for her had seen her achievements.

The encounter with the countess, Victoria, and the others had soured everything. Dagmar's skin crawled like she was back at school, surrounded by those same sneering faces. She shuddered. Now she was alone, brave words rose in her mind, things she wished she'd said to them. Not to mention all the ways she could imagine getting revenge. Not that she ever would. She'd never be that bad.

'Fuck's sake.' She slammed her hand on the wheel, then knocked off the rosettes from the dashboard. Pointless, useless things. They should have been symbols of her hard work and dedication, but no. Didn't they just prove how sad she was? Exactly as Victoria had been hinting. She had nothing in her life apart from horses.

Horse girl through and through.

The countess's condescending smile, Sherri's dismissive gaze, and Victoria's thinly veiled insults played on a loop as she wound around the lochside. And James. Well, he and Ophelia were the only ones who'd stood up for her, but he'd also pretended not to know her. Was she really that bad? Fury bubbled up inside her like acid eating her from the inside out.

'Why the hell did I even bother?' Her instinct was to push harder on the accelerator, but she didn't. Zephyra was in the trailer and didn't deserve the brunt of Dagmar's fury. Zephyra, her only true friend. The one she could rely on. Horses had been her constant companions through thick and thin.

Her thoughts raced back to school. The teasing, the exclusion, and the loneliness. Now this. Normal service resumed.

What did it matter? James wasn't for her anyway, and Victoria was so delighted by him he wouldn't need any more lessons to win her. Dagmar could part company with him and forever this time.

The sun was setting beyond the hills, but she barely noticed.

'Forget them,' she muttered. 'Just forget them.' But the words felt empty. She couldn't just forget. Not when the memories were so vivid, the pain so fresh. She turned onto the drive leading to Glenvorneth and slowed down, taking a deep breath. Parking the trailer wasn't easy, and she needed to concentrate.

I'm stronger than this.

She had to be. She'd got this far, and she could keep going. But what was the point? She wasn't sure any of this made her truly happy anymore. Her heart was empty and cold.

She stepped out of the trailer. Birdsong and the gentle whisper of wind in the trees filled the cool May evening, but it didn't soothe or calm her. If anything, it was irritating that pleasant things existed while her mind felt so dark. She grabbed the wheel blocks from the storage compartment and placed them under the trailer's wheels.

'Come on, Zephyra,' she said softly, opening the trailer door. Zephyra's head appeared, and she stepped out carefully. Dagmar led her up the bridle path towards the stable. They'd done this so often together. Dagmar had got her when she was young, trained her herself, and together they'd had so much success. It was such a beautiful evening. The people who'd been at the horse trials were probably enjoying it in the pub or sitting out in their gardens. Ophelia and Brann were likely back at the Boathouse, the beautiful property they'd done up on the estate. No doubt they were sitting out on the balcony, all loved up with champagne, looking out over the little lochan and enjoying the peace. Who knew what James and Victoria would be doing? Dagmar steered her mind well away from every scenario her brain threw at her. Possibly his whole family had stayed on at the castle. Perhaps they were all still talking about her – or more likely they'd forgotten she even existed.

She opened Zephyra's stall, and Zephyra walked in, immediately nosing the hay. Dagmar stroked her neck, then pulled out a little box of chopped watermelon. Zephyra instantly turned her attention to that. 'Here you go. Your favourite. That's for being such a good girl. At least I can count on you.' She gave her all the melon remaining in the box, made sure she had enough water, then closed the stall door behind her. With one last quick check on the other horses, she headed back down the hill to the trailer.

Before going inside, she went for a quick wee and a shower. As she did so, she spotted headlights up at the car park. She squinted, holding the towel tight around her, trying to make out the vehicle. Probably Ophelia or someone making a late call to feed their horse. On a day when a lot of owners would have been at the trials, that wasn't unexpected.

Climbing inside the trailer, she shut the door firmly. She rummaged through the pull-out storage box, retrieving her night-clothes. And James's sweater. Was it ridiculous that she liked wearing it quite so much? Somehow it had brought comfort on cold, lonely nights, but tonight she wanted to burn it. She stared at it, then let out a sigh. *Ah, to hell with it.* Who would ever know? And it was warm.

She slipped it on. It smelled faintly of him, a mix of pine and something she couldn't quite place.

'What a mess.' She sat on the edge of the bed, the sweater's sleeves long enough to cover her hands. Pulling her knees up to her chest, she reached over and turned on the small lamp by the bed, its yellow glow filling the trailer. The long Scottish dusk meant it wasn't completely dark yet, but the light was comforting.

Lying down, she pulled the blankets up to her chin and stared at the ceiling, her mind a whirlwind of thoughts. The events of the day replayed in her head, bringing sharp stabs of pain and irritation rather than the thrill of winning. Her mum would want to know how she got on though. Dagmar pulled out her phone and messaged her. If anyone was always happy to hear from her, it was her mum. She would have something kind to say, even if no one else did. After hitting send, she flicked off the light and lay back, closing her eyes.

She wasn't even sure what she was more upset about. The fact that James hadn't let on he knew her or him and Victoria being so close. Despite Victoria hanging on his arm, he'd still stood up for Dagmar – and in front of the earl and countess. That had to count in his favour, but none of it appeased the restlessness in her soul. Because it made no difference what he said or didn't say. The bottom line was, he wasn't for her. And the pain in her heart seemed to stem from that more than anything else.

The sound of footsteps outside made her tense. She listened, holding her breath and lying completely still. Who the hell would come walking about down here at this time of night?

A knock on the door.

She froze, her heart pounding in her chest. No one ever came down here. She stayed silent, praying whoever it was would just go away. But the knock came again, more insistent this time.

'For fuck's sake,' she muttered, slipping off the bed. Grabbing her riding crop from its hook by the door, her hands trembling, she cautiously opened the door and peered around.

It was James.

'What the hell are you doing here?' Her voice shook. How dare he think this was ok? Especially after the day she'd had. She thrust the door open and shoved her riding crop into his chest. All the burning rage from the day – maybe longer – boiling over. 'You scared the shit out of me!'

James stepped back, his hands raised in surrender. 'I'm sorry. I didn't mean to—'

'Didn't mean to what? Pretend you didn't know me because Victoria is more important?' She jabbed the riding crop into him. 'You haven't changed one bit!'

'Listen, I'm sorry.' He didn't try to stop her, taking the prods without flinching. 'I did what I could, but I realise I was stupid not to admit I knew you. It wasn't because I'm ashamed of knowing you or anything like that. It was only because I didn't want to mention the lessons. But I've been thinking about it ever since because it didn't sit well with me. I came to apologise. I was wrong, and I know I've hurt you.'

'Too late for that.' She lowered the crop, her breath coming in short, sharp gasps. 'Just go, James. Leave me alone.'

'Dagmar, please, let me—'

'Go away!' She shoved him with the crop and turned on her heel, storming back into the trailer and slammed the door shut, locking it behind her. As she leaned her hands against it, her body trembled, and her breathing was blocked. Tears welled and she let them fall. She pressed her forehead against the cool metal of the door, willing them to stop.

'Dagmar,' James's voice said softly. 'Please, please, let me talk. I beg you.'

She couldn't bring herself to say anything. What was left to say? Nothing could change what he'd done or not done. Or take away the fact that any day now he'd ride off with Victoria and she'd never see him again – except at shows, when he'd be sitting in the earl's box, a hundred leagues above her. She should be rejoicing that day, but her heart cracked even more at the thought.

'I know I'm an arsehole. It was all so I could keep up the front with Victoria, but that's no excuse. I wanted you and I to be friends, but I haven't acted like a friend. All I've been is a dick. Please. I know you're hurting in there. Let me see you. Let me fall at your feet and you can slap me about some more. I deserve it. I'm so, so sorry.'

Tears streamed down her face, and she bit her lip to stifle the sobs. 'I said go away. Go.

If you don't get off this land, I'll get a rifle from the gunroom and shoot you.'

She listened until his footsteps receded up the path, then fell back onto the bed.

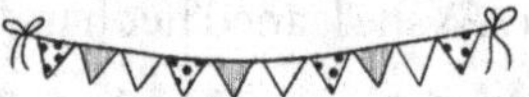

Dagmar was up early the next day, even though she'd barely slept a wink. Keeping to her routine, even though it was Sunday morning, might be enough to keep her sane and her mind off James.

After mucking out, she propped the wheelbarrow up against the wall, and turned, dusting her hands together. Caitlin and Kristi were walking across the yard.

'Morning,' Kristi said. 'Sorry Caitlin's a bit late. It's my fault. One of my sisters needed me to drop something off, and it took longer than I expected.'

'Don't worry.' Dagmar gave her a little smile.

'See you later, Mum.' Caitlin gave Kristi a hug and headed straight into the stables.

'I hope it doesn't mess things up too much. I'm really sorry.' Kristi walked over to Dagmar.

'It's not a problem. I didn't even notice to tell the truth. My head's such a mess.'

'Oh? Has something happened?'

Dagmar sighed. Much as she hated talking about herself, she wanted to offload, and Kristi seemed like a safe person.

'How long have you got?'

Kristi gave a little shrug. 'As long as you need.'

Dagmar nudged her head towards the office and moved in that direction. Kristi followed her.

'What's going on?' Kristi was watching her. 'Is it Ophelia?'

'No. It's James.'

'Is he the bloke you were talking about before?'

'Yep.'

'What's he done?'

'I don't know where to start. I'm a mess thinking about it. Yesterday, at the trials, something stupid happened.' She explained about him pretending not to know her. 'But he did stick up for me. So did Ophelia. And I know he didn't want to say he knew me...' She glanced at Kristi. 'I'm not supposed to say why.'

'Ok.' Kristi sucked on her lips, still eyeing Dagmar. 'Why is his opinion so important to you?'

Dagmar huffed and looked away. 'Good point. I guess that's the problem. I used to have a crush on him and I don't think it ever went away. But he's... Well, he has someone else on his radar.'

Kristi put her hand on Dagmar's shoulder and sighed. 'Hey, that's tough. But if he's not actually with this person and you fancy a shot, why not go for it? This is the twenty-first century. You don't have to wait for him to ask you. Go ask him. Get in before the other one.'

'I don't think that would work.'

'Why the hell not? I refuse to believe you're any less than this other woman.'

'I definitely have less money... And experience.'

'Hmm, if he's only out for her money, then he's a twat, and experience of what?'

Dagmar gave a little shrug. 'Relationships. I've never really made time for them.'

'Well, most of them are overrated, so you probably haven't missed anything. Everyone's got to start somewhere, and you've got plenty of life experience. Running this place on your own isn't exactly easy. I'm telling you, if you want more from him, go for it. Even if it's just a fling. Have it and be done with.'

'Are you serious?'

'Sure.' Kristi grinned. 'Give him a test run and see if he's worth it.' She winked and squeezed Dagmar's shoulder.

'I wish I had your confidence.'

'I'm not sure it's confidence,' Kristi said. 'I've just got to a stage in life where I don't really care what people think, though it doesn't always work. I'm as susceptible as anyone, but in this instance, if you want something to happen, then make it happen.' Kristi put her arm around Dagmar's shoulder and Dagmar leaned into her, allowing herself to relax into the friendly hug.

She needed to keep these words with her, even though most of it was stuff that was easier said than done.

It gave her lots to think about as she went about the rest of the day as she went about her work. She wasn't sure she had the nerve to do any of that or even speak to James again. Maybe he wouldn't need any more lessons. But what about the café? So much felt unresolved.

She hadn't thought James would show face here again that day, but she was wrong. As she nipped out of her trailer just after lunch, she saw him leaning on the fence not far up the path. Taking a deep breath, she steadied herself.

She marched up the path towards him, channelling the energy Kristi had instilled her with – though she wasn't going to ask him out or anything like that. He straightened up and looked around.

'Why are you here?' she asked.

He held up his hands. 'I... I don't know. I'm trying to think.'

'Then can you go back to your own house and think? I don't want you standing around here.'

He huffed out a breath. 'Fair enough. But I just want to know you're ok.'

She shook her head and met his eyes. 'I'm sure that's exactly what you want, then your conscience can rest easy, but I can't give you that satisfaction. I've had it with you and... I want to know what you're doing about the café and then you can go back to Victoria.'

'Everything is fine with the café. I've handed my proposals to Henry, and things should be finalised within the next few weeks.' He held up his hands and backed off. 'Please don't hate me.

You're a great person and you're important to so many people, and—'

'Important? For what?'

'For your mum, the horses, yourself... Me.'

'Just stop. I'm not important to you.'

'You are.'

'Oh yeah, I forgot, so you can learn to ride.'

'More than that. You're my friend. Please, let me make amends. I'm happy to go to Victoria and tell her you and I already know each other. We can go together if you want.'

'I don't think she'd like that.'

'Well, tough shit. Because you're my friend and no matter what kind of relationship I have with Victoria in the future, I want to keep our friendship. Victoria will have to deal with that.'

Dagmar stared at him. 'But she hates me.'

'She's jealous of your riding skills.'

'And you think it's a good idea for you to be friends with someone she's jealous of? When you and she are practically en-gaged?'

'So my parents think. But turns out, I'm not the only person on her list. After I praised your ride yesterday, both Victoria and her parents took great delight in telling me so. Good to keep their options open and all that.'

Dagmar sucked on her lower lip. She'd heard that rumour from Ophelia. 'Does that mean you're giving up on her?'

He nodded. 'I think so. My parents won't be happy, but for me, it's a get out of jail card. I really didn't feel anything for Victoria.'

'What about...' She wanted to say "me", but she couldn't bring herself to do it. Kristi's voice might be urging her to, but it wasn't possible. 'What about the horses?'

'I want to keep doing the lessons... If you were up for it. That's what I came here to talk to you about.'

She glanced away with a little shrug. 'You've paid for them, so you may as well keep going, and who knows, they might come in handy with some other rich woman.'

He gave her a wry smile. 'Yeah, that's a good point, one that my parents would certainly see as beneficial.' He moved a little closer and put his hand on her arm. 'But I'd rather do it because I enjoy it, and I enjoy your company.'

She frowned, not quite able to take in what he'd said.

'Anyway, I'll leave you in peace. I just wanted to check you were ok, and let you know I didn't want to stop the lessons.'

As he made to walk away, she grabbed his arm. 'James.'

'What?' His eyes met hers and for a moment, they just looked at each other.

'I...I don't know.'

'I appreciate everything you've done for me, really.' He gently placed his hand on her upper arm.

She gave him a little smile. 'Yeah.'

'Friends?' He raised an eyebrow.

She nodded, swallowed, and, remembering Kristi's words, reached out and placed her opposite hand on his arm. It was the boldest move she'd ever made, and, with his hand still on her, it was like they'd formed a cage. She kept her eyes on him, aware of how handsome he looked, how warm he felt, and how divine his fragrance was.

Never taking his gaze from her, he pulled her a little closer and gave her the smallest of hugs. Holding still, her breath caught in her throat. She'd never been hugged by a man before. The sensation was overwhelming, causing a storm in her chest. Was it terror, excitement, pleasure?

But before she could get used to it or relax into it, he pulled back. 'I'll see you tomorrow for another lesson. You take care.'

And that was that. She watched him walking up the bridle path and stopping to chat to one of the horses before he made his way to the stables. Her head still felt messy and uncertain, but something else was there now too.

Hope.

She needed to hang onto it. Crazy it may be, but it was exciting and new. Maybe, just maybe, she had a tiny chance to do something different. Have a little fun and move out of her comfort zone. And why not? She'd been stuck in one place for a long time.

The main problem was, she wasn't sure what to do next.

Chapter Seventeen

James

James returned to the stables the following evening for his lesson. After his chat with Dagmar the previous day, he felt like they'd cleared the air. Discovering Victoria wasn't as keen on him as she'd made out was such a relief, but he was pretty sure his parents wouldn't think so. He'd managed to avoid them since the trials and wasn't in any rush for a discussion. Right now, he just wanted to spend time with Dagmar and the horses.

He got Conker ready, brushing the horse's coat with deliberate strokes, easing the tension in his own limbs as well as relaxing the horse. He hadn't seen Dagmar when he arrived, which was odd as she was usually about, but hopefully she wasn't avoiding him. Not now. Had he done enough to get into her good books?

'There you go,' he said gently, laying down the brush and collecting the saddle pad.

When Conker was ready, Dagmar still hadn't appeared. Normally, she'd come into the stable to check his progress.

Leading Conker out, he spotted her by the gate, talking to Brann's daughter. Dagmar avoided his gaze – or it seemed like that was what she was doing.

'Hey,' he said.

She looked up briefly, then back at Brann's daughter. 'Hi.' She carried on talking for a few minutes and James stood by like a loose end. This was how it felt to be overlooked and shunned. The way she'd obviously felt all through school and even now when she was in the company of the countess and Victoria. In fact, this was only the tip of how it must feel. He wasn't being ridiculed or talked down to. If this was even a little painful, then he deserved it.

Finally, Brann's daughter moved away, and Dagmar strolled up to him. 'I'll be another few minutes. You'll have to wait for a bit.'

'Ok. Shall I just hang about here? Or go into the field?'

'Out here will be fine. I won't be long.'

He walked Conker across the yard towards the bridle path, standing by him, looking out over the hills. If his parents had had their way last year, he and Ophelia would be together, and all this would be his. He sucked in a little breath – very glad it wasn't. He didn't need this kind of responsibility along with Duchan Fayre. Victoria was a far safer option as she had nothing to inherit, but still had the name his parents so desperately craved. But if she wasn't a hundred per cent committed, and he certainly wasn't, then it seemed crazy to continue.

'Ok, let's go.' Dagmar appeared behind him on Zephyra.

He mounted Conker, and together they headed for the bridle path. 'Where are we going today?'

'We can go up to the lochan near Ophelia's house. The path goes right around and there's a good place where we can separate and you can ride by yourself, but I'll still be able to see you.'

'Ok. I'm up for that.'

She met his eyes at last, then shook her head. 'Is there anything particular you still want to learn? The lessons could go on indefinitely, but if you have a specific goal you want to work to then we could work to that.'

'I'm not sure. I'm just enjoying the process… and your company.'

Dagmar's cheeks flushed scarlet, and she turned away, staring straight ahead. 'Oh.'

'I mean it.' He kept his gaze fixed on her. 'I enjoy being around you. This may sound wild, but even years ago when we were at school. I always hoped to bump into you. Sometimes I tried to talk to you, but you were hard to find.'

She finally looked at him, her eyes searching. 'Is it any wonder why?'

'No. I fully understand now. If I could go back, I'd change so many things'

'Yep.'

'But I can't do that. All I can do is focus on the present and try and make amends now.'

She gave him a little smile. 'Careful. You never know what I might make you do.'

That was more like it. He let out a laugh and shook his head. If he could keep her in this mood, they'd get on just fine.

The temperature was pleasant, and it made for an easy ride through the woods, where Stroman had escaped into. Thankfully today he'd been relaxed in his field. James smiled – so nice to see some progress had been made there, much the same as with Dagmar. She also seemed a lot more chill today. A little way through the woods, the path emerged and joined another path that led to the boathouse – the gorgeous property on the estate where Ophelia lived with Brann. They rode up a short and rather steep hill. When they got to the top, he saw the boathouse below, sitting on the edge of a small lochan, its rather curious tower rising on one side. The rest of it was a modern extension that afforded great views from the inside. Ophelia's red BMW and Brann's van were both parked outside.

'That house is incredible.' He gazed down at it. 'That was the kind of place I wanted to build near Loch Briar, but the plot I bought wasn't right. I need somewhere a lot more secluded. Exactly like this.'

'Yeah. It's amazing what they've done to it. It was a mess for years.'

As he watched, he spotted Ophelia and Brann coming out of the house and sitting at a table on the terrace that was right on the side of the lochan.

'Shall we go say hi?' Dagmar glanced at him. 'It's down there that I thought we could try the solo riding.'

'Yeah, sure. Let's do it.'

They walked on, approaching the gate to the boathouse garden. Clearly, Ophelia and Brann had heard them as they appeared at the gate.

Brann lifted the latch and he and Ophelia came out.

'Hi. What brings you here?' He looked up at them both.

'We're going to refresh James's solo riding. I'm sure he remembers how to do it.' She cast him a look, and he tried to keep his face straight. 'I'll ride around the side of the lochan and wait over there. He can follow. That way, I can see him the whole way round.'

Ophelia smirked as she scratched Conker. 'Good idea. We can watch too. This should be fun. I hope you're being a good boy for James,' she added to her horse.

'Yeah, he's the best,' James said. 'I've grown rather attached to him.'

Ophelia raised an eyebrow at him. 'Who'd have thought it?'

'Who indeed.' And now they were going to be watching his every move. Only this time, he wasn't too bothered. He and Conker had developed mutual respect, and he trusted Conker to do as he was asked. Conker was clearly very pleased to see Ophelia though. Would that make him want to get back to her rather than do as James said?

'You wait here,' Dagmar said. 'I'll wave to you when I'm ready for you to follow. Happy with that?'

'Sure.'

They watched her amble along the path that skirted the edge of the lochan.

James let out a sigh. 'She's such a great rider and a good teacher too.'

Ophelia looked at him with a slight frown. 'She most certainly is.'

'Have you heard about Victoria?'

'What about her?'

'Apparently, she's keeping her options open.'

Ophelia shrugged and held out her hands. 'All's fair, or so they say. But really, James, unless you are one hundred per cent madly in love with her, you should let her go.'

James glanced out at the serene water. 'You think?'

'I know. Remember what happened with us last year? I couldn't commit to anything with you because I didn't feel it.'

He nodded. 'Yeah. I get that. Thing is, I know Victoria is a good person. But—'

'Something's missing?'

'Exactly. But how did you do it?'

'Do what?'

'Go against your parents?'

'It wasn't easy, but I decided it was my future, not theirs, and if I wanted to be happy, I had to follow my heart.' She glanced at Brann, and he squeezed her shoulder.

Could James do that? It wasn't quite as simple with his parents, not when he'd made a promise. And he hated going back on his word. What if they lost all trust in him and that filtered into his career at Duchan Fayre?

Dagmar was almost on the other side of the lochan.

'You and Dagmar seem to be getting on well,' Ophelia said. 'If you can persuade her to move into one of the cottages, that would be great. I hate seeing her living in that trailer and I don't understand her resistance.'

'I don't think she's used to trusting people,' Brann said.

'I think you're right.' James spotted Dagmar waving. 'It's hard when you've been let down so often in life.'

'Do you mean by me?' Ophelia frowned at him. 'Is that how she feels?'

'She's never said that to me, no. But she definitely feels like that towards me and I'm sure I'm not the only one.'

Ophelia was watching him with her steely eyes, and he looked away.

'I should go. That was her waving.' He waved back and, without thinking, nudged Conker, and said, 'Walk on.'

Conker moved off straight away, ambling around the path. James smiled and relaxed. This was actually a lot of fun and the sense of achievement filling his veins was next to nothing. He was riding a horse – on his own. And sure, there were other people nearby, but right now, it was just him and Conker, and they were doing just fine.

'Well done,' Dagmar said as she reached him. 'You did that really well, and you looked very confident.'

'It felt great.'

She nodded with a little smile. 'Good. Let's head back. It's been a long day, and I'm knackered.'

'Yeah, sorry. I'm taking up your evenings now too. I could do early mornings again if you preferred.'

'We don't really have enough time then and I don't mind an evening hack when the weather is good.'

They headed back to the stables and spent some time getting the horses ready for the night. When James went back outside, Dagmar was standing in the yard, looking a little lost.

'Are you ok?' he asked.

'What? Oh… Yes. Fine. I wonder… Have you eaten yet?'

'No.'

'I've got some lasagne left over. We could sit out and eat it if you want.' Her eyes were wide, and she was fidgeting with her fingers. James cocked his head. This wasn't like her, but she was clearly making a big effort.

'Sure. If you don't mind.'

'I don't mind.' She led the way to the trailer, walking ahead and almost making a point of not talking to him. 'If you wait out here. I'll get the food. Grab a seat.'

He lifted a camping chair that was propped up at the side of the trailer under the awning and popped it open, then did the second one. In this weather, it must be quite pleasant sitting out here in an evening, but surely in winter it was awful. He remembered what Ophelia had asked him to do, but was it his place? Dagmar could be stubborn.

She appeared a few moments later with a couple of plates. 'If you hold them, I'll grab some drinks and cutlery.'

He waited until she returned, then they juggled the plates, cutlery, and cups until they both had what they needed.

'Ophelia wants you to move into a cottage,' James said. 'Apparently, it's ready if you want it. Don't you fancy it?'

Dagmar shrugged, and he took a mouthful of lasagne, which was rather tasty.

'I suppose I should. It just feels like I'd be indebted to her. Kind of like how I feel about you and the café.'

'I understand that, but I think it would make a big difference to your life. This kind of setup is ok at this time of year.' Though he wouldn't fancy it for himself. 'But don't you freeze in the winter?'

She nodded. 'Yup. I guess if I'm going to do it, it would be smart to do it before then.'

'We're only in May, so you have plenty of time before that, but I wouldn't leave it too late. Take Ophelia up on the offer. She wants to help.'

Dagmar looked at him, and he maintained eye contact. All sorts of feelings woke inside him, and his heart trembled. He'd like to lean in and kiss her, tell her everything would be ok, and make her smile, but he wasn't sure she'd like any of that.

'I'll think about it.' She took the empty plates and disappeared inside.

James let out a sigh and ran his fingers over his forehead. It felt a little achy. Probably due to tiredness. He'd been burning the candle at both ends recently. Dagmar was possibly washing up; she definitely didn't seem in any rush to return. He leaned his head to the side, yawning, and closed his eyes.

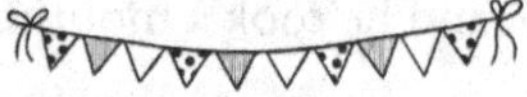

When he woke, he blinked a little and rolled his shoulders. 'Ow.' He ran his hands up his neck. He must have fallen asleep and cricked it. His eyes landed on Dagmar. She wasn't sleeping, but she was very still, staring into the distance.

She looked so peaceful, but what was she really thinking? Was she worried about the café? The cottage?

'Hey.' He sat up.

She turned to him. 'Hi, sleeping beauty.'

'Don't know what happened there. I just relaxed and the next thing I know I'm waking up. What time is it?' He shuffled around to get his phone out of his pocket.

'You haven't been asleep that long. Just about twenty minutes.'

'Oh, right.' He checked the time. It was half-past eight. 'I should get going. We've both got early starts tomorrow.'

'We sure do.' She turned to watch him.

'Thanks for the food... and the company. I had a great time riding.' That word had a way of sounding suggestive when he really didn't mean it to.

'Yeah. It was good, and you're getting much better. If you're looking for your next conquest, you'll certainly find a lot of horsey people with money and status.'

He looked away and shook his head. 'I'm not.' Even thinking about stuff like that made his skin crawl – though his parents would be, though not until they found out about Victoria. That was a conversation he still had to face.

Conflicted thoughts churned in his mind. Victoria was still perfect on paper. She fit into his family's plans so seamlessly. But in front of him was someone who fit with what he wanted. Someone whose company he enjoyed, and he had a shared interest with – an interest he'd never meant to become so real.

'Maybe you'll let me return the favour one day,' he said.

'What favour?'

'By letting me take you for dinner.'

'Oh... Well, maybe.' She got to her feet, lifting the chair and folding it up. Sometimes she seemed so uncertain around him. Had she ever had anyone truly close to her? Or was it just him she was like this with? She was so passionate and dedicated to her horses. She never took time for herself. Maybe she'd never pursued a relationship, or maybe she'd just never found anyone who cared enough to be there for her.

Could he be that guy? He'd like to, but he wasn't sure she'd want that. His parents certainly wouldn't, but what if he did what Ophelia had done? But he was getting ahead of himself. Dagmar still had so many walls, and he wasn't sure she'd ever let him in.

'I'll get going then.' He folded up his seat and propped it next to hers. 'Thanks again.' He looked at her for a long moment, and she held his gaze. It would be the easiest thing in the world to dip down and place a kiss on her cheek. But he didn't. He gave her a gentle pat on the upper arm before heading off. Halfway up the bridle path, he turned back, looking over his shoulder.

Dagmar was at the edge of the field, leaning on the fence, watching him. He gave her a little wave, keeping his focus forward and didn't look back again, though he felt certain her eyes were boring into him.

He returned to the wing of his parents' house that he lived in, showered and got ready for bed. Sleep didn't come easily that night – not that it did at all these days. Switching off his brain with everything that was going on was almost impossible. Even when he felt exhausted, his body didn't play along, and he lay awake for hours.

When he woke, it was just after five. What was the point in forcing himself to try and sleep for another hour? Instead, he got up and went for a run. He had a mountain of emails to get through that day and decided doing it from home would be better than the office. This way he could start straight away and finish up at a more reasonable time, maybe even go early to the stables and spend some time with Conker... And Dagmar, if she didn't think he was in the way.

A knock on his door sometime later dragged him away from his screen into the moment. He quickly checked the time. How had it gone twelve thirty already?

'James, dear?' his mother's voice called, and she peered into his room.

He rolled his eyes. Nothing like waiting for him to let her in.

'Are you working?'

'Yes.'

'Oh. I thought you were maybe taking time off today when I saw your car.'

He shook his head. 'Just thought I'd get more done working from home.'

'So...' She put her hands together and beamed. 'I noticed you've been out a lot in the evenings. Have you been with Victoria?'

'What? No.' The word blurted out faster than he meant. What the hell was he going to tell her? Presumably she hadn't picked up on Victoria and the countess's remarks about other "suitors" on her radar.

'No?' A frown creased her otherwise immaculate brow. 'Where were you then?'

'That's not something I want to talk about.'

She pursed her lips; he knew that look so well. She always thought it was ok to snoop in on his life like this, even when he asked her not to. But his parents had managed his whole life. Even his career, in which he was very successful, had been mapped out for him. They'd decided it all, and he'd gone along with it, rarely questioning it as it always appeared they'd set him on the sensible path. But now a rebellious streak he'd never known before was writhing inside him. Why should he accept their chosen path? Not without a little bit of defiance anyway.

Even though he was heavily aware of the promise he'd made to his father. Aware and somewhat concerned. He didn't want to do anything that might upset his father so much that it brought on another heart attack.

'But there is something I want to tell you about Victoria.'

'Oh yes?' She took a seat on the little sofa in his office, smiling. 'What about her? You and her seemed to be getting on so well. I hope this is the start of something wonderful.'

James shook his head. 'I don't think it is. In fact, I'm pretty sure it can't be.'

His mother tilted her head. 'Why not?'

'Didn't you hear her and the countess talking on Saturday? I'm not the only one Victoria is interested in. She's got at least one other person lined up.'

Sherri let out a sigh. 'Well, yes. But I don't think it's a big cause for concern. If anything, it was a friendly warning, telling us not to hang about too long. I get that you don't want to be too forward and scare her, but I'm not sure you should waste time. She looked very keen on you, so if you act fast, you won't miss out.'

He ran a hand through his hair. 'I'm not sure I want to. Maybe we should forget about her. If she has other people lined up, then it probably means she's not that interested. She's from a family that are well trained to make a good impression, so of course she'll act like she is.'

'But they've been so genuine with us.'

His mother would see it like that, but he didn't. He knew they were putting on an act and he was doing exactly the same. 'I just don't feel anything for Victoria. Dad says I should treat it like business, but I'm not sure I can.'

'Why not?'

'Did you? Is dad a business deal for you? Did you judge him solely on money and connections?'

She pursed her lips and looked out of the window. 'No, I'm not sure I did.'

'Exactly.' They used to judge people on other values until they'd started earning money, then they'd started desiring to grow their friend circle to match their income and the status they wished for. Now it seemed like that was all they could see.

'I just worry,' his mother continued, 'about your father and the future. But I wouldn't want you to be hurt either. It's so difficult.'

He got to his feet and took her hands in his. 'Try not to worry. I'll speak to dad about it and hopefully he'll understand.'

'I'm not sure he will. He's so dead set on Victoria. And she seems so perfect. I just wish it could work.'

'Leave it with me.'

A flicker of hope registered in his mum's eyes, but he wasn't sure he could appease her. Not yet anyway. He wanted to do something else first. Something he'd never done. He wanted to kiss a girl of his own choosing.

CHAPTER EIGHTEEN

Dagmar

Dagmar switched off her phone and put it down. She'd told her mum that James had set plans in motion for saving the café and now they just had to wait for the money. Apparently buying the property from the landlord was not out of the realm of possibility. Probably as it was small and not in the best condition, though it had a great location on the main street in Glenbriar.

She took a deep breath and stepped out of the office into the yard. After her talk with Kristi the other day, she felt like she was on the cusp of something with James. Especially as he didn't seem that interested in Victoria anymore. But did Dagmar really stand a chance? And what exactly did she want? Kristi had suggested a fling, and that seemed by far the most sensible thing. She could play this casually. Why not? Her time had come. She just wasn't sure how to approach it with James without looking stupid. Flirting was definitely not her strong point.

And what if he said no?

A groan escaped her, and she hurried inside the stable block. The idea of doing anything with James other than the lessons was possibly so crazy she should just drop it. Yes. That was what she had to do.

'Hey.'

Dagmar jumped, recognising James's voice. 'What are you doing here?' she asked, spinning around. 'It's not time for your lesson yet.' The words tumbled out because she felt she had to cover herself, as though, somehow, he might have broken into her brain and heard what she'd just been thinking about him.

His lips curled into a smile. 'I know, but I finished early, and I fancied spending some time here. With the horses... And you.'

She swallowed and took a step back. 'Me?'

'Yeah, you. I don't mean I want to get in your way or anything, but I like being with you.'

'You do?' Her heart raced, her thoughts a tangled mess. Had he actually read her mind? Could he know that moments ago she'd been desperately trying to figure out a way to take what they had to another level? She'd talked herself out of it, thinking he might not want to... But here he was, pretty much telling her outright it was exactly what he wanted.

'Of course I do,' he said. 'And I still have to repay you for dinner. When are you free?'

'Free? Oh... I, um, will have to check.'

'Just let me know when suits. Am I allowed to ride Conker on my own on the bridle path, or is it still too risky?'

She pulled a side pout. 'It would probably be fine, but as Conker's Ophelia's horse, I don't think you should. If you want to tack him and Zephyra up, I could come with you. I have a couple of things to get ready for tomorrow's lessons, but after that, I'm flexible.'

'Ok. I'll do that.'

She left him to it, muttering to herself as she went into the field to set up the fences. Really, it was now or never. He'd practically asked her on a date.

Be brave. You can do this... Whatever it was.

When she returned to the stables, James had the horses tacked up and was chatting to them in his soft voice. His tone was so low and mesmerising that Dagmar wouldn't mind listening to it all day.

'Ready?' she said.

'Yeah, all good here.' He turned and smiled.

'Let's go then.' They headed outside, and Dagmar led Zephyra alongside the mounting block before getting on. She kept Zephyra ahead of James as they headed across the yard, giving herself time to breathe, to think. It wasn't like he was ever going to choose her as a forever partner, but what about that fling? Maybe if she agreed to the dinner, things would progress from there. That was what happened in films and on TV.

'Have you had a good day?' James asked, catching up to her.

'Yeah, it's been ok. I did some lessons with three of the High School kids who use riding as a kind of therapy.'

'Does it work?'

'It does while they're here, but the teacher told me as soon as they get back to school, everything goes back to normal. She also said there was a lot of resentment from other pupils who didn't get why the "naughty" ones should get perks like horse riding. And to be honest, I get where they're coming from.'

'Not ideal, but hopefully it's doing something for them, even if the results haven't shown up yet.'

She kept her gaze ahead. 'I hope so too.'

'I know some nice places we could go for dinner, by the way. But if you don't want to, just tell me and I'll shut up about it.'

She glanced at him and held her breath. Even in his riding hat, his dark eyes and sharp features were strong and alluring. 'I... Well, I suppose so. I mean... Yes, ok. If you're definitely not seeing Victoria.'

He shook his head. 'Definitely not. I think my parents are still holding a candle for her, but I can't. She does nothing for me.'

'Oh.' She looked forward. 'And I do?'

'Yes, you do. I know we didn't start out on a good footing, but I'm always happy when I'm with you. It just feels... Relaxed. Not like the way I was around Ophelia and Victoria when everything is tense and stressed.'

Dagmar took a deep breath. 'Thing is... I've never... Well, you know...' Her voice trailed off, her cheeks burning. 'I don't have a lot of time for relationships. It's never bothered me too much before, but now...' She looked away, a lump rising in her throat, constricting her and stopping further words from coming out.

'Now?'

She didn't look at him or reply.

'When you say you've never had time for relationships...' He paused. 'Do you mean...? Look, I think I get what you're trying to say. And in that case, I didn't mean I was trying anything on or forcing you into anything. I literally meant dinner.'

'I see.' She shook her head, turning her eyes back to him. 'Nothing more.'

'Well... Not unless you want more. I don't want to push you into anything.'

Her pulse was now drumming so loudly in her ear she was convinced he would hear it. 'Yes, I want more.'

'Do you?' His voice was a little shaky. 'What do you want?'

'I want to have a fling. You can teach me whatever I need to know. Just like I taught you with the horses. We'll keep it casual, let it run its course until we're ready to move on.'

He opened his mouth for a moment, then closed it again. 'Are you...' Conker's head twitched as he shook off a fly and James made much the same movement, like he was trying to shake himself. 'Is that really what you want?'

'Yes. Just a casual relationship. You can do that, can't you?'

He raised his eyebrow. 'I... I think so.'

'Good.' Though she wasn't sure she could. She'd fancied him forever, but if stories were to be believed, first times were always hideous, so maybe this experience would turn her off to him. Assuming he agreed. His dark eyes watched her, and her insides turned over. If he could do this much damage just with a look, she was in trouble.

'If that's what you want.'

Her heart stopped, and she could hardly breathe. Maybe she hadn't really expected him to say yes, or maybe the reality was sinking in. The euphoria she'd expected to feel didn't hit. Instead, a wash of worries and practical considerations swept through her so quickly she couldn't catch any of them and put them into words.

'Let's start with dinner,' James said. 'We can take things from there.'

'Ok. Where?'

'Anywhere you like.'

'But what if someone sees us?'

He gave a little shrug. 'Does that matter? I'm not ashamed to be seen with you, if that's what you're thinking.'

'No. I just thought you might be worried about meeting Victoria or her parents.'

'Why should I be? But if you think it'll be a problem, how about I get a takeaway, and we eat at my house?'

'Ok.' She blinked, then a smile twitched at the corner of her lips. 'Sounds good.'

This was it. She was going on a real date – with James Charlton. Her teenage self wouldn't believe it.

James smiled. 'Let's stop here a minute.' He steered Conker into a clearing and dismounted. 'Come here and let me show you something.'

'Show me what?' She rubbed Zephyra's neck, taking a deep breath.

Still holding Conker's rein, James moved closer. 'Come here.' He held out his hand.

Dagmar hesitated for a moment, then swung her leg over and slid off her horse, landing lightly beside him. James stepped closer still; his eyes locked on hers. Warmth radiated from his body, along with his trademark scent.

'Can I kiss you?' he asked, his voice barely more than a whisper.

Dagmar's heart pounded in her chest. She clung tightly to Zephyra's rein, not because she was worried she'd bolt, but because she needed something to hold on to. Before she could think, she found herself nodding. 'Ok... Though we should probably take off the hats. Won't they get in the way?' Maybe she only mentioned it because her brain was pushing practical things at her to avoid the moment she knew was coming.

'Oh, sure.' James unclipped his hat, pulled it off and laid it down on the ground. Dagmar clung onto hers, not sure what she'd do with her hands if she didn't. Her eyes were on James, and he was watching her. Gently, he lifted her chin with his free thumb and forefinger. The contact sent tingles soaring to her nerve ends. He leaned in, holding her face softly. The moment his lips touched hers, her breath caught. His lips were smooth, the kiss tentative at first. Something instinctive took over, and she closed her eyes, relaxing into his mouth, pressing closer. She pushed her hat under her arm, still clutching Zephyra's rein, and her free hand wound around his neck. The kiss deepened, sending a shiver down her spine.

James's tongue grazed hers, and she gasped at the shock of sensations ricocheting around her. Why had she never done this before? It was so lush.

When they finally pulled apart, she was breathless, a smile tugging at her lips. The euphoria she'd expected earlier had arrived, and her veins were overflowing with happy hormones.

James brushed a strand of hair from her face. 'There, how was that?'

'I... Um...' She wasn't sure how to put it into words. 'It was... perfect.'

'Perfect?' He nodded, still smiling. 'Let's hope we haven't peaked too soon.'

'Indeed.' She let out a little laugh.

'So, are you good for Friday night? I'll come for you around six if you are.'

'Yeah... I'm good for that.'

'Good.' He lifted his hat off the ground. 'We'll take it easy. No pressure, no rush.'

'Ok.' Dagmar's heart and mind raced each other at breakneck speed as she and James rode back to the stables. The kiss. Oh god, that kiss. Now she'd had a taste, she wanted more, and soon. Her insides burned raw. James rode close beside her, catching her eye every now and again and smiling.

Once they reached the stables, Dagmar dismounted and led Zephyra into her stall, her heart still spiking with every little glance from James. He followed her, a glint sparking in his eye, and a wolfish smile on his lips. As she turned to leave the stall, he grabbed her hand and pulled her into a darkened corner of the stable.

'James, what are you—'

'Nothing... Unless you want to.'

'Want to what? Kiss you again,' she whispered, glancing around. 'In here?'

'No one's watching. Except Zephyra, and I don't think she minds.'

Dagmar let out a little giggle. 'Ok then.'

With a smile, James leaned in and kissed her again, pinning her up against the stable wall. This kiss was urgent, all-consuming, and Dagmar melted into it, her hands finding their way into his hair.

His lips were so warm and soft. Heat flooded through her at the contact, and James groaned, hauling her closer, deepening the kiss, tangling his tongue with hers. His hands slipped round her hips, and he ground against her. She'd not expected this, but it didn't feel strange. Something about it was all so natural, and even as she was savouring the moment, it occurred to her that it probably felt like this at any time of life... As long as you were kissing the right person.

'You have no idea what you do to me,' James murmured.

'Oh, I think I do,' she whispered with a little grin. She had power over him. The power to make him lose control, to desire her. An inner goddess woke at the thought, like Epona the horse goddess riding free and wild, and Dagmar tugged his head close, bringing him in for another kiss. He held her firmly against him and she was goo in his arms.

When they broke apart, his eyes were dark with desire. 'It's going to take all my willpower not to have you right here and now,' he murmured against her lips.

Dagmar's breath hitched, a shiver running through her. 'Then don't leave.' Did it really matter if they had dinner or whatever first? The only thing she was hungry for was him.

He groaned, resting his forehead against hers. 'I have to. There are people talking outside. It's too risky. Plus, I can't stay late. I'm working tomorrow, and I have an important meeting. This is important too and I don't want to rush it.'

'But...'

'I know. I don't want to go either.' His thumb brushed her cheek. 'But let me come back on Friday. We'll make it a night to remember.'

Dagmar sighed. 'Ok. Friday.' She'd waited this long. Another few nights wouldn't hurt, though she guessed they would be the longest of her life.

James smiled, stealing one more quick kiss before stepping back. 'See you Friday.'

'Ok, see you then.' She watched as he reluctantly left the stables.

She leaned against the wall for a moment. Friday couldn't come soon enough.

CHAPTER NINETEEN

Dagmar

Was there a more exquisite form of torture than this? Waiting two more days until Friday would be impossible. But with time seeming to slow down, it gave Dagmar a moment to think. The estate cottages were ready and in move-in condition. She had so little possessions other than what she kept in the trailer that it would only take a few hours to move in – maybe not even that. All she needed to do was say the word to Ophelia.

With all the changes in her life, this was just one more. Her mum was all for it, and Dagmar knew it was the sensible course of action. The only thing stopping her was her stubborn wish not to be in anyone's debt.

'I can't afford to pay the full rent,' she told Ophelia when she tracked her down in the office to chat to her.

'I don't expect you to pay rent. I told you before. Those rates are for tenants coming in, but you work here. This is part of the deal. If I'd realised sooner that you were living permanently in the trailer, you could have had the cottage I did up last year.' She pulled a face. 'The one Jacinta rented to her friend, Camilla, the mad artist.'

'Oh, her.'

'Yeah. And don't think I'm being rude. She's the one that christened herself that, not me.'

Dagmar took a deep breath. 'Ok, so... When would this start?'

'Right now, if you want. There are six cottages in the row. I can give you the one at the end furthest from Camilla, so hopefully she won't bother you too much. They're all furnished and ready to go.'

Dagmar's insides squirmed a little at the thought of living that close to someone, but still, she needed to do this. She'd long outlived the trailer.

'Ok.'

Ophelia smiled and gave her a pat on the arm. 'You want to do it now?'

'Only if you can spare me here for an hour or so.'

'Of course. In fact, I'll help you.'

Dagmar's instinct was to decline, but why not? Ophelia looked eager.

'I don't exactly have a lot to move.'

'Tell you what. You drive the trailer down and I'll meet you there and help you unload.'

Settled. She headed to the trailer and packed away the camping stuff. It would be so nice not to shower and go to the loo in the horrible little booth. She grabbed all her toiletries and shoved them into the trailer before hooking it up to the truck.

Ophelia was already at the cottage when Dagmar arrived.

'Here you go.' Ophelia dangled a set of keys before Dagmar. 'Your very own cottage.'

'Thanks.' Dagmar took the keys and walked up the little path to the cottage door. It was the end one in a terrace. None of them were large, just two small bedrooms and a bathroom upstairs, with a living area and kitchen downstairs, but Ophelia had decorated them beautifully. As she was an interior designer, the results were stunning. Dagmar felt like it was almost too good for her as she looked around the perfect shabby chic living area with its comfy sofa and small wooden dining table by the window. 'It's gorgeous.' Her eyes fell on the table where there was a bottle of wine. 'What's that?'

'I snuck in and left it.' Ophelia grinned. 'Welcome to your new home.'

Tears prickled at the corner of Dagmar's eyes. It already felt like a home. A place she wouldn't be ashamed to bring people. 'I can't wait for my mum to see this.'

'Invite her round. Invite anyone you like. It's your house to do with as you please... Within reason, of course.'

'Don't I have to sign agreements and things?'

'I'll get Barbara to sort out all the paperwork, but for now, just relax and enjoy it.'

Ophelia helped to offload all Dagmar's belongings in the house, and they chatted as they made the trips back and forth. For someone Dagmar had always been a little in awe of, she was actually easy to talk to.

'I've noticed,' Dagmar said, 'that Stroman has a particular dislike of greys. We should watch him carefully when greys are in the neighbouring paddock. His owners told me yesterday there was a nasty incident at his last livery where Stroman and a grey had come to blows with teeth and hooves.'

'I wish they'd mentioned that before,' Ophelia muttered. 'I don't want any aggro here.' She glanced at Dagmar. 'Do you remember that time—'

'How could I forget?' Dagmar didn't need her to finish. Years ago, not long after Dagmar had started, a horse had killed another one. It had been so unexpected and shocking it had shaken everyone for months. Nobody wanted an incident like that ever again.

'I think we should keep Stroman on his own for now.' Ophelia drew in a breath and held it for a moment. 'In sight of the other horses, but separate. I don't want to risk another tragedy.'

'Agreed.'

'Listen, Brann's away on Friday. He and his son are travelling to a highland games in Morayshire. I can't go as I'm in Edinburgh on Saturday for my friend's birthday, but I'll be free on Friday evening. Do you fancy having a drink? Or we could take the horses out for a hack if the weather stays nice.'

Heat burned Dagmar's cheeks. Everyone knew she *never* did anything in her free time, but Friday was the one time in her life she really had something on. Ophelia wouldn't believe her. This would sound like such a copout. Seriously? Social events were worse than London buses.

'I, um, can't on Friday. I mean, thanks for asking, but I've actually got a date.'

Ophelia raised an eyebrow. 'Aw, that's lovely.' She patted Dagmar's upper arm. 'Anyone I know?'

'Oh... No.' What a lie. But how could she tell the truth?

'Well, enjoy.'

That was the general idea, but her nerves were frayed.

'I'll leave you to settle in here.'

Living in the cottage was bliss compared to the trailer, though she found it odd not having the horses in sight. It was just a short walk up the path, but because of the layout of the land, a hill blocked the view from here. When Dagmar chatted to her mum, she seemed to think that wasn't a bad thing. And maybe she was right. The horses were always going to be important to her, but that didn't mean she had to spend every second with them.

She messaged James and told him she'd moved, so he should pick her up from here on Friday.

He replied quickly.

JAMES: That's so great! I'm so pleased for you. See you on Friday. Can't wait xx

She smiled at the message and the kisses. Suddenly, her life felt new and fresh – if a little strange. Now, every free moment she had was taken up with making herself as presentable as possible. She even bought some new make-up, even though she was only going to James's house. It seemed necessary though as the only stuff she had was so old it had dried up and was useless.

She spent ages moisturising, shaving, plucking. On Friday afternoon, she clocked off early to make sure she had time to de-horse in her wonderful new shower in the cottage. She caked her hair in a new conditioning balm she'd bought and left it in for ten minutes.

Now, she just had to wait. While she did, she applied her new make-up, following a tutorial she'd seen online and hoping she hadn't made herself look like a waxwork. Tilting her head in the mirror on the pretty dressing table in the dormer window in her bedroom, she checked herself... Not too bad. Was it?

Her heart leapt at the sound of a knock. She squinted out the window but didn't see a car. Had James walked from somewhere? Maybe he'd parked at the stables. She rushed to the door, a smile already forming. But when she opened it, it wasn't James standing there.

'Caitlin?' Dagmar blinked. 'Why are you still here?'

Caitlin shifted from foot to foot. 'Mum was supposed to pick me up, but she hasn't shown up yet. My phone battery's dead. Can I charge it here? And maybe use your phone to call her?'

'Of course.' Dagmar stepped aside, her stomach knotting. What if James showed up now? This could be all kind of awkward. 'There's a charge point just there.'

Caitlin unravelled a charger from her bag and shoved it into a plug in the living room

'Thanks. This cottage is so cute.' Caitlin glanced up at Dagmar and opened her mouth slightly. Oh god. Dagmar never wore anything other than horsey clothes, so this dress and the make-up must look completely sus. 'Do you mind if I use your phone now? I just want to make sure Mum's ok.'

'Oh, yeah.' Dagmar opened her phone. She had Kristi's number in case she needed to call her about Caitlin, but she'd never used it. She hardly ever called anyone. Her eyes scanned for a message from James, then flicked to the window. Where was he? And how was she going to explain what he was doing there if he showed up? Surely it would be blatantly obvious. What would Caitlin make of it? Would she gossip?

Dagmar handed the phone to Caitlin, who hit the call button and pressed the phone to her ear. 'Hi Mum, it's me. Where are you?' She paused, listening. 'Ah, ok, that's fine. I was just worried. My phone died, and I'm at Dagmar's cottage... Yeah, she's in the end one. You know the terraced ones on the main drive... I'm charging it now. See you soon.'

She ended the call and handed the phone back. 'She got held up behind a tractor, but she should be here soon. She's still not that confident a driver.'

'No problem.' Dagmar smoothed out her long black dress, glancing at the door. When would James be here? Should she offer Caitlin a drink?

Caitlin checked out the window. 'I didn't want to hang about at the stables. Stroman's owner is in the tack room and he's a bit weird sometimes. That's why I didn't want to use the charger in there.'

'He's a bit abrupt at times,' Dagmar agreed.

'Are you going out? You look nice.'

'Thanks. I, um, yeah. I'm on a date later.'

'Really? Cool.'

Dagmar sat on the sofa but couldn't help tapping her feet. Where was James? Would he arrive before Kristi?

'I had a date with this boy the other week, but he was strange. He had this totes annoying habit of flicking his hair.' Caitlin demonstrated, then laughed.

'Oh dear.'

'Yeah. Anyway. I'm not seeing him again.'

Fussy girl. Dagmar chuckled internally. But Caitlin was young and very pretty; she could afford to be fussy.

A car door banged outside, and Dagmar spun around, but it was Kristi's car not James. As she got to her feet, a message came in.

JAMES: So sorry, running late. Be there soon as I can xx

Dagmar let out a sigh. At least she would have to explain his presence to Caitlin and Kristi.

Dagmar opened the front door as Kristi jumped out of her car, waving. Her outfit wasn't dissimilar to Dagmar, but she wore the black dress with more style. Perhaps it was her curves or the fact the dress laced down the front like a bodice. Her shock of red hair begged to be seen. Her arms were bare, and she had tattoos that looked both pretty and a little scary.

'Sorry I'm late.' Kristi strode up the path to them, her tartan Doc Martens crunching on the gravel. 'There were so many tractors, and I hate passing them on those roads. I'm too chicken.' She hugged Caitlin briefly before turning to Dagmar. 'Wow, you look stunning. Going somewhere special?'

Dagmar's cheeks heated. How could someone who looked as good as Kristi think *she* looked stunning? 'Oh, just a date,' she mumbled.

'A date.' Kristi's eyes lit up, and Dagmar could almost see her putting everything together after their chat the other day. 'How exciting. Well done, you.' She patted Dagmar on the arm. 'And you've moved? This cottage looks amazing.'

'Have a look if you like.' Dagmar stood back to let her in.

Kristi came in and scanned around. 'I love it. This is what I need. My flat is tiny and falling to bits. The lock on the front door is a total menace.'

Dagmar smiled. 'I think the other cottages are still available. You could ask Ophelia.' The idea of having Kristi as a neighbour was quite fun.

'It's a nice thought, but I like living in Glenbriar. It's handy for work.' Her eyes roamed over Dagmar's outfit again. 'So, who's the lucky guy?'

'Good point,' Caitlin added, grinning. 'You didn't say who.'

Dagmar laughed, tucking a loose strand of hair behind her ear. 'It's nothing, really. Just a casual thing.'

'That's my girl.' Kristi gave her a wink, and Dagmar had no doubt she'd worked out who Dagmar was seeing. 'That's exactly what I needed to hear. You look amazing. I love your dress. Very elegant. He's a lucky man and don't let him forget it.'

'Who?' Caitlin frowned at her. 'Do you know something I don't?'

'Of course I do. I'm much older and wiser.' She winked at her, then grinned at Dagmar. 'You go kick up a storm, girl.'

'I'll try.' Dagmar let out a laugh, glancing towards the window. When would James get here?

'Just enjoy it.' Kristi patted her arm. 'And remember, you have my number. I'm sure nothing will go wrong, but don't think twice about calling me if you need an out.'

'Thank you.'

As Dagmar turned to leave, Caitlin called out, 'Have fun.'

Dagmar waved and went back to the living room, her mind racing. How long would it take James to get here? She took a deep breath, trying to steady herself. Maybe he was stuck behind a tractor too. Or maybe he was in a meeting that would go on for hours. The tension might crack her head open at any second. She let out a groan.

Horses were so much more reliable than humans, but if she wanted to get out of her perpetually single, constantly celibate rut, then she needed people. So far, she'd made inroads by getting new friends in Kristi and Ophelia – even Caitlin, despite how young she was. But men were still a mystery... Hopefully, it wouldn't stay that way much longer.

Chapter Twenty

James

James cursed under his breath as he glanced at the clock on his dashboard. He'd had meetings all day, which was crap enough for a Friday, but they'd dragged on far longer than expected, and now he was running late. Even when he'd tried to excuse himself, there was always just one more thing. He'd wanted to go home, shower and change first, but there was no time for that now. He just wanted to get to the cottage and see Dagmar. The fact she was there at all was amazing news. Surely that had to be better than living in the trailer.

In the boot, he had the best of Duchan Fayre's restaurant leftovers. The chef there knew how to cook up something tasty and had assured James it was easy to heat up.

When he finally reached Glenvorneth, the main house loomed in the distance and he took the track that led to the stables, but stopped before that outside the row of cottages he'd often passed but never been in. Dagmar's truck wasn't parked outside, but maybe she'd left it with her trailer. It wasn't a long walk to these cottages from the stables and was probably quite enjoyable at this time of year.

He knocked on the door and waited, but there was no answer. He knocked again, harder this time, straining to hear any movement inside. Still nothing.

'Damn it.' He ran a hand through his hair. Had she given up on him? Maybe she hadn't got his message. He checked his phone. She'd seen it according to the little blue ticks, but there was no reply. Maybe she was in the bathroom.

He hesitated for a moment before peeking through the front window. It looked very well done up inside, but nothing was moving.

Stepping back, he hit call on his phone and waited. No answer. Where was she? He turned, scanning the area. There was a car outside the cottage at the far end of the terrace, but other than that, just the estate grounds, long swathes of grass, and wooded areas. The stables were just over the hill; maybe she was still there, finishing up some last-minute chores.

He walked up the path to the top of the little hill. From here, he could see the stable yard. In the paddock, the horses grazed quietly. He carried on towards the stables. A large black car was just visible in the car park. He was pretty sure that was Stroman's owners' car, but he couldn't see either of them. In fact, no one was about. Stroman was in the furthest away part of the paddock, eating from a hay net hung at the side of a wooden shelter.

James headed into the yard and strolled up to the fence, letting out a sigh. Something nudged him. 'Oh, hey, Conker.' Turning, he rubbed him gently on the neck. 'I'm not here to see you tonight. It's Dagmar I'm looking for.' He continued to absently stroke Conker until he heard voices from inside the tack room. He frowned and squinted towards it. The door opened and Dagmar emerged in a long black dress that emphasised her upright column figure, followed by Maurice, Stroman's owner. Neither of them looked too happy. Maurice glanced at James and pulled an odd face partway between a greeting and an expression of irritation. Dagmar hovered at the door until Maurice was out of earshot. Then she turned to James and smiled. He gave Conker a last pat, then made his way over to Dagmar.

'Hey. Sorry I'm late. I got held up. You look stunning.' He checked Maurice wasn't watching, then put his hands on her hips and gazed at her. She smiled, but it didn't quite reach her eyes. 'Is everything ok?'

'He's a strange man.' She indicated Maurice, who was getting into his car. 'Sometimes he agrees with everything we say he should do with Stroman, then other times he wants to go against that and have Stroman being treated as "normal".' She air-quoted and rolled her eyes. 'He called me and made it out that it was an emergency. I should have known this kind of thing would happen the minute I moved out of sight.'

James stroked her hair behind her ears. 'Hopefully it was just a coincidence.'

'Honestly, it feels like it happens every time. If I went back to stay with Mum for a bit, that was always when something would happen, and I'd have to come back.'

'And has that happened recently?'

She shook her head, and a wry smile appeared. 'No. This was before Ophelia came back, but I still find it so hard to switch off from this place.'

'I get it. Work can be all-consuming at the best of times and when it involves your passion too, it must be a hundred times worse.'

'It is.'

'Do you have things you need to do? Did Maurice want something done for Stroman just now?'

'No. It's just annoying that people think I'm always available.'

He raised an eyebrow.

'I know, I know.' She held up her hand. 'I've made my own bed.'

'I didn't say that, but everyone knows how dedicated you are. It's nice for them having that, but sometimes they need to respect boundaries.'

'Especially on Friday nights.'

'Yeah, especially then.' He squeezed her upper arm.

'Maybe if we get more staff here... The idea still scares me, but I can see that it might be useful at times.' She met his eye, and a smile grew on her face.

'You're so beautiful, but even more so when you smile like that.' He dipped in and claimed her lips. She was still smiling as he kissed her, and it made him smile too. 'Do you still want to come back to my house? The chef gave me food. It can be heated up anywhere, so if you wanted to hang out at your lovely new cottage, we could do that.'

'That sounds good... Because...' She eyed him over. 'I'm not even that hungry. Only for you.'

'And you can have me. Any way you like.' With a little wink, he took her hand and led her towards the path. The evening air was cool, and a gentle breeze rustled the trees. 'Are you sure you're done here?'

'Yep. All done.' She tightened her grip on his hand. 'So, what food did you bring?'

'You'll see.' James cast her a little smile. 'The chefs at Duchan are all great, but Manolo is the best.'

'Then I'd be silly not to try something.'

'You can always have a starter first. Work up an appetite. Whatever you like. The evening is all yours.' And he was determined to make it special. He gave her hand a little squeeze, then looked at where their fingers were linked and grinned. They carried on back to the cottage. 'Let me get the food from the car.' He let her go and headed to get it. When he returned, she was in the cottage already, sitting on the little sofa bed in bare feet.

She reminded him of an elf princess with her long dress and braided hair. Would she allow him to take it out of the plait and set it free? He caught the sweet scent of her perfume, and it sent spikes of lust through him. Laying down the food, he sat beside her.

'This place is perfect. I love it.' He scanned around. 'Do you like it?'

'It's so much better than the trailer.' She covered her face. 'I was so stubborn in refusing to move out, wasn't I?'

'You're a determined person. Nothing wrong with that.'

'I think I've been channelling my determination in the wrong places.'

He let out a little laugh. 'Not all of it, though clinging onto trailer life was maybe a little bit mental.'

She nudged him and laughed. He mocked being knocked over. When he sat back up,

his gaze locked onto hers. 'I really want to kiss you.'

Dagmar's eyes widened. 'You do, do you?'

'I do... and I mean really kiss you.'

'Um... Isn't that what we've done up until now?'

'Can I show you?'

She nodded, and he slid his arm around her waist and pulled her close.

'I've been thinking about this all week.'

'Me too. I can't think about anything else. That's what made me finally decide to move. It took my mind off you.'

He chuckled. 'I'm not sure if you're thanking me or blaming me.' He dipped his head, capturing her lips with his. 'I always liked you. I wish I'd tried harder at High School.'

'You were friends with people who hated me.'

'More fool me. None of us kept in touch. I can't even remember most of their names. But you? I never forgot you.'

'Me neither. I assumed you hated me at high school. Everyone else did. And I was still annoyed with you for leaving primary school and taking my favourite Schleich horse with you.' She smirked. 'I hold a grudge for a long time.'

'So I see.' James stroked her cheek. 'I didn't steal it, you know? I found it and meant to bring it back to you, but my sister started playing with it and I forgot. Then we moved and, well... It wasn't as important to me as it obviously was to you. I'm truly sorry.'

'It's ok. It's not like it matters now. I was just explaining why I didn't trust you at high school, and I guess it all snowballed from there.'

'Then let me make it up to you.' He ran a thumb over her cheek. 'I can cook you the fanciest meal in the world, courtesy of Manolo.'

'Can you... maybe kiss me some more first? I'm still not hungry.'

'Of course. Anything you want.' He kissed her again, and she responded eagerly, winding her arms around his neck. The kiss deepened, and all thoughts of food vanished. James pulled her close, his hands tracing the line of her back.

Dagmar's breath hitched as his lips moved to her neck, dotting kisses on her soft skin.

'James,' she murmured.

'Hmm?' he hummed against her skin, his hands finding their way to the small of her back.

'Are you...?'

'Am I what?' He pulled back just enough to meet her gaze.

She took a shaky breath, her hands resting on his chest. 'Are you sure you're ok with this? Or would you prefer to eat?'

James eyed her. 'I'll do whatever you want. The food will keep.'

'Ok. Let's keep doing this then.'

'Good, because the only taste I fancy right now is you.' He resumed kissing her, their breaths mingling as the intensity built. He couldn't get enough of her, the softness of her lips, the way she melted into him.

'Dagmar,' he murmured against her mouth. 'Can I take out your plait?'

Her eyes fluttered open and met his. She nodded. 'If you really want to.'

'I do.' His fingers found the end of her braid, slowly working the elastic free. He took his time, unravelling each twist with a gentle touch. As the plait loosened, her hair cascaded down her back in silken waves.

'Beautiful,' he whispered, running his fingers through her hair, letting it spill over his hands. The scent of her strawberry shampoo mingled with her perfume, creating an intoxicating blend that made his head spin. He tucked a strand behind her ear and kissed her just below the earlobe.

Dagmar sighed, her hands moving to his upper arms, pulling him closer. Her hair was free now, and she tossed it over her shoulder. James cradled the back of her head, deepening the kiss, allowing the softness of her hair to tickle his fingers.

He pulled back slightly, his forehead resting against hers. 'You're so beautiful.' He breathed deliberately. Making this last would be a tough ask. He was so hot for her already, but this wasn't going to be a rush. It was her first time, and he wanted to make it good.

'I could say the same about you.'

He laughed softly, kissing her once more. 'Me? Beautiful?'

She giggled, the sound light and infectious. 'You're very handsome.'

'Come here.' He tightened his grip on her and scooped her onto his lap. She adjusted her dress and straddled him. 'My turn,' he said.

'For what?'

'To give you some riding lessons.'

She swatted him. 'Really, that's terrible.'

'I'm hoping it'll be rather good actually.'

She nibbled her lush bottom lip, which increased the ache in his groin.

'How about we take this to a new level? Let's start with this.' He gave her a wolfish grin, then tugged up her dress, letting his hands linger on the warm skin on her thighs and hips as he did so. She looked like she'd stopped breathing momentarily as he ran his fingers around the elastic of her knickers. He took a deep breath. Easing the dress off, he drank in how beautifully lithe and toned she was. She had on what looked like a brand-new underwear set, consisting of a black lacy bra and pants with white embroidered flowers. Her eyes gleamed wide, like she was worried he wouldn't like what he saw. Raising his hand to her breasts, he grazed his fingertips over the lace. Her breasts weren't large, but they were pert and rose to his touch. He carried on toying with her until he felt her nipples rising.

Her wide eyes burned with desire, and he gave her a smile. 'All ok?'

'Very ok.'

'Good.' He stood up, taking her with him. Her legs wrapped around his back. He pressed his hand into her lower back and down, smoothing over her bum, drawing her against him.

'Oh,' she squealed. 'I hope I don't disappoint you.'

'You won't. No way. I just don't want to hurt you. First times can be a bit sore.'

'I'm ready.'

'I know, but not yet. Let's get you good and relaxed.'

She ran her hand over his shirt, down his chest, touching the ridges of muscle.

'Do you want to stay down here or take this upstairs?' he asked.

'Upstairs. And I think I should lock the door.'

'Ok. Do people normally come barging in here without knocking? If they do, you have my sympathy. My mother does that to me.'

She shook her head, moving into the small hallway and turning the key in the door. 'No one has so far, but I've only been here a couple of days. The woman in the first house is a bit mad – by her own admission – so I wouldn't like to leave anything to chance.'

'Fair enough... Lead the way.' He followed her up the stairs, ducking slightly as the upstairs ceilings were quite low where the roof cut in.

As soon as they were in her room, he took her face in his hands and kissed her. Then he scooped her up and lay her gently on the bed.

'Are you keeping your clothes on?' she asked.

'For a bit. If they come off right now... Well...' His gaze locked with hers, his mouth inches from hers. 'I might not last.' He was ready, too ready, and he needed to hold back. He drank in the sight of her on the bed. Her pale skin was rosy with the flush of arousal. Her blonde hair, freed from its plait, spread across the broderie anglaise pillows on the soft bed. It was a double bed, not as big as the king-size one he had at home – and needed as he was too tall for smaller beds, but in this case, he didn't care. In this bed, they could get very close. He sat beside her, looping off her bra straps and exposing her breasts. They rose and fell with every ragged breath. Her nipples were bright pink and looked edible. The ache in his crotch was painful. *Cool it. Get a grip.* Tugging off his shirt, he tossed it away, then hesitated before undoing his trouser button. He didn't remove them. He just needed some room to breathe.

Sliding onto the bed next to her, he cupped her breast and gently smoothed his fingers over it. In her eyes he saw her vulnerability, felt her tremble a little, but he'd be gentle. He swallowed the raging desire to take her and bury himself inside her.

'Is this still ok?'

She nodded, biting into her lip. 'Can I touch you too?'

'Sure. Just go easy for now. I want this to last.'

Her smile was adorable. As she brought her hand to his chest, he had a moment of raw male satisfaction. Then she dipped in and pressed a kiss on his left pec. He held his breath, not expecting such a bold move on her part, but he couldn't deny how good it felt. She didn't stop kissing around his shoulders, then his neck.

'You're killing me,' he groaned.

She glanced up. 'Am I doing something wrong?'

'God no. It's great.' If she lowered her hands to his boxers, she'd find out just how great. He propped himself up on one arm. 'But it's my turn to give you something.'

He traced the top of her lacy knickers with his fingertips. Her breathing intensified, and he gently rolled his palms back towards her breasts, cupping them, and smoothing his hands over the soft flesh, then leaning in to kiss her again. She let out a little squeal as his tongue met hers. His body slid over her, and everything became more urgent, but he held himself together, trailing his mouth over her breasts, then making his way lower. When he reached the scrap of lace covering her most intimate place, he placed a kiss on top of it.

'Still ok?' He met her wide eyes and saw her nod. It was the consent he needed.

Chapter Twenty-One

Dagmar

Dagmar could hardly breathe, knowing something big was about to happen. Something she'd only dreamed of. The soft kisses on her heated skin had turned sinful. James's lips and fingers were busy on her most intimate area, and she no longer felt the need to hold back. If she just relaxed...

The second she did so, all the sensations doubled, tripled, then detonated.

She let out a cry, jolting like she'd been hit by lightning. She'd never known anything like this. James crawled back up to her, lust blazing in his bright blue eyes. Dagmar panted, not sure where to look or what to say. She was completely exposed and kind of lost. Cold and shaky.

Was that all he was going to do? Would he leave now?

'Are you ok?' He raised an eyebrow as he looked at her.

She nodded, then wrapped her arms about herself. A second later, a wall of heat surrounded her. James's strong embrace held her close, and he kissed her brow. He'd removed all his clothes, and she felt him hard against her.

'You're so beautiful. Are you enjoying yourself?'

'It's better than I imagined.' Dagmar's head and heart might explode. How did people do this casually? Maybe it was like everything else: the more you did it, the more you got used to it. She couldn't see herself ever taking moments like these for granted. Her breathing calmed and the rush of serotonin spread out, filtering through her nervous system, as James gently kissed her and soothed her.

His breath fluttered across her skin. 'I feel so much,' he said. 'Normally, I'm good at detaching myself, but Christ. You're too good.'

'Am I?'

'Yes.'

'But we haven't even...'

'When you're ready.'

'I'm ready now.' Readier than she'd ever thought she would be. 'I really want it.'

'Ok.' He lay down, taking her with him, and shifted one of his legs between hers. Wiry hairs tickled the inside of her thighs, a deep heat building again.

'I thought this was just going to be sex.' She gazed into his eyes.

'That's what we're doing.'

'Are you sure?' She fixed him with a hard stare. 'This feels like more... I don't know. It's a lot more fun than I imagined. I thought it would be more serious.'

He ran his fingertips down her cheek. 'No point in it being serious if you want to enjoy yourself.' He moved off her for a moment and she wondered what he was doing, then she realised he was sheathing himself.

'I get it. You want to ruin me for everyone else?'

'Something like that.' He came back to her, grinning. His mouth found hers and the urgency returned.

He moved in between her legs, pushing her thighs wide, and smoothing his palms over her. She wasn't worried about him encountering any physical barriers; horse riding had seen to that, but he was big, and she tensed. 'It's ok. We can do this. Just relax... if you can.' He lowered his face to hers and kissed her, slipping his hand between them and teasing her until she relaxed and was ready. Then he inched in.

At first, she winced a little, not sure if the burn was painful because of the touch, or because she was so desperate for it. Slowly and surely, he filled her, and she panted, adjusting to all the new sensations.

'Still ok?' He watched her.

She smiled, emotions rising inside her. 'It's good. You're in.' He was the first person who'd ever done it. She wished he could be the last. Maybe he would be, not because he was planning on sticking around, but even if he went off with some rich woman, Dagmar might not want anyone else doing this.

He blew out a breath. 'Tell me to stop if it's too much. Ok?'

'Ok.'

He groaned as his hips drove into her, gently at first, then faster. Pinned beneath his hard body, she started to enjoy the friction. Even the sound was oddly erotic. Her inhibitions dissolved and she let out a long moan, embracing fully the raw energy surging through her. She was desirable and invincible. Epona, the horse goddess, was in a different saddle now, a new and very hot one. The pleasure coiling inside her was like nothing she could describe or explain. No one could have prepared her for this. She tightened with every thrust.

'I'm not sure I can... oh James. I think I'm—'

He ground into her until she shattered again, a wild groan escaping her. Following a few more thrusts, James's body stiffened. 'Oh god,' he moaned, collapsing on top of her.

She savoured the solid weight of him, the heavy thud of his heart pounding against her chest. Heat radiated from him, surrounding her, and she wanted to stay like this forever. But all too quickly he rolled off her, staring up at the moulded ceiling as he lay on his back. Had she done something wrong? He jumped off the bed.

'Let me get rid of this. I'll be back. Here.' Grabbing the duvet, he covered her with it, then disappeared out of the door.

Dagmar lay still, not quite sure what to do or think. Her legs were still shaky, but her core felt full to the brim. She wasn't a virgin anymore. That thought made her smile. But where was James? Was this his way of keeping things casual? Would he leave now they'd done the deed? The door swung open, and he returned.

'Hey.' He slipped under the cover with her and smiled at her. 'How does it feel?' He raised an eyebrow. 'Down there.'

'Ok.'

'Not too sore? I can get you a warm flannel or something, if you want?'

She smiled. 'I'm fine. I guess horse riding has its uses for other things too.'

He let out a little laugh and pulled her into an embrace. 'I guess. Do you like cuddling?'

'I think so.'

'Then let's do it.'

'Do you like it?'

He stroked her hair as she placed her head on his chest, loving his slightly coarse hair against her cheek. 'Normally, no. My ex probably thinks me the coldest lover she ever had.'

'Why?'

'You want me to tell you about an ex right now?'

'Yeah. Why not? It's not like talking about her will make her appear or anything.'

'Well, she and I didn't really feel that much for each other. We had an arrangement, kind of friends with benefits and kind of faking it for our families. We never cuddled. I think she wanted to, and I always felt bad because I didn't. I couldn't. It wasn't like that for me.'

'I don't know how you do this casually,' she said, voicing her feelings from earlier.

'I'm struggling to remember myself.' He planted a kiss on her forehead. 'Let's just cuddle for a bit. Then I might need some food.'

'And… Will you stay after that?'

'If you want me to. We could even go for round two if you're up for it.'

She grinned. 'I think that's more of an issue for you than me.'

'I'm sure it won't be a problem.' He winked, and she buried her face in his chest, letting all the joy of the moment seep into her.

A thrill ran through Dagmar as she walked with James towards the stables the following morning. Holding hands in public wouldn't be sensible, but their little fingers brushed every so often, bringing a smile to her face. A hint of rain hung in the air, but it hadn't come to anything yet.

'It's great, this,' he said. 'We can spend the whole weekend together and no one will know we're not just innocently going riding together.'

She smiled, feeling her cheeks warm. 'Indeed. Even if we continue riding later.'

'Oh, you're naughty.' He ticked his finger at her. 'That didn't take long to convert you.'

She let out a laugh. Everything looked different somehow. It was stupid to think she was seeing the world through fresh eyes, but she was. She'd done something new and incredible. After hearing so many stories about first times being awful, she'd almost talked herself out of ever having sex. But now she'd tasted it, she wanted more. Though a painful stab reminded her this was borrowed time. Still, she didn't need to think about that just now.

They reached the stables and started preparing the horses. Zephyra snorted softly as Dagmar approached, and she scratched her neck. James started on Conker, whistling a jaunty tune. Since when had he been this cheerful?

'I never thought I'd enjoy riding this much,' he said. 'It's actually a lot of fun.'

'You've definitely taken to it,' Dagmar replied.

'I had a good teacher.' He snuck into her stall and put his arms around her from behind. She giggled, and he placed a long kiss on her cheek. She turned, wrapping her arms around his neck and meeting his hot mouth. Zephyra snorted, but Dagmar ignored her. She could stand by and watch for a moment. This was too good an opportunity to miss.

Voices at the door made them leap apart. James staggered backwards a little, but wasn't able to get out of the stall before two people came in. Francesca Chattan-Blythe and her mother,

Jacinta, entered the stable. Dagmar froze. Jacinta was the estate owner's wife and although Ophelia pretty much managed everything, her stepmother still had some power and could probably get rid of Dagmar if she wanted.

Jacinta's eyes narrowed as she looked at Dagmar and James.

'Morning,' Dagmar said.

'Hi.' Francesca gave her a little wave, but even she had a slightly raised eyebrow. Dagmar guessed she and Caitlin would have their heads together, gossiping, as soon as they got together, but that was only a small concern next to Jacinta, who hadn't taken her eyes off them.

'Morning.' Jacinta shifted her focus to James. 'Are you here to see Ophelia?'

James shook his head. 'Er, no. I ride here.'

'You do?' Jacinta raised both brows. 'I don't recall you being a rider.'

Dagmar's stomach tightened. 'He's taking refresher lessons. Didn't Ophelia tell you?'

Francesca's gaze was still curious as she busied herself at the feed box. 'I'm sure she mentioned it to you, Mum.'

'Well, that's very interesting,' Jacinta said. 'She may have mentioned it, but I must have misunderstood her.'

'Um...' Dagmar swallowed.

'I doubt it.' James leaned on the edge of the stall. 'It's surprised everyone. But now when I'm in the saddle, I feel great.'

Jacinta gave a tight-lipped smile. 'You never mentioned a thing about it when you were here last year. I feel like it would have been the ideal conversation starter for you and Ophelia.'

'Good point. That was a bit silly of me.' He eased his way out of the stall. 'Should get this lad ready.'

Jacinta moved back to let him pass. Her eyes turned back to Dagmar. No words left her lips, but they didn't have to. Her eyes told Dagmar she'd seen all she needed and suspected a whole lot more. Eventually, she moved on. Francesca glanced back, giving Dagmar an odd, almost pleading look, like she really hoped what she'd seen wasn't true.

Dagmar couldn't wait to get the saddle on Zephyra and get her out of the stables. The sun was poking through the clouds, and the threat of rain had eased. James mounted Conker with a lot more confidence than he had just a few weeks ago. He looked almost assured enough to pass as someone who'd been riding for a long time and had indeed only needed a few refresher lessons to get him going.

As they headed for the bridle path, James glanced over at Dagmar, his brow furrowed, and she met his gaze. 'That wasn't good, was it?'

'Meeting Jacinta, you mean?'

'Yup. She'll make mischief out of what she saw in there. I just know it.'

'Yes, I expect she will.' Dagmar sighed. 'She's a major gossip.'

He pulled a face. 'Like my mother. I just hope it doesn't get you into trouble.' He checked around. 'We should be a little more discreet. Well, I should be. You've done nothing wrong. I need to get a hold of myself.'

'I could take a hold for you.'

He burst out laughing. 'You really are a naughty one. But, easy tiger, you can take hold of anything you fancy later on.' He winked.

A smile tugged at her lips, and she let the worries about Jacinta slip away. For now. 'I look forward to it.'

He'd learned to ride quick enough, and she could learn how to be a goddess in the bedroom just as fast.

'Come home with me later,' he said. 'You missed seeing my house yesterday. I think you'll like it.'

She sucked on her lower lip. Should she? Why not? She deserved a night off, and she could only begin to imagine what James's house would be like. Not just his house, but his bed.

'Ok.'

Late in the afternoon, Dagmar tossed a few essentials into a bag before jumping into James's car. Ophelia was still at her friend's party in Edinburgh, and Dagmar felt weird leaving the stables completely unattended. She messaged Barbara, the estate manager, to say if anyone needed her to call straight away. Wouldn't it just be the thing for something to happen tonight? But hopefully with CCTV now installed, everything would be fine. She hadn't been called to an emergency for a long time.

'Ophelia will be back soon.' James squeezed her thigh. 'So try not to worry.' But that would be difficult.

He drove the other way up the lochside than she was used to. Normally she'd drive towards Glenbriar to see her mum, which she really must do soon. She needed to talk to someone about what had happened and if she couldn't talk to her mum, then who? Ophelia? Kristi? She classed them as friends now. Kristi had said to drop her a message any time. Why not?

As James drove, she tapped out a text.

*DAGMAR: Hey! Hope you don't mind me messaging like this. I'm going to someone's house tonight *wink emoji*... You can probably guess who, but I'm feeling nervous about leaving the stables. I'm sure everything will be fine, but argh!! Sorry... Just need to get it off my chest.*

She sent it, then cringed. Did it sound totally stupid? A few seconds later, the ticks turned blue and the word *typing* appeared at the top. Dagmar waited, watching the scenery, until a message pinged.

KRISTI: Ooh! You didn't waste time. Don't worry about the stables. Caitlin wants to go up and get something she left there yesterday, so we'll nip up later and check everything's ok. You enjoy yourself x

'Oh god,' Dagmar said.

'What?' James frowned.

'I didn't mean for Kristi to go up and check.' She explained what was in the message.

'But she's going anyway.'

Dagmar hoped that was the truth. Kristi was so nice Dagmar could well imagine her driving up just to help out.

James turned into the driveway of a modern mansion with sleek lines, white paintwork and expansive windows gleaming in the afternoon sunlight. Dagmar's breath caught.

'Wow.' It looked very similar to Duchan Fayre and had clearly been built around the same time.

'You like it?'

'It's huge.'

'It's not all mine. My parents built it. I've got my own wing, so it's like my own place, but with familiar neighbours.'

Dagmar could see both ups and downs with that arrangement.

He parked around the back and glanced up at the windows. 'My mum technically can't see this part of the building from here, but let's get in quickly, just in case. She's very nosey.'

He led her through a side entrance that was grander than most people's front doors. As soon as they stepped inside, Dagmar's jaw dropped. Polished wood floors, high ceilings, and elegant furniture filled the space. Compared to her humble cottage – which was a mansion compared to the trailer – this place was Buckingham Palace. No wonder James was on the chase for a rich wife. How much better suited to him were the likes of Ophelia and Victoria? *So much more than me.*

'Would you like a tour?' he asked.

'Yeah… I guess.' Though every step she took made her feel even worse about herself. She and James were the same age, but he had all this.

'This is the living room.' James opened the door. 'And across here, we have the kitchen.'

She nodded, trying to focus on his words but feeling increasingly out of place. They climbed a sweeping staircase, and he led her down a corridor. 'There are two bedrooms up here and my office.' He pushed open the door to his room and Dagmar's inside contracted.

A plush white room with subtle duck egg and navy contrasts unfolded before her. She could imagine posh suites in hotels looking like this. But she'd never been in one. It was a world away from what she was used to.

James furrowed his brow. 'Hey, are you ok?'

'Yeah, it's just… a lot to take in compared to where I live.'

'It's just a house, and one that my parents handed to me on a plate. I don't intend to stay in it forever.' He smiled, pulling her close. 'You make it special by being here.'

She smiled back, and he pushed the door behind him. The large bed with its plush duvet looked soft and comfortable. Dagmar's mind had already raced ahead to visions of them entwined in the sheets. That was exactly what she craved, his hot body inside her again. James leaned in, his lips brushing hers, and she responded eagerly.

Just as their kiss deepened, the doorbell rang.

James groaned, pulling back. 'Stay here. I bet that's my mother. She has a habit of just walking in on me, so I better answer it.'

Dagmar nodded, watching as he left the room. She took a deep breath, trying to steady herself. His mother? Much as she loved her mum, she wasn't sure she'd like this level of interference. She moved to the door and put her head to it.

What were they saying? An urge to know seized her and she pushed open the door to listen.

CHAPTER TWENTY-TWO

James

J ames took a deep breath as his mother breezed into the hallway. She didn't look at him but scanned around with a slight frown. He had a deep sense of unease similar to how he'd felt when he'd watched *Chitty Chitty Bang Bang* as a boy and the child catcher had sleazed onto the scene, trying to sniff out the hidden children. Sherri wasn't that sinister, but her nose was just as tuned in, and he was sure she could smell Dagmar's perfume, or she'd spied something amiss.

'Mum, what are you doing here?' He kept his voice level.

'I've been worried about you.' Sherri moved past him, still scanning around. 'I noticed you've been out a lot. Where have you been and what are you up to?'

'Really? It's none of your business.' He shut the door and followed her into the living room. 'If I didn't live here, you wouldn't know one way or another where I was. We might have to reassess this arrangement. I'm not sure I want this kind of third degree every time I go out.'

Sherri glanced around again, and James ground his teeth. What did she hope to find? He guessed it wasn't Victoria. That would have made her a lot happier, and right now, she didn't look too amused. 'I had a strange call from Jacinta Chattan-Blythe this morning. You know, Ophelia's stepmother from—'

'I know who she is.' James's stomach tightened. Like he couldn't guess why she'd called. She was a renowned gossip and a busybody who liked to stir up trouble and drama. 'I didn't think the two of you were that friendly.'

'We're not exactly best friends, but we got to know each other quite well when you and Ophelia were...' She pulled a face, knowing, of course, that he and Ophelia had never really been anything.

'Just get to the point, Mum.'

'I am. So, she was asking if you were still interested in Victoria which, naturally, I told her you were—'

'Why did you tell her that? When I told you we're no'

'I'd like to think you're not going to give up that father has set so much on this. You promised him want to hold that promise to your head like giving up so quickly seems silly to me. Th what's really happened.'

James folded his arms and raised h

Sherri pulled a face like this

said she thought their stable

you.'

James couldn't hold back his eye roll. Bloody nosey parkers. Couldn't they just mind their own business?

'What stable girl? The stable girls are kids.'.

'Some woman called Dagmar.'

'Dagmar is the yard manager.' If his mother wanted to accuse her, she could at least get her title correct.

'Isn't she the one who won all the events at the horse trials? I think someone mentioned her working at Glenvorneth. But it dawned on me I'd heard that name before. Didn't you go to primary school with a Dagmar? It's not a name I've heard very often.'

James ground his teeth. 'Yes, the woman who works at the stables is the same Dagmar I was at school with and the same one who won all the competitions. She's the woman who has been teaching me to ride.'

'Really? It is actually her?' Sherri raised an eyebrow.

'I needed the best rider in the area to teach me, so it made sense to approach her.'

'She was a strange child.' Sherri picked absently on her nail. 't not as odd as her mother. Dotty. That's what everyone called Not sure it was her real name though. Suited her. Dotty by Dotty by nature.' She laughed.

'ge of irritation raced through him. 'Dotty's actually a 'an.'

'n't have thought you could even remember her. You out seven when we moved away.'

'Yeah, but I ended up at the same high school as Dagmar too. And Dotty owns the Cosy Bean Café. She's a nice lady.'

Sherri's eyes narrowed, and she watched him for a moment. 'The Cosy Bean Café? The place that's on the list of community projects.'

'The very same.'

Sherri pouted, then narrowed her eyes. 'And this is all above board?'

'In what way?'

'You and this Dagmar woman aren't doing anything you shouldn't be, are you?'

'Such as?'

'Did you put the café on the list in return for... Well, favours?'

'No... Not what you're thinking anyway. I suggested it on its own merit, but I admit, I wanted to sway Dagmar into helping me.'

'You shouldn't have done that.'

'Look. Dad and Henry both agreed it was a good idea *before* I approached Dagmar. I would have suggested it anyway, whether she helped me or not. And now Dagmar is a friend. She's helped me a lot with the riding, which is exactly what you and Dad wanted.'

Sherri let out a sigh. 'Yes... We did. So you and Victoria could get together. But it doesn't look like that's going to happen now.'

'That's because I want to have the freedom to decide for my-self.'

'How do you mean?'

He closed his eyes and rubbed his forehead. 'All these women are people you've chosen for me. That's why nothing ever comes of them. I need to choose for myself.'

'So, what are you saying? That you won't choose Victoria just because your father and I think she's right?'

Up until now, he'd gone along with all their schemes and believed one of their matches would suit him and be exactly what he needed. That was before Dagmar. Now she was upstairs, in his bedroom, waiting for him. All he really wanted was to go to her and stay with her. Would it really be so bad if he chose her? Would she choose him?

'James.' His mother glared at him. 'Are you going to answer me?'

'I don't think Victoria and I are right for each other.'

She let out a sigh. 'Then you need to tell your father. He sees this as the chance of a lifetime. A chance to be related to the Earl of Dairvin and Duchan Fayre will have links to the best family in the area. Our legacy will be preserved forever. You have a chance to be a father to children who'll be part of the aristocracy.'

'Listen, Mum. I don't really care about any of that. Duchan Fayre can exist without a big family name behind it. Our family name is good enough. You and Dad didn't use to judge people on their titles or how much money they had. What about their other qualities? What about trusting me and Eloise to carry on the family legacy in our own way?'

Sherri swallowed. 'I hear what you're saying, darling. I agree, and maybe I've been blinded by money. Your father won't be so easily swayed, and I'd rather you told him this than me.' She patted his upper arm and placed a kiss on his cheek. 'I'm not trying to force anyone on you, but Victoria always looked so happy when she was with you. I suppose I don't want her to be disappointed, but if you don't like her, then there's no point.'

'I like her... I just don't love her. And I don't think I ever could. Dad thinks a marriage can be like a business arrangement, but I don't. Is that really what your marriage has been like?'

His mum shook her head. 'No. I suppose some of it maybe. I mean, all relationships need compromise. Your father is very good at making comparisons... Even when there aren't any.'

'Yeah. Well...'

'Will you speak to him?'

'Yes. But not now. I'm actually right in the middle of something, but I will speak to him as soon as I can.' He escorted her out of the house, mainly to make sure she actually went.

As soon as he was sure she was gone, he locked the door. Taking the stairs two at a time, he returned to Dagmar.

The bedroom door was open, and Dagmar stood just inside, twisting her fingers.

'Did you hear any of that?' James tried to gauge her expression. She had her competition face on. The one that gave nothing away.

She bit down on her lower lip, glancing away for a moment before meeting his eyes. 'I heard most of it. I didn't mean to eavesdrop, but...' She took a deep breath. 'I couldn't help myself.'

'It's fine. I don't mind if you heard. My parents are such meddlers. I'm truly sorry about what she said about your mum though. That was out of order.'

'I'm sure it's nothing she hasn't heard before. People have always called her strange. Mostly ones who don't know her.'

'My mother is such a snob. Both my parents are. Maybe I've been guilty of it too, and I'm sorry.'

'Listen, I'm a bit worried about what she said about the café. Do you think she'll stop the money going through?'

'I'll speak to my father about it. It wouldn't look good for the company to go back on its word, so I don't think he'll stop it. I can go now if you want, but nothing will get done over the weekend.'

'Stay here then.' She opened her arms. 'I think I need a hug.'

'Me too. This has all got messy. But I need to talk to my father about other things too.'

'Such as?'

'Us.'

She pulled back a little. 'Is there an us?'

'I'd like to think so. We deserve a shot, don't you think? But I made a promise to my father some time ago and I hate breaking my word.'

'A promise to marry Victoria?'

'Not exactly. But when my dad was very ill a few years ago, I promised I'd marry into a big-name family to ensure the future of Duchan Fayre. But even in those few years, Duchan has come so far and I don't think that's necessary now. It shouldn't ever have been, but that's how my father thinks.'

James kissed the top of her head, then she reached up and met his lips. The heat of her drew him in, and his insides burned. She stiffened for a moment, then melted into him, her arms wrapping around his neck. 'I just want you. Nothing else.' He breathed the words onto her neck.

She kissed him again, their bodies pressing closer as the tension between them ignited. Warm desire flooded his veins, and his hands roamed her back, pulling her even tighter. Dagmar's fingers tangled in his hair, her breath quickening.

Their lips parted briefly, both of them gasping for air. James looked into her eyes, his heartrate picking up.

'I can't think about anything else right now but you.'

She looked up, her eyes wide and searching. 'Same.'

James kissed her again, more urgently this time. The world outside faded away. The intensity of the connection was raw and unbridled, and they clung to each other.

James pulled back slightly, his forehead resting against hers. 'Time for your riding lesson for the day, I think.' He raised an eyebrow.

'That sounds so crude.' Dagmar stroked his hair absently, her breath warm against his skin. 'But I'm ready.'

'Good.' Slowly he undressed her, taking his time, giving her all the attention she needed. She'd grown brave, urging him to take off his shirt, then removing his belt and exploring inside his jeans with her fingers, until he had to stop her.

'Not too much yet.' He smiled, catching her eye.

When they were fully naked, he laid her on the huge bed, her hair billowing across it. Now she was laid bare for him to worship with his lips until she was quivering around him. Such a delicious pleasure. Then he lay alongside her, kissing her and running his fingers through her hair.

'Still ok?' he asked through kisses.

'Yes.'

He lay on his back, reaching for a condom and rolling it on. She sized him up for a moment, then straddled him. Their eyes met as she lowered herself slowly onto him. The sight made his breath catch.

She smiled, leaning forward and rocking. Hot sparks of pleasure darted through him. Her cute little breasts peaked as she increased the tempo and her eyes closed.

He pushed himself up, so he was sitting, bringing him closer to her, and wrapped his arms about her. Pressing his lips to hers, he groaned, and gently thrust, allowing the hot intimacy of the moment to percolate into every cell. Their tongues met, heightening the sensations coursing through their linked bodies. The friction and erotic energy were so powerful James couldn't remember anything except how to give and receive pleasure.

'Dagmar,' he whispered, sliding his hand into her hair. 'Open your eyes. Look at me.'

She did, and their gazes connected. Keeping his eyes on her, he thrust a little harder, her hips answering him, until she raced ahead, chasing the final jump like her life depended on it. He captured her breasts, rolling his palms over them. Like he'd hit a magic switch, she cried out, shuddering, still looking at him, her eyes wide and bright, almost fearful. But she had nothing to be scared of. She deserved this pleasure. He held her as she panted and gasped for air, but his own release was close. Nestling his forehead in the crook of her neck, he took a few deliberate breaths before looking back at her.

This was what being in love felt like. None of the fake stuff he'd been exposed to so far.

She smiled, and his hunger intensified. He pounded into her, his body supercharged, his mind desperate. She slipped her delicate arms around his neck to brace herself, the dreamy smile still etched on her face.

'Christ. Oh. Dagmar.' The words came out in stilted breaths as his climax hit. A few aftershocks made him twitch, and he held tight to her, his skin suddenly hypersensitive. She kissed his neck, and he smiled as it tickled him, then he turned to her and joined the kiss. It was warm and wholesome, affirming everything they'd just done, and begging to be done again and again. Which he would in a heartbeat. Except an unpleasant obstacle shaped like his father stood in the way. If he and Dagmar were going anywhere, he had to sort that out.

Chapter Twenty-Three

Dagmar

Dagmar parked her car outside the Cosy Bean Café, her mind swirling over everything that had happened that weekend. James was in a meeting that morning to talk to his colleagues about the café. No doubt his father would be there too, and Dagmar had a funny feeling things wouldn't go smoothly there. The idea of driving to Duchan Fayre clawed at her mind. She could crash the meeting and say her piece. Though she wasn't sure that would help.

She pushed open the door to the café, the familiar scent of coffee and pastries welcoming her in. A couple of people were seated near the window. That was the first time Dagmar had seen anyone in here for ages. Her mother was behind the counter, lifting a pastry from the glass cabinet with a pair of tongs, her brow knitted. She glanced up and saw Dagmar, and her expression softened, but the worry lines didn't disappear.

'Hi, Mum.' Dagmar forced a smile and made her way in behind the counter. 'How's it going?'

Dotty sighed. 'Let me get these to the customers, love, then I'll chat.' She took a tray to the table at the window, placed the cakes and drinks before the customers, then headed back to Dagmar. 'Things are not going well,' she said.

Dagmar's heart sank. Dotty looked tired, more so than usual, and her eyes were a little red.

'What's wrong?'

'It's the landlord.' Dotty checked the customers couldn't hear her. 'He's just been on the phone, and he's given me an ultimatum. Either I pay up the back rent by the end of the week, or I'm out.'

Dagmar's stomach churned. 'The end of the week?'

Dotty nodded. 'I think he's looking for any excuse to get rid of me.'

Dagmar reached out and squeezed her mother's hand. 'Oh god. I'll have to tell James. He's in a meeting talking about things right now.'

'I don't know what he can do.' Dotty placed her hands on her cheeks.

'I'm sure he'll do what he can.' Dagmar pulled out her phone and typed a message.

'I'm not sure what he can do. Not unless he moves very fast.'

'Let's see what he says.'

Dotty's shoulders slumped. 'This ultimatum has hit me so hard. I might be better just giving up. Maybe my café owning days are done.'

Dagmar shook her head. 'No, Mum. We'll sort this out. This is you. It's not your fault the landlord has made the rent so extortionate.'

'But maybe the rest of it is. This place has got away from me. I should have made more of an effort to update it. I sat back and rested when I should have been working.'

'If it's really too much, then of course I don't want you to do it, but if you still enjoy it, then we'll find a way. I'm seeing James later; I'll talk to him then.' Her heart squeezed at the thought. What might happen at the meeting? Would his father pull the plug on things? James's mother had made a comment like that. The rush of love Dagmar had felt over the last few days was replaced with a gnawing dread. Everything was imploding around her, and she didn't know how to fix it.

Later, she returned to the stables. James hadn't replied to her message yet, and it didn't look like he'd even seen it. He was due about six, so she only had a short while to wait – assuming he wasn't held up again. Caitlin was being so helpful, coming around every day even after exams, perhaps still hoping to get the job, and Dagmar hoped she would. She should speak to Ophelia about it. But it was a fine line she wasn't sure how to navigate. She wanted to help Caitlin, but with so many big personalities involved in Caitlin's life, Dagmar didn't want to take sides or cause problems.

Once she'd parked her truck, she headed for the stables. Despite being here in body, she was still engrossed in thoughts about the café and James. This was when mistakes happened, and she had to focus. What if she left gates open or something equally as stupid? She passed a very posh car in the car park that she didn't immediately recognise. A Ferrari? She'd surely have spotted one of them before, but the owners who used this livery were all minted, so it wouldn't be a surprise if one of them owned a Ferrari. Dagmar wasn't into cars, so it was possible she'd just never noticed.

As she entered the stable yard, she spotted a woman hanging about near the entrance. No way. It was Lady Victoria Bruce. What the hell was she doing here? One thing was certain, she wouldn't be here to see Dagmar. Most likely it would be Ophelia she wanted to see or James, but did she even know he came here? That was a secret, wasn't it? Had someone blabbed?

Jacinta probably.

Oh god.

After what she'd overheard James's mum say, that seemed so much more likely and if that was the case, then Dagmar really didn't want to be here. She looked around. She could get back in her truck, drive around the estate, and park down at her cottage. Victoria wouldn't know she'd ever been here. But before she could execute her plan, Victoria looked her way. A flicker of recognition registered on her face.

'Dagmar. Oh god, I forgot you worked here. That's a stroke of luck.' Victoria strolled over, flicking her dark hair over her shoulder.

'Is it?' Dagmar stood very still. If she moved, something might give her away, though she wasn't sure what.

'Yes, indeed. I'm looking for a bit of intel, and you might be just the person to fill me in.'

'Me?'

'Sure. So, my mother had the strangest call from Jacinta.' Victoria held out her hands with dramatic flair. 'She said she didn't want to gossip, but she wanted to give us a bit of a heads up.'

'About what?'

'James.' Victoria glanced around as if checking for him. 'You know he and I have a little thing going? Only he's been rather reticent lately, which could be my fault. He maybe thinks I've led him a bit of a merry dance. I had this other man in London... But that's by the by. I've had it with him. James is so much nicer. Anyway, I've completely digressed. Jacinta seemed to think James has been riding here quite a bit. I wondered if maybe his interest had strayed back to Ophelia.'

'Ophelia is happy with Brann. I don't think either she or James ever—'

'Oh, I know they were never that close.' Victoria waved an airy hand as she cut in. 'But he doesn't actually keep a horse here, does he?'

'Well, no, he doesn't own one. He uses the horses here to ride.'

'Interesting.' Victoria's gaze swept over the stable yard. 'That sounds like he's still quite chummy with Ophelia.'

'She's nice, so I don't see why they shouldn't be friends.'

Victoria made a little snort laugh, which was rather unkind as Ophelia had always had a humane side, in spite of her status and her implacable façade. If she gave as good as she got from Victoria and the countess, then who was Dagmar to complain?

'Jacinta also mentioned that James had an admirer.'

Heat rose in Dagmar's cheeks and her heart missed a beat. Was all Victoria's preamble a ruse? Was this her getting ready to strike? 'Oh really?'

'Some stable girl, apparently.'

She forced a smile. 'Oh?'

'I mean, it sounds terribly clichéd to me. But Jacinta implied he was having a romp in the hay with her. Which naturally I don't believe for a second.'

Dagmar tried to agree with a nod that was more like a nervous tic.

'But out of curiosity, are there any young stable girls here? I saw someone in there mucking out. Does she work here, or is she an owner?'

'Caitlin?' Dagmar's throat tightened. 'I, um, don't think she would be interested in James. She's very young.'

Victoria's gaze lingered on the stable door before she turned back to Dagmar. 'I hope that's true. I'm not giving him up for some stable girl.'

Dagmar managed a tight smile, but she'd quite like to slap Victoria. How dare she? *Some stable girl!*

Victoria narrowed her eyes a little then added, 'It would be quite ridiculous for him to get involved with someone that unsuitable, don't you think? I mean, with his EP, he can do much better.'

Dagmar barely held back her eye roll. All the pony club girls had talked about EP as teens – earning potential. Some had even extended it to EPNL. Earning potential, not looks. None of it had ever seemed to have a point to Dagmar, so she'd kept away from conversations like that, but this brought it all back. 'No doubt.'

'Well, I shouldn't hang about too long. I've got so much to do. Tell James I was here, won't you?'

'Sure.' Dagmar took a deep breath, willing Victoria to go – and quickly. But she didn't move. Her gaze was fixed on something over Dagmar's shoulder. Before Dagmar could check what she was looking at, a smile crept onto Victoria's face.

'No need. He's here. I can talk to him myself.'

Dagmar turned to see James approaching. His eyes widened when he clocked who she was talking to. He froze, but he hadn't managed to say a word when Victoria marched up to him, took hold of him and kissed both his cheeks, one after the other.

'James, hello! I was just talking about you.'

'Oh, really?'

'Indeed. How was work?'

He stepped back a little. 'Busy as always.' He glanced at Dagmar. 'So, ready for the ride?'

Dagmar nodded, almost surprised he was even giving her the time of day when Victoria was around. 'Yeah, sure.'

Victoria narrowed her eyes. 'No need to interrupt Dagmar's work. I'll go with you. I'm sure Ophelia will lend me a horse.'

A rush of heat surged up Dagmar's neck. 'I'm not sure our insurance covers you riding one of the horses unless you're a paying customer. I'll have to check the terms.'

'Pardon?' Victoria gaped at her.

James stepped towards Dagmar. 'I can't ride with you,' he said to Victoria. 'I'm going with Dagmar.' He gave Victoria a winning smile.

Her own smile faltered for a moment. 'Why don't we all ride together? If Dagmar really feels the need to come along, then I suppose it'll be fine.'

'We already had this planned,' James said.

'And it doesn't change the insurance issue,' Dagmar added.

'I'm sure that can't be right. Where can I find Ophelia?' She glanced around, perhaps expecting her to appear like a servant she'd summoned to attend to her needs.

'She's probably at the boathouse.' Dagmar exchanged a look with James, who was fiddling with the neckline of his sweater.

'Can you call her?'

Dagmar let out a little sigh. 'I can, but she'll say the same as me.'

'Victoria, this isn't the right time.' James appeared to be trying to flash her a smile again, but this time it looked more like a grimace. 'I'm not sure why you want to ride with me anyway.'

'Because we need to talk. I just wish I'd had someone bring my own horse. I had no idea the staff here were so obstinate.' She turned away from Dagmar and added to James. 'And rude.'

Her cold shoulder didn't hide the words, which Dagmar heard quite clearly.

James shook his head. 'That's unfair and uncalled for.'

Victoria patted James's arm and chuckled like she thought he was joking.

'If you're unwilling to abide by the yard's rules, you'll have to leave,' Dagmar said. 'I need to call Ophelia.' She gave James a little shrug, then turned on her heel and stalked off. She didn't need to listen to anymore, not after the day she'd had.

CHAPTER TWENTY-FOUR

James

A sharp pain stabbed James in the ribs, almost like Victoria had prodded him with a nail, but it was seeing Dagmar walk away that increased the ache.

'I need to go.' He made to walk away, but Victoria caught his arm, pulling him back. 'You should leave. This is helping no one.'

'I need to talk to you. Leave Dagmar. She's got work to do. And anyway, I've been meaning to talk to you about next year's horse trials. Mother is very keen to discuss the sponsorship you and your father mentioned, but we need to set the ball rolling, and soon.'

James breathed through his gritted teeth. 'This is not a good time for this because—'

'Of course I get that,' Victoria interrupted. 'But we can't waste too much time. We're talking about significant exposure for Duchan Fayre. And having that allied with Dairvin castle. Well, you see the significance, don't you?'

'Of course.' He forced a smile. It was precisely what his father wanted and what James had promised to do – a promise his father wasn't likely to forget, especially if today's talks were anything to go by. It had been a gruelling day, all in all. 'But I really need to—'

'Mother is hosting a dinner next month. You and your parents will be invited of course. It'll be the perfect chance to solidify the deal.'

James glanced in the direction Dagmar had gone, the tension in his chest mounting. 'Listen, I can't talk now.'

'Why the hell not?' Victoria took his hand. 'Let's get out of here and go for dinner or something.'

'I can't. I need to find Dagmar.'

'Dagmar?' She screwed up her face. 'Why do you need *her*?'

Her tone was as disparaging as ever.

'I really don't like the way you talk about Dagmar.' James frowned, struggling to keep his tone polite. 'She's not just some "stable person". She manages this livery and riding school. Plus, she's an extremely talented horse woman and a very pleasant individual. I think a little more respect is in order.'

'Oh, good gracious.' Victoria pressed her hand to her chest. 'Don't think I'm disrespecting her. Far from it. If anyone knows how good a rider she is, it's me. I just think it's wrong for us to bother her when she's obviously so busy. And we've finally got this opportunity to be together. I feel like I hardly ever get to see you.'

'That was your choice. You had someone else on the go... And so I... Well, what was I to think?'

'Oh gosh, yes. That's exactly what we need to discuss.' She pulled a side pout. 'I've ditched him completely. He was a mistake. I think it's time you and I fully committed to each other.'

'I can't do that, Victoria... The thing is—'

'Hello!'

James glanced around to see Ophelia and Brann approaching.

'Hey,' James said.

'Hello.' Ophelia smiled at them both, and Brann nodded. 'I didn't expect to see you here, Victoria.' Ophelia's eyes bored into her like she was trying to extract her reasons for being there without asking.

'So Dagmar hasn't grassed me up yet, has she?'

Ophelia frowned. 'No... Why? What have you been up to?'

'Disturbing the peace.'

'Oh dear. Well, I'm glad you're here. I've got some stuff for you.'

'For me?' Victoria raised her eyebrows.

'Jacinta left some books and things in the tack room and ordered me to deliver them to you, but needless to say, I'm not her servant and I simply haven't had time, so this is rather a happy chance.'

'What kind of books?'

'Honestly, I have no idea. Perhaps you'd like to come and look for yourself.'

Victoria hesitated, glancing at James. 'I... Well—'

'You should,' James said. 'I have other things to do.'

Victoria gave him a dirty look, but he ignored it.

'I heard Duchan Fayre was getting an extension.' Ophelia said, her eyes lingering between Victoria and James. He had the distinct sense she was trying to suss out what was going on with them.

'There are always rumours like that going about, but we don't have any expansion plans at present.'

'But they might be sponsoring the horse trials next year,' Victoria said.

'That makes sense.' Ophelia caught James's eye, and he gave her a brief smile, making sure not to betray anything.

'I'll leave you to discuss it,' James said, not looking back. 'I need to find Dagmar.'

The voices of Ophelia, Brann, and Victoria chattered as they went towards the tack room. James nipped into the stable block and looked around. Where was she?

He pulled out his phone and saw several messages. He'd been so busy all day, he hadn't replied to any of them. Some of them were from Dagmar. Opening the thread, he read some she'd sent that morning about her mum's café.

Shit.

Zephyra shuffled her feet in her stall as she ate. James took a deep breath; the scent of hay and horses had become like old friends but couldn't ease the squeezing sensation in his chest. This ultimatum made his plans for the Cosy Bean Café almost impossible. After his discussions with his father today, he was already in a state of flux. He was having to tread so carefully around his father that getting the finances sorted by Friday would be near impossible.

Victoria's voice floated into earshot. 'Where's James? Is he still here?'

'Not a clue,' Ophelia replied.

'This is so annoying,' Victoria huffed.

James held his breath, waiting until the sound of footsteps retreated, followed by the murmur of voices fading away. He peered around the door to make sure the coast was clear. Seeing no one, he cautiously stepped out of the stables.

Victoria was heading back towards the car park. He needed to find Dagmar.

'James.'

The voice made him jump. He turned to see Ophelia standing just outside the tack room, her eyebrows raised.

'Oh, hi.' James forced a would-be casual smile.

'Is Dagmar in there?' Ophelia gave him a long, penetrating look.

'No.' He raked his hand through his hair. 'She might be in the office. I think she went to call you.'

'What about? Was Victoria actually disturbing the peace?'

'Well...' His eyes strayed across the field. 'She was being rather demanding and pretty rude.'

'To Dagmar?'

'Yes.'

She put her hands on her hips and sighed. 'She can be very entitled, and she likes getting her own way. Why was she here anyway?'

James half rolled his eyes and sighed. 'I'm not even sure I know. I think Jacinta might have had something to do with it. She was definitely stirring up trouble with my mother.'

'That sounds like Jacinta alright.' She looked back into the tack room at a clattering sound. 'What's Brann doing in there?'

'Not sure, but I should head… I need to talk to Dagmar.' He didn't make eye contact with Ophelia. 'I'm not sure where she went though.'

'How are the lessons going?'

'Extremely well.' Though he wasn't talking about the horses. Dagmar was riding like a pro these days – a totally crude thought, but he couldn't stop it from flitting through his head.

'Well, that's something.'

His gaze met Ophelia's, and he had a weird sense that she'd guessed what he was thinking.

'I'll go find her. Nice seeing you.' He walked toward the office and looked in the door. Was Ophelia still watching him? He didn't dare look back to check.

Maybe Dagmar had gone to the cottage. He darted up the path in that direction. When he got to the crest of the hill, he looked down at the row of cottages. Dagmar was outside, hanging washing on a pull-out line to the side of her cottage. Without hesitation, he jogged down the path.

'Hey,' he called as he opened the gate.

'James. What—'

'Listen, I'm so sorry. I just saw all your messages. Today has been hellish. That ultimatum will make everything a hundred times worse.'

'Does that mean you can't do anything?' Her eyes were wide and fearful.

'I'll try my best.' He shook his head. 'But my father is not in a good place.'

'How do you mean?'

'Apparently, he's not feeling well and finding out that I don't want to see Victoria has made him worse. He thinks I'm not trying hard enough... and... I don't want to repeat it all, but I need to tread carefully. He could pull the plug on the whole café business, so I need to keep him onside.'

'It's such a nightmare.'

'I'm sorry. I never thought time would run out like this. These deals usually take a while to go through. I've done everything I can. I hope you believe that and don't think I've been slacking. Everything is in motion, but this changes things.'

'I believe you.' Before he could utter another word, she pushed onto her tiptoes and her lips were on his, urgent and demanding.

He responded with equal intensity. 'I'm not giving up,' he whispered between kisses.

Her hands gripped his shoulders, pulling him closer. He slipped his tongue into her mouth, deepening the kiss, and heat burned through him.

'I know you'll do what you can.'

He broke away, his breath ragged. 'I'll do everything within my power,' he murmured against her lips. 'I promise.' The word echoed in his mind. He'd made a promise to his father too, and it looked like he'd have to break it. What if he couldn't save the café either?

Dagmar's chest heaved, the outline of her bra showing through the thin white cotton t-shirt, and James barely mastered the urge to rip it off. 'Did you get rid of Victoria?'

'For now. I tried to tell her I wasn't interested anymore, but Ophelia showed up, and I had to stop talking.'

'Victoria reckons it's Caitlin who's sweet on you, not me.'

'What?' He looked away and frowned. 'Isn't she just a teenager?'

'Yup.'

'I'm going to have to either meet Victoria or message her and tell her she and I aren't ever getting together.'

Dagmar shook her head. 'Are you sure?'

'Yes,' he said, his voice low. 'I only want to be with you.'

'You what?'

'You heard me.'

'But... I thought this was just a fling.'

'Is that what you want?'

She smiled. 'I thought I did, but... Well, I'd like to think we had a future. I assumed you'd need to go and find someone richer than me for the long run.'

He shook his head. 'That's what my father wants, and it's what I promised to do, but I'm working on a way to let him know I want to be with someone of my own choosing.'

'And that's me?' She stared at him like she could hardly believe her ears.

'It's always been you. I just didn't know how to bring it about. Even now, I'm not sure, but I'm determined to find a way.' His mouth found hers again. 'You are the future I want.' Though getting it wouldn't be an easy task. His father was bound to find obstacles even Zephyra would have difficulty clearing.

The kissing continued, growing more passionate. 'Let's go inside,' Dagmar said. 'Camilla, the mad artist, might be watching, and god knows what she might say to Jacinta or Ophelia.'

'I think Ophelia suspects already.' James followed her in.

Dagmar's eyes widened. 'You think?'

'Yep, she's sharp.'

Dagmar bit her lip. 'Are you sure we're doing the right thing?'

'Yes. We just need to keep quiet about it for a little longer, then it doesn't matter who knows.'

He captured her lips once more, sliding his hands under her top and popping her bra open. Their kisses grew more frantic.

'I need a shower.' Dagmar pulled back. 'I can't do this when I'm in such a state. I feel sticky from working.'

'Let's clean up together.'

'Are you serious?'

'Deadly.' He wanted her, needed her, and every fibre of his being screamed for more. 'Come on,' he murmured against her lips, tugging her up the stairs.

They stumbled inside the little bathroom, barely managing to close the door behind them, before James started undressing her, then himself. His body was so ready and thankfully he'd prepared by shoving a couple of condoms in his wallet. He retrieved it from the pocket of his trousers and rolled one on.

Dagmar looked a little uncertain, standing wholly naked in the small space, which was pristinely white with grey accents on the tiles and a potted plant at the window. James kicked their clothes into the far corner and reached for the handle, turning on the water. It flowed out in a somewhat unenthusiastic trickle.

'It takes a moment to work up.' Dagmar glanced at it.

'Me too.' James stepped under the water in the glass cubicle and drew Dagmar towards him, turning her under the flow. 'God, you're beautiful.' His hands slid up her wet skin.

'Am I?'

'You always have been.' He flipped up the lid of a shower gel bottle, squeezing some creamy white liquid onto his palm and smoothing it over Dagmar, lingering longest on her breasts, watching them rise to his touch. She tossed back her head with a moan. He dipped in and kissed her neck.

'Oh, god, James.' She put her hands on his shoulders. 'I have to ask you something.'

'What?' He lathered around her shoulders and her upper arms.

'Will your parents ever accept me? I mean, if we do end up having a future together.'

'My mother will, I'm sure.' James gently massaged her shoulders.

'But my father will take some work. Leave it with me. I'm working on it.' He put his hands under her bum and lifted her. She wrapped her legs around his waist. 'But, right now, I'm working on you, and only you.'

CHAPTER TWENTY-FIVE

Dagmar

Dagmar brushed Zephyra's sleek coat, enjoying the steady, repetitive rhythm. She needed something to keep her mind and body occupied because her life was unravelling, and she wasn't sure how to stop it.

She sighed, pausing for a moment. If she closed her eyes, she could still feel James's touch, the warmth of his embrace, the way his lips moved against hers. She'd ridden horses for as long as she remembered and was used to sore legs and hips, but the exquisite aches she had now weren't like that. They might be around the same area, but these carried memories. She'd crammed so many into such a short time. Each memory was hot and brought pleasant little jolts to her nerve ends. A vivid contrast to the cold reality that was waiting beyond the stable doors. She was living in a dream, a blissful bubble that could burst at any second. The future of the café was on a knife edge. James had gone to work to try and sort things out, but Dagmar could tell his hopes weren't high.

'I wish I knew what was going to happen,' she whispered to Zephyra, who nuzzled her shoulder. How was James going to get around his father? And could he do it quick enough to help her mum?

Her heart ached at the thought. She'd finally tasted love, a kind of love that made her feel whole. She'd never felt so cherished, so wanted, but she couldn't celebrate it or embrace it with the café's future hanging in the balance like this.

Zephyra tilted her head, her dark eyes watching Dagmar. 'If only I was sure it would be ok.'

She ran her hand down Zephyra's back. 'I just want mum's business to be safe,' she murmured, her voice breaking slightly. 'But it's not looking good, and she really has nothing else. This is what she's always done.'

With a final stroke of the brush, she finished with Zephyra and packed up. Her mind was a constant whizz of thoughts and doubts, and she couldn't settle to anything. Even just the new relationship with James had given her enough to be going on with, but adding the café had pushed her to the edge. The fact she couldn't do a thing about it and had to rely solely on James wasn't helping. She trusted him now to do what he could, but things had got complicated.

She stepped out of the stable and walked towards the paddock. Ophelia was at the exit to the car park talking to Caitlin, Kristi, and another woman with a little girl resting on her hip. Dagmar couldn't help doing a doubletake every time she saw Kristi. She

'Hey,' Kristi approached them and both Ophelia and Dagmar turned to her. 'Sorry.' She held up her hands. 'Am I interrupting?'

'Not really,' Dagmar said.

'I was just telling Dagmar about Caitlin and the job,' Ophelia said. 'But I just need to convince Brann.'

Kristi snort laughed. 'Sorry, but I don't see you having any trouble there. You've got him eating out your hand.'

Ophelia glanced away, smiling. 'Yeah. I reckon I can bring him around.'

'I'm sure you can.'

'And I was moaning about Jacinta for a change,' Ophelia said.

'She's been telling stories about me,' Dagmar said. 'Ophelia was about to tell me.'

'Well, yes.'

'I can go,' Kristi said.

'I really don't mind if you hear.' Dagmar gave her a little smile. 'I just want to know what she said.' Was it the same thing she'd told James's mum and Victoria?

'She seems to think you and James have more than just horse riding going on.'

Kristi patted Dagmar on the arm and winked. 'I should hope so.'

Heat bloomed in Dagmar's cheeks.

'Am I missing something?' Ophelia's eyes widened.

'Oh my god, sorry,' Kristi clapped her hand to her mouth. 'Have I put my foot in it?'

'Not exactly.' Dagmar covered her face, and bizarrely tears pricked at the corners of her eyes.

'Hey.' Kristi put her arm around her. 'It's ok.'

'No, it isn't. Because he's... Well, we can't tell anybody anything yet.'

Ophelia stroked Dagmar's arm. 'Does that mean you and James...?'

'Yes, but... Well, he promised to help my mum save her café as part of a community programme at Duchan Fayre, but if his dad finds out we're in a relationship, he could pull the plug on it, and it might not matter anyway because my mum's had an ultimatum from her landlord, so James might not be able to do anything fast enough.'

'Oh, wow. I can see that's difficult.' Ophelia was looking at her with that searching gaze of hers. 'But I'm sure James will do his best. If he can't save the café, I'm sure there are other ways.'

'Not before the end of the week.'

Kristi gave her a little squeeze. 'The end of the week isn't the end of the world.'

'Exactly.' Ophelia rubbed her chin. 'There will be a way, I'm sure.'

Dagmar let out a long breath. 'Will there? Even for me and James. What if his parents don't accept me or cut him off? I'd hate to cause a family breakup.' Forming a relationship with James was bad enough. She hadn't even considered his parents, and she didn't have the first clue how she would go about meeting them, let alone convincing them she was a good person, not when they clearly had their hearts set on Victoria. How could she compete with an earl's daughter?

'Yeah, I hear you,' Kristi said. 'But if he's worth anything, he'll find a way.'

'I've met James's parents,' Ophelia said. 'His mum will probably come around before his dad, but don't think you have to impress them or anything like that. All you can do is be yourself.'

'Totally.' Kristi winked. 'If they don't like you, they can take themselves out. It's James's opinion that matters. I know it's easier said than done, believe me. I've come up against prejudice and judgement all my life, and sometimes it gets to me; I'm not going to lie. But if you're good enough for James, you're good enough for them.'

Dagmar glanced between Kristi and Ophelia, and randomly, completely unexpectedly, she smiled. Even when the path looked dark, she saw two friends. It had taken her a long time to find her people and perhaps they were strange friends, all things considered, but they were friends nonetheless and that made the road ahead seem a little less daunting.

Chapter Twenty-Six

James

James stood by the conference table in the private boardroom at Duchan Fayre, tapping the mahogany top and glancing out of the floor-to-ceiling windows over the lush woodland and hills beyond. This area was reserved for confidential meetings away from the activity of the shopping centre. He checked his watch. Where were his parents? Maybe his father was too ill to attend. Maybe seeing him at home would have been better, but this was business, and James wanted to keep it that way.

About ten minutes later, the door swung open, and Laurence and Sherri entered. Laurence took the seat at the head of the table, looking every inch the corporate businessperson he was and not the slightest bit unwell despite his recent complaints. James frowned. It didn't seem his father's style to make something like that up.

Sherri sat next to her husband, wiping invisible lint from her smart skirt.

'So, what is it we need to discuss so urgently?' Laurence clasped his hands on the table. 'Is it about the sponsorship opportunity at the Dairvin Castle Horse Trials? Because I think we should be all over that.'

'That is on my radar to talk to you about.' James took a seat. 'But before we do that, there's something more pressing.'

Laurence arched an eyebrow. 'Which is?'

James squared his shoulders. 'We need to speed up the funding for the Cosy Bean Café from the community fund. The owner has received an ultimatum and could be thrown out by the end of the week.'

'Ahh, interesting.' Laurence glanced at Sherri. 'That might be just what we need.'

'How do you mean?' James looked between the two of them.

Sherri tilted her head, giving him an almost pitying look. 'We can't do anything with that café.'

James's jaw set. 'What do you mean? We made a deal. It was approved weeks ago. I've met with the owner and discussed it. We can't back out now.'

'Yes, that was indeed my issue.' Laurence folded his arms, his expression stern. 'I didn't want to withdraw the money from the project as it would reflect badly on Duchan, but this ultimatum means we won't be able to fulfil the conditions in the timeframe, so it gives us the perfect way out.'

'And why do we need a way out?' James ground his teeth, but he had a horrible idea of what was coming.

Sherri exchanged a glance with Laurence, then turned back to James. 'Oh dear.'

James mouthed 'what?' but before he could say anything else, his father let out a huge sigh.

'Because you made that deal with a vested interest.'

'I did. Because I needed riding lessons. I'm not denying that.'

His mother shook her head. 'It's not just that though, is it?'

'What do you mean?'

'That riding instructor has drawn you in. It's as Jacinta said. She's developed a thing for you. I guess it must go two ways and that's why you agreed to help her.'

'A relationship like that was unwise at the best of times, but with this deal in the background, it could have put us in a very tricky position.'

'Listen, my relationship with Dagmar had nothing to do with this deal. That happened after and—'

'It doesn't matter when it happened.' Laurence's gaze bored into James. 'How on earth do you know this woman isn't using you? Her interest in you is purely financial.'

James clenched his fists. 'Isn't that exactly the kind of relationship you want me to have? All the women you've introduced me to only want me for my money. Dagmar is the first one who doesn't.'

'And yet she wants you to save her mum's café.' Sherri gave a little shrug. 'Actions speak louder than words. Will she still be interested in you if you don't?'

James frowned. 'Of course she will.' Or at least he hoped so. His parents' words drummed in his mind, making him doubt himself... Doubt everything.

'I'm not so sure.' Laurence placed his palms flat on the table. 'I think it would be a good idea to keep away from her for the time being.'

'Why?'

'Because the business with the café is problematic enough.' Sherri gave him a pointed look. 'If you're hanging around her, she'll do nothing but pester you to take action.'

James let out a sigh and rested his head on his hand. 'And so what if she does? I need to take action. I need to do something. We made a deal. A promise.'

'Like you also made a promise to me.' Laurence stared at him.

'I did, but I regret that now.'

Laurence sat back and rubbed his chest. 'You what?'

'I made it at a time when you were very unwell and when Duchan Fayre wasn't as successful as it is now. We don't need to align with another big family to ensure its continued success. It'll endure with me and Eloise – when she's back from maternity leave. We'll keep it going ourselves.'

Sherri pursed her lips. 'That may be so, and it is very admirable, but I don't think you should give up on Victoria so quickly.'

James dropped his forehead into his hand. 'I'm not going to date Victoria.'

'That's ok. No need to think about that just now. But I've arranged for the countess to meet us for lunch today, and I suspect Victoria will be with her. You will have to be there too, as we want to discuss the sponsorship plans.'

'You made these plans without even discussing them with me?'

'I checked your calendar,' Laurence said. 'You have nothing on.'

Wasn't that just great? James needed to speak to Dagmar, but before he did that, he might have one last trick up his sleeve. He had several private investments, not to mention the land at the end of Loch Briar he'd bought years ago. None of the funds were easy to access. They were long-term investments, but he might be able to tap into them if he made some phone calls. That didn't look like something he'd be able to do today if he was being forced to have lunch with the countess though.

He definitely didn't need the land anymore. The idea he'd had for putting a house there had died a death, and these days, he didn't fancy a home so close to the town, but if he sold the land, that would easily cover the café cost and then some but selling land wouldn't happen quickly.

He sent a message to Dagmar, telling her he was so far hitting a brick wall with his parents, but would get in touch when he knew more. Trouble was, he couldn't see an easy way out of this... Or a way at all. Whatever happened, it didn't look like he would be able to raise the funds quickly enough to save the café.

CHAPTER TWENTY-SEVEN

Dagmar

Dagmar fanned her face as she watched her riding students lead their mounts back to the stables. The late afternoon sun cast long shadows across the riding arena, and the heat was making her sticky.

James had messaged her, saying he was having no luck with his parents. Dagmar's insides curdled at the thought. She was helpless. Nothing she said or did now could save the café, and it seemed like James couldn't either. Her mum would have to give up her life's work and do something else. Dagmar let out a sigh. Why had she ever thought that social media campaign was a good idea? It had seemed so hopeful all those weeks ago and James had been the knight in shining armour, but he'd been knocked off his horse and there was no coming back from it.

'Thanks, Miss Dagmar!' One of the younger girls waved as she walked away with her parents.

'You did great today. See you next week,' Dagmar replied with a smile despite the niggling worries preying on her mind.

As she turned to gather the equipment, her phone buzzed in her pocket. *Please let it be James.* She pulled it out and saw her mum's name on the screen. Her heart sank, not because she didn't want to talk to her mum, but because she was so ridiculously desperate to hear anything from James.

'Hi, Mum.'

'Hi, love. I just wondered if there was any news. The landlord called in with someone looking to buy the building. I didn't like to ask, but I wondered if it was someone working on James's behalf.'

Dagmar bit her lip, glancing around. 'I don't know. Maybe. He messaged, saying he wasn't getting on too well, but maybe that's changed. Maybe they sent someone around to look.'

'I think he would have messaged to say so.'

'Yes, I would have thought so too.'

'Oh dear.' Dotty sighed. 'You know my faith in men is very low, and this isn't helping. I'm so afraid of what's going to happen.'

'Me too. It's not James's fault though. This ultimatum has made everything so much worse. James has done what he could.'

'Yes, I'm sure he has. I'm sorry to have said anything. Sometimes I can't help myself. It's just my café... it's everything I have really, apart from you.'

'I know. And I'll call you as soon as I hear anything, I promise.'

'Ok. I'll keep my fingers crossed.'

'Me too.'

As she ended the call, she checked her messages again. Still no more from James. She sent him a quick message explaining what her mum had just told her, then slipped her phone back into her pocket and took a deep breath.

She tidied up after the riding lessons, stacking helmets and folding rugs and saddle pads. The stable was quiet with only a few of the students still hanging around with their horses. As she returned to the paddock, she noticed a couple, arm in arm, coming in from the car park. They were older than her and the woman was adjusting large sunglasses.

Dagmar squinted, trying to place their faces, which were vaguely familiar. Her heart froze when she realised it was Sherri and Laurence Charlton. What were they doing here? Had James had an accident? If he had, why would they be here? This didn't make any sense, but her insides churned. Them being here couldn't be a good thing, could it?

They approached Dagmar, their expressions stern, and Dagmar's body temperature dropped below freezing despite the heat.

'You're Dagmar, aren't you?' Laurence frowned at her.

'Yes.'

'It's good that we found you so quickly.' Sherri glanced around. 'I'm Sherri Charlton, James's mother. And this is Laurence, my husband. We're the owners of Duchan Fayre. I wonder if you have a moment. We need to talk. Somewhere quiet if you don't mind.'

'Um… ok.' Dagmar nodded. 'But why?'

'Not out here. Where can we go?' Laurence raised an eyebrow.

'Into the office.' She led them to the small room next to the tack room. This so obviously wasn't good, but what the hell could she do about it? She closed the door behind them and turned to face them, fiddling with her fingers. 'What's this about?'

'Let's cut straight to the point, shall we?' Laurence's eyes were cold. 'Duchan Fayre won't be financing the Cosy Bean Café.'

Dagmar's blood ran cold. 'But we had an agreement. He promised to help save the café in return for the riding lessons.'

'Indeed. We are aware.' Sherri shook her head. 'And you've been paid for the lessons. That's quite enough. We understand an ultimatum has been put on the café and, unfortunately, that makes the timing impossible for us.'

Dagmar's mouth went dry. 'And there's nothing you can do?'

Laurence's lips thinned. 'We're not going to anyway,' he said quietly. 'Your relationship with James has put us all in a ridiculously awkward position.'

Dagmar gaped at him. 'I don't get—'

'It looks like you've been providing goodness knows what services to get his backing.' Laurence straightened his tie.

'I absolutely have not. It was nothing like that.'

'James won't be coming back here, and I urge you to stay away from him. Obviously, we can't force you, but if you care about his future, then leave him alone.'

'We understand this won't be easy.' Sherri was clearly attempting to be empathetic, but her words were like poison. 'It won't be for him either, but it will not look good for anyone if the two of you are caught together just now. We need to distance ourselves for the sake of both our business and your mother's. I'm sorry if the café can't be saved, but we can't have Duchan Fayre being hauled over the coals for that.'

Dagmar shook her head. Her words barely made sense. All she was doing was saving their own skin and trying to keep Dagmar away from James. She didn't want to stay away from him. Did he even know his parents were here?

'Where is James?'

Sherri gave her a brief and very curt smile. 'James is busy. He's with Lady Victoria Bruce just now. They have a lot to discuss.'

'What?' Dagmar's jaw set. Her heart was bleeding out. What was he doing with Victoria?

'We wish your mother's business no ill will.' Laurence pushed open the door. 'I hope she can find another investor before the end of the week.' He and Sherri left without looking back. Dagmar sank into the chair behind the desk and put her head in her hands. She should probably cry, but tears weren't there. Something more akin to rage was battling in her mind. What was James doing with Victoria? Why would he go to see her now?

How much of this had come from James and how much from his parents? It was impossible to know. But she trusted him. Even now when it would be so easy to believe he'd abandoned her. She couldn't and she wouldn't. Yes, she was naïve when it came to relationships. Of course she was going to think the first man she'd slept with was love, but if he'd given up on her this quickly, she needed to hear it from him and not his parents.

Slowly, she got out of the chair and forced herself to move towards the door. She still had work to do, but as soon as she could, she needed to go and see James. The day passed in the slowest, strangest way, almost like her insides were lagging and unable to keep up with her mind. Her thoughts were now so far ahead they were lost and scattered, and she couldn't get them back to properly weigh them up or make sense of them.

When she finished up, she checked her phone and saw a message from James. She almost dropped it in her hurry to open it.

JAMES: hey, sorry for the radio silence. Today has been crazy. I've had a lot of meetings and calls to make and I'm still working. Hopefully, I'm getting somewhere, but it means I won't have time to come over tonight. I'll see you as soon as I can. Keep your fingers crossed. XX

Dagmar frowned at the message. Did that mean he was still trying to save the café, even though his parents said no? And he'd had meetings all day? What meetings? His parents said the meeting was with Victoria. Surely he wasn't going to ask her to help. Dagmar's stomach lurched. Being in Victoria's debt would be awful.

She tapped out a message as she walked back to the cottage.

DAGMAR: Can you explain? Are you trying to get funding for the café?

She'd just got in the door when a message pinged in. Assuming it would be James, she opened it and was surprised to see her mum's name on the screen.

MUM: The landlord came over today and said he'd accepted the offer on the building. The buyer wasn't James or anyone from Duchan Fayre. x

Dagmar stared at the message, not sure what to make of any of it. One thing she was sure of though, was that her mum needed her.

She jumped into her car and drove to her mum's ramshackle but cute little cottage; the garden and ivy-covered walls looked like a postcard in the evening sun. So adorable and homely.

She parked her car, pushed open the creaky gate, and walked up the short path. As she stepped inside, the familiar scent of home enveloped her – flowers and baking. But the sight of her mum sitting at the kitchen table with tears streaming down her face cracked her heart in two.

'Oh, Mum.' Dagmar rushed to her side.

Dotty looked up, her eyes red and swollen. 'Oh, Dagmar, it's terrible. The cafe's finished. Nothing anyone can do will help now.'

Dagmar's heart sank. Her phone vibrated in her pocket, and she pulled it out.

JAMES: Don't get your hopes too high, but I have some ideas x

Ideas that had come too late in the day.

Dagmar wrapped her arms around her mum, holding her tight. 'We'll figure something out. We always do. Haven't we got this far?'

'Yes, yes. That's so true. We do know how to survive.' Dotty patted Dagmar's back. 'I just don't know where to start this time.'

Tears finally came, silent and unstoppable, rolling down Dagmar's cheeks. 'I'll help. Whatever it takes, we'll find something.'

She'd like to think whatever she found for the future would involve James, but she suddenly felt so distant from him, and after what his parents had said to her that afternoon, she wasn't sure what to think.

Chapter Twenty-Eight

James

James raised his eyes to the ceiling and ground his teeth to stop himself from yelling. He'd come in very early that morning and seemed to have already spent hours on calls to solicitors and land agents. Why was everything so slow? He still had his usual work to do, but he was desperate to raise some capital before the end of the week, though it was looking less and less likely. Yesterday, he'd been thrown by the lunch with the countess and Victoria. He could see the sponsorship deal being thrown up as a "carrot" by his parents to entice him into seeing more of her. They just wouldn't get it into their heads that he's committed to Dagmar and had no interest in Victoria.

Before he was off the call, his father poked his head around the office door and gave James a wave. James used it as the excuse he needed to bring the call to a close. His father had disappeared, which was fine. It gave him a moment to check his messages. He'd barely flicked onto his phone screen when his father opened the door again. James frowned. His mother was there too, and she looked serious, a little upset even.

'Mum, Dad. Is something happening that I should know about?'

Sherri gave him a brief, tight smile. 'Yes. We need to talk. It's very important.'

James frowned, registering a message from Dagmar. He pulled it open.

DAGMAR: sorry I didn't message last night. I was with mum. She's really upset. The landlord has accepted an offer for the building. I guess no matter what you do now won't work. Xx

'Oh god.' He pressed his fingers into his forehead. Whatever his parents had to say was unlikely to make him feel any better.

'Is everything ok?' Sherri asked him.

'Not really.' He sighed. 'But what do you want to speak about?'

Laurence pulled out a chair for Sherri, then sat himself opposite James. 'We went to speak to Dagmar yesterday and now we need to discuss the situation with you.'

A jolt like an iron rod hit James in the gut. 'You did what?'

'It was fine,' Sherri said. 'She was a nice woman. We explained the situation to her, and she seemed to understand.'

'We can't afford a scandal.' Laurence adjusted his cufflinks. 'Duchan Fayre has a reputation to uphold, and we can't put the community fund to use for businesses that present a conflict of interest.'

'Before you go on.' James held up his hand. 'I understand all that, but I didn't set out to have a relationship with her. That happened after and now I feel like I've let her down—'

'You haven't.' His father looked him straight in the eye. 'She understands, and I'm sure she'll be able to do something else.'

'It's too late. Someone put in an offer for the building.'

'Well, I'm sorry to hear that, but it's not our concern. If her mother is jobless, I'd be happy for her to apply for a position here. I assume she can cook if she runs a café, and we always have vacancies in the kitchen.'

'It's not quite the same, is it?'

'No, but it's an option.'

James shook his head and looked out the window. It wasn't something he'd be comfortable suggesting to someone who'd spent the last thirty years running her own business. He doubted working in the kitchens at Duchan Fayre would be what she wanted.

'The good news is that Victoria and the countess are coming in later.' Sherri gave him a little smile, perhaps hoping he'd return it, but how could he? 'They were very excited about the sponsorship plans and want to talk more about it.'

'Today?' James's fists clenched at his sides.

'Yes, I'm happy to talk to them, but it would obviously be best if you were there,' Laurence said. 'We have a real chance here to forge ahead with a strong deal.'

'Ok. Just let me clear something up though. I'm not against a sponsorship deal. It's a great idea and could definitely be mutually beneficial, but if you think this is going to somehow lead me to a personal relationship with Victoria, then you're wrong. I'm seeing Dagmar. She's the one I want.'

Laurence shook his head. 'Don't cause any more unnecessary grief to the poor woman.'

'Let her go,' Sherri added. 'She'll have her own issues to sort out. She doesn't need you.'

James stared at his parents, his rage simmering just below the surface. 'This is exactly when she needs me. It isn't your decision to make. I won't leave her to face this alone. I'm not going to stop trying to help her now. If the building for the café has been sold, then I can't do anything about that. But I'm going to do something. I'll find away and make it work – not just for the café, but for the two of us. And I'd like you to be onboard with that. She may not be the woman you would have picked for me, but she's the one I've picked for myself, and I hope you'll respect that.'

Sherri tilted her head, giving him a sad look. 'Ok, son. Let's see what happens.'

'And can we at be assured of your presence at the meeting with the countess and Victoria?' Laurence eyeballed him.

Angry heat rose in James's neck, but he knew better than to argue this or make a scene. He'd told them how he felt, but they obviously didn't want to hear it. Maybe the best way to get the point across would be to attend this meeting and make sure everyone knew exactly where he stood.

He turned away, unable to look at his parents. 'I'll see you at the meeting then.'

'Great.' Sherri's chair scraped across the floor, and he caught her standing up in the reflection in the window. 'We'll see you then.'

Laurence followed her to the door, pausing to look back at James. James stared out at the countryside, trying to ignore his reflected father's eye. 'This will all work out for the best, you'll see.'

James didn't respond. He waited until they were gone before collapsing onto his seat, his head in his hands. If it worked out best for them, he didn't want any part in it. If it worked out best for him, he'd like them to be involved.

He opened his phone to message Dagmar and saw a message on the screen from his sister. She used to message him a lot, but since the baby had arrived, she'd been so busy. James smiled at the photos she'd sent of his nephew before reading the message.

ELOISE: Hello! Sorry I've been off radar for so long. It's mad here. I've been hearing you're in all sorts of trouble. Dear, dear, naughty brother!! What's this I hear about you ditching the earl's daughter for the stable wench? Let's have the whole story straight from the horse's mouth (ha-ha, you like that?). What is going on and what have I missed? I never trust the parents to tell the story properly... You know what they're like for putting their own spin on everything, so spill.

He smirked as he read in spite of himself, then carried on to another one she'd sent straight after.

ELOISE: also, Mum said the stable woman was Dagmar. As in the girl who was in your class at primary school! Small world, huh? You won't believe this, but I still have that Schleich horse of hers. I found it in a bundle of old stuff just the other day. Do you want it back? You could give it to her... though she's probably forgotten all about it.

James's smile grew. She hadn't forgotten. And actually, he'd love to give it back to her. Maybe he couldn't save the café, but he could return the treasured possession he'd lifted all those years ago and always meant to give back to her. A little thing maybe, but better than nothing.

CHAPTER TWENTY-NINE

Dagmar

Dagmar lay in bed, staring at a large damp patch on the ceiling of her mum's cottage. The whole place was rundown and needed a massive cash injection to get it sorted. Cash they didn't have and were unlikely ever to have. Money didn't grow on trees, or in cafes or stables, for that matter. Closing her eyes, she wished she could open them and everything would right itself. Her mum would still have the café, and customers would flock to it. This house would get the renovations it needed. And she and James would have a chance together. She squeezed her eyelids shut, then popped them open. Maybe they still did, but her head was too sore and filled with such topsy-turvy and uncertain thoughts she couldn't see how. The only things she knew for sure was that she couldn't face the stables in this state. Rarely in her life had she called in sick to work, but today she'd have to. Ophelia would have to sort out the horses. Between her, Caitlin, and Francesca, they'd no doubt manage something. Guilty acid burned in Dagmar's stomach as she reached for her phone. Her head pounded at the movement, and she could hardly focus on the screen. Back in her high school years, she'd have taken days off all the time if she could. But Dotty had been a single parent with a café to run and wasn't always able to be around. When Dagmar was older and allowed to stay home by herself, she felt constantly guilty if she was off sick, though it was often better than facing the bullies. She knew in her heart some of the times she'd complained of headaches or tummy aches was because she didn't want to face certain people.

But this was horribly real.

She typed out a message to Ophelia.

DAGMAR: Sorry I can't come in today. I've got a thumping migraine.

She hit send and put the phone down. *Done.* Hopefully, Ophelia would see it soon and wouldn't feel the need to call her about anything. Dagmar didn't fancy having to explain herself or speak at all. The pain was so bad she might throw up. The thought of missing the horses made her insides ache. Would Caitlin remember to check the fences? What if she forgot and Stroman got out? Wouldn't that just be the thing to happen when Dagmar wasn't there?

Perhaps she should message Caitlin too and remind her.

She sighed. No. She couldn't do that. She couldn't face looking at the screen at all. Plus, this was good practice for Caitlin – assuming she definitely wanted the job and that she got good results in her exams.

But that was a thought for another time. Dagmar needed to stop thinking and try to get some balance back in her mind.

Downstairs, the clatter of plates and clink of cups told her Dotty was up and about. Dagmar closed her eyes, willing everything to go blank and for the pain to stop. She lay like that for some time, breathing deeply as waves of nausea rolled over her.

A creaking on the stairs was followed by her mum's voice. 'Morning, love. Are you ok? Shall I make you some breakfast before you go?'

'I'm not going today. I can't.' Dagmar held her arm over her eyes.

'Oh dear.' The door slid open. 'What's wrong?'

'A migraine, I think.'

'Let me get you some painkillers.' Dotty bustled off and returned a few moments later with some tablets and a glass of water. Dagmar didn't even ask what they were but knocked them back.

'I'll come down,' she said. 'I need some air.'

She followed her mum down the stairs and opened the kitchen door, standing beside it and letting the fresh air hit her cheeks and forehead.

Piled on the table were the café's finance books, and stacked all around were all the small pieces of equipment Dotty had rescued from the café. Unfortunately, the large coffee machine had been too big to get out, so she'd had to leave it. She insisted it was a temperamental old thing anyway, but Dagmar hated the fact the buyers would probably trash it. Her mum had spent a small fortune buying that – though a long time ago.

'Oh, sweetheart.' Dotty looked her over with sad eyes. 'Try not to worry. I'll go through the numbers today.' Dotty opened an old ledger. 'And see what's left, if anything.'

Dagmar let out a sigh. 'I'll help if I can.'

'No, you should rest.' Dotty watched her for a moment. 'This isn't something you want to be looking at with a migraine. I'm going to a church meeting later this morning, so I want to have a look at these first. If all else fails, I'll ask the minister to pray for me.' She grinned, and Dagmar let out a little laugh. Her mum was a great churchgoer, but clearly didn't really believe prayers could save her now. 'Please don't worry. I can always get a job working in one of the other cafés in town. I have lots of experience and it might be fun just doing the nice bits and not having to worry about all the management bits.'

'Maybe.' Though Dagmar wasn't convinced.

Dotty stared at the ledger in silence for a while, every so often glancing at her laptop screen. The old kitchen clock ticked tirelessly. Dagmar sat at the table with a cool drink. Her pounding head was subsiding little by little.

'I wonder, if we sold some of the equipment that we saved,' Dotty suggested, breaking the silence, 'that might help.'

Dagmar sighed, rubbing her temples. 'Maybe.' Though she didn't see that making much.

Dotty smiled weakly. 'We seem to be back to where we were a few months ago, before James appeared and got our hopes up.'

'I need to message him.' Dagmar closed her eyes. 'I don't think he's replied to my message about the building being sold. I couldn't face looking at my phone anymore. My head was too sore.'

Dotty got up and put on the kettle. 'He seemed like such a lovely lad when he came around here.'

'He is... I'm just so worried.'

Dotty let out a sigh, lifting a mug from a hook on the dresser. 'I hope I haven't misjudged him. I'm not good with men. I've not had positive experiences with them... In relationships anyway. I know some good men, like Grant the lovely minister, but your father was the only man I ever had a relationship with, and he put me off for life. He promised me the world only to vanish at the first sign of being asked for anything real. Charmed me, then left me. At least I got you, but I've never wanted a man since.' She popped a tea bag into her mug, keeping her back to Dagmar. 'I'm sorry if I've put my feelings about relationships onto you. It was never my intention, but I'm very aware that you never seemed interested... I hope that's not because of me.'

Perhaps indirectly it was, though Dagmar had never seen it like that. She'd never actively sought a relationship or met anyone she liked enough.

Until James.

'It's not your fault. I never wanted...' The words wouldn't come. A lump had risen in her throat, obstructing her speech. Her desires had changed so much over the past few weeks, and what she'd suddenly wanted so desperately had been snatched from her. How could she ever go back to the way she'd been before?

'Dagmar?' Dotty came over and put her hand on Dagmar's shoulder. 'Are you ok? What's wrong? I'm so sorry I've upset you.'

Dagmar shook her head, wiping away a stray tear. 'You haven't.'

'Oh, my love. You're in a bad way. Please, try not to worry. I'll find something. Maybe it's time for me to have a change. Change doesn't have to be bad.'

'I know. But it's not just that.'

'Then what?'

'James.'

'What do you mean? Has he done something wrong?'

'No. He's tried so hard. I know he wanted to save the café. But he and I... Well, we...'

'Oh no. Did you have a relationship with him?' Dotty gripped Dagmar's shoulder.

'Yes.' Dagmar swallowed. 'And maybe it was stupid. Originally, it was only meant to be a fling, but it became so much more. Then yesterday his parents came around and said some nasty things to me. I'm so confused and worried. His parents are desperate for him to be with Lady Victoria Bruce. What if he decides he wants that too?'

'Well, if he does, he's not worth it. If he's promised you anything, then he needs to keep it. If you don't trust him—'

'I do. I think I just miss him. And all this uncertainty with the café is making me doubt everything.'

Dotty sat beside her and took Dagmar into her arms, holding her. 'Believe me, I know how this feels. At least you're not pregnant.' Dotty stroked her hair. 'Thank your lucky stars for that. I haven't regretted you for one second of my life, but I'm not denying how difficult it was at times.'

Yes, that was one thing, but Dagmar couldn't process it as a positive. Her head and her heart hurt too much.

She drew away from her mum. 'It's pathetic letting a man affect me like this.'

'It's human nature, but don't give up on him yet. Be kind to yourself.'

Dagmar's phone buzzed, and she lifted it.

OPHELIA: Sorry you're not well. I went to the cottage to see if you needed anything, but you weren't there. Give me a shout if I can help in any way. Hope all's ok x

Dagmar groaned. 'Does that mean she thinks I'm skiving?'

'No.' Dotty read the message. 'She sounds worried about you. I used to think she was rather snobby when she was younger, but she actually seems like a nice person. She's changed and grown into someone a lot nicer than most of her family, though that's probably a little unkind. Her mother is very pleasant.'

'Yes.' Dagmar sighed. 'Ophelia isn't that bad. She was a bit snooty when we were kids, but she always stood up for me and she's been kind. Maybe I should have been more open with her from the start. It's just hard for me to know if people like me. I never think anyone will want to be my friend.'

'Why?'

'I don't know.' Tears pricked again. 'I just assume people are going to hate me.'

'Then we need to change that.' Dotty patted her on the back. 'You are such a wonderful girl. You work hard and you're kind. It's time you recognise your own value. I want you to see it. Let's go and do something for you.'

'Such as?'

'Anything you like. Message Ophelia and explain. Then we can do whatever you want. You said once that you fancied having your hair done. Why don't we arrange that?'

Dagmar pulled her long plait over her shoulder. 'Yeah... I kind of fancy something new, though I don't know what.'

'Then I know just the place. There's a wonderful hairdresser on the High Street. We can make an appointment. I can call them right now. They might not have anything for today, but it's worth a try. And if you don't fancy sitting in the house alone, come to the church with me. It's lovely and peaceful there. The perfect place to sit and think.'

A hairstyle wouldn't change the world just like that, but maybe it would lift her spirits while she waited to hear from James.

CHAPTER THIRTY

James

James tapped his fingers on his desk, holding the phone to his ear. Where was Dagmar and why wasn't she picking up? He needed to talk to her now – before his meeting with the countess and Victoria.

Nothing. She must be at the stables, maybe teaching a lesson. Ending the call, he ran a search on his computer and pulled up the number for the Glenvorneth livery.

Perhaps she'd be in the office.

'Hello, Glenvorneth livery and stables.'

He knew from the voice that it wasn't Dagmar but Ophelia. He didn't really want to talk to her, but maybe she'd have some answers.

'Hi, it's James.'

'James.' Ophelia's voice sounded surprised. 'What can I do for you?'

'I...Um. I'm looking for Dagmar. Do you know where she is? I need to speak to her.'

A pause followed, and James looked up at the clock. 'She's not here today. She called in sick this morning.'

James's heart sank. That didn't sound like Dagmar at all. Not the woman who lived onsite, so that she was here for the horses twenty-four-seven. 'Sick? Did she say what was wrong?'

'A migraine,' Ophelia said, and despite not being able to see her, he had the distinct impression her steely eyes were dissecting him and analysing the results from afar. He could almost hear the cogs of her brain turning.

'Oh dear. I'm sorry to hear that.' Even sorrier that she hadn't told him. Had his parents scared her away? Or maybe she was too ill to message. 'I didn't know she suffered from migraines. They're awful.'

'Indeed they are,' Ophelia said. 'I've never known her to have one before, bless her. She's one of the healthiest people I know. So this must be bad.'

James hesitated for a moment, taking a deep breath. 'Is she at home? Does the cottage have a landline I could call? She's not answering her mobile... Though she might be asleep.'

'She isn't at the cottage.'

'Where is she then?'

Ophelia let out an audible sigh. 'Listen, before I tell you any-thing, maybe you should tell me why you're so desperate to talk to her. I know there's something going on with the two of you. She told me as much, and maybe it's none of my business, but if you want me to help, I need to know the facts. If something has gone wrong between the two of you, I'm not helping you find her if it's to cause her more grief.'

James ran his fingers through his hair. So this wasn't awkward at all – having to explain his current predicament to the woman he'd unsuccessfully courted last year. 'Look, nothing's gone wrong. Not like that. Dagmar and I are in a relationship. We also had an agreement.'

'An agreement?'

'Yes. I wanted to use money from the Duchan Fayre community fund to help her mum save the Cosy Bean Café in return for...'

'Yes?' Ophelia's tone was sharp.

'For doing the lessons.'

'Even though you paid for them?'

'Well, yes... But I knew she didn't like me. We had a history, and I needed her to come round.'

'So, you bribed her?'

He took a deep breath and looked away, shaking his head. 'Yeah, ok. It does sound like that. That's certainly what my parents think. But I needed her to give me lessons, so I could fool Victoria and make her believe... Well, that I could ride.'

'I knew that was a ruse. It was so obvious you hadn't ridden before.'

'Yeah. I was paranoid you'd tell Victoria, and I wanted to persuade Dagmar to teach me on the fly. When I read about her mother's issues with the café on social media, I said I would save the café in return for the lessons. But that's fallen through anyway and I really need to talk to her, but I can't get hold of her. I think I've upset her... Or my parents have.'

'Dagmar is a friend of mine and if you or your parents have hurt her in some way, I'd like to hold you accountable.'

A smile twitched at the corner of his mouth, and he was glad she couldn't see him. Ophelia ran a very successful business, but it was amazing how people forgot that about her and viewed her as someone who'd been born into her success. She definitely had some balls though. James would pay good money to see her up against his father in the boardroom. 'I haven't intentionally hurt her, but I'm sure the closure of the café will have upset her.'

'Why did it close? Why didn't you hold up your end of the deal?'

'I tried, but the landlord put in an ultimatum which complicated things, and then my parents discovered my relationship with Dagmar and decided they couldn't back the deal anyway.'

'I see.'

'They still want me to go after Victoria. That's what this was all meant to be about. But it's not anymore. Dagmar is the one I want, and the riding isn't for anyone now, other than myself. But I'm having a hard time convincing my parents. They went to speak to her yesterday, which was really fucking irritating; pardon my French. But they've properly messed up a situation that was bad enough already.'

'I assume they disapprove of your choice.'

'Yup.'

'Well, let me tell you something. If Dagmar's the right person for you, then stick with her. You won't regret it. Look at me and Brann. You know my father wanted me to make a good match – you. But I chose who I wanted to be with. It wasn't easy going against what my father wanted, but I'm glad I did. I'm happy with Brann and I couldn't bear living my life as a lie, just getting by with someone. Not when I see how great life can be with the right person.'

'Yes, I know. And that's what I'm trying to do.' Even though his parents were still pushing Victoria at him. His eyes strayed to the clock. She'd be here any minute, and he still hadn't reached Dagmar.

'Good. Well, she's at her mother's house. I don't have the number, sorry. I'm not even sure where it is.'

He blew out a long breath. 'Ok. I'll message her again, because I have an idea for the café, but I need to speak to her about it.'

'Well, good luck.'

'Thanks.' James clenched his fists. Time was ticking on. The meeting was due to start any minute. He pulled out his phone, but too late.

The door opened, and people were talking. James got to his feet as his parents came in with Victoria, the countess, and

'Eloise!' James headed around the table to hug his sister. 'What are you doing here? Don't you want to enjoy every second you don't have to be here?'

She chuckled. 'Yes, I do, but Dougie is off, and he's taken Alfie out, so I thought I'd nip in and join the fun.'

He gave her a look, hoping to impart the message that it was unlikely to be any fun at all.

'Let's all take seats,' Laurence said.

James resumed the seat he'd be on before and Victoria sat beside him, smiling.

'Well, hello, James. This is a lovely office you have. What a stunning view. This must be the best office view in the county.'

He took a deep breath. 'Yes, I'm sure it is.'

'Right, let's talk through the sponsorship proposals,' Laurence said. 'We can make the draft of an action plan with the understanding that it's all very informal for now.'

James joined in when needed, aware of the time ticking on, and also Victoria's constant glances in his direction. His mind had no doubt that she saw this as a prelude to a more personal relationship.

'There's something I need to say before we continue.' James closed the lid of his laptop and looked up.

'What's that?' Laurence frowned.

'It's a little bit delicate, but I don't want to go on with any ambiguity or chance of misunderstanding.'

'Oh?' The countess eyed him over.

'It's to do with any proposed personal relationship for Victoria and I.' He looked directly at her. 'I know there's been some hopes, perhaps even assumptions, that you and I will get together. And while I can see the business and financial benefits of that, and I also think you're a great person, I'm afraid a relationship beyond business and beyond friendship is out of the question.'

'Wow, ok.' Victoria looked at her mother.

'Better to go on without false hope, I suppose.' The countess gave James a cutting look.

'False hope?' Victoria shook her head. 'Is this because you believe I'm seeing someone else? Because I assure you that's finished.'

'No. It's not that. You're just not the right person for me. I've met someone else, and I'm fully committed to her.'

Victoria narrowed her eyes. 'Someone else? Who?'

'Dagmar Ingenfeld.'

'What?' Laurence let out an audible huff that made James snap around to look at him. His father was red faced, but hopefully his obvious fury wouldn't result in another heart attack.

'Dagmar?' Victoria gaped at him.

The countess's eyes had almost popped. 'Goodness gracious.' Her hand flew to her chest. 'So, it's not enough winning all the competitions over Victoria, but she's also won you.'

'I'm not a prize to be won. Neither are you.' His eyes met Victoria's. 'You're a person, not a commodity. I don't want to have a manufactured relationship with you just to appease our families. I'm in love with Dagmar.' James met the countess's gaze. 'I'm afraid I don't feel that way about Victoria.' He scanned the room. His father still looked like an overripe tomato, but his mother and Eloise both had softer expressions. He turned his attention back to Victoria. 'You're worth better than this. I hope you find someone better suited to you than me, someone who'll love you the way you deserve.'

'Nice words, I'm sure.' Victoria pulled a tight-lipped pout. 'No point running after someone who's not interested. It's not like I don't have other offers.'

'Exactly. And I hope one of them works out for you.'

The countess drew in a long breath through her nose, her mouth poised in a very fine line. 'I suppose, if this is how you feel, you should do what's right. A lesser man might not have spoken up. I'm acutely aware this can't have been easy to say.'

'Thank you.'

The countess sighed. 'Well, I'm glad you let us know, unfortunately this means we'll be calling off our dinner date with you on Saturday.' She looked over at Laurence and Sherri. 'I'm sure you'll understand under the circumstances.'

'Indeed.' Sherri blinked several times. 'I hope it won't affect the sponsorship deal.'

'We'll have to think about that and not here.'

'That's your call, of course.' James gave her a rueful nod. 'But the offer is still on the table, should you wish it.'

She raised an eyebrow. 'We'll consider it carefully. But right now, I don't feel like talking anymore. We're leaving.' She stood up, and Victoria followed.

'We'll show you out.' Sherri nudged Laurence, who got to his feet looking a little dazed.

As the door shut, James stared at it, just breathing.

'Well, that was dramatic,' Eloise said. 'I wasn't expecting that. So, you are chasing the stable wench.'

'Don't call her that.'

'Sorry.' She grinned. 'Listen, before they come back in here and give you a bollocking, I need to give you this.' She handed over a little gift bag.

'What's this?'

'You'll see. Something you might want to return to your new girlfriend.'

He peered into the bag and frowned. 'Is that the—'

The door burst open, and his parents returned.

'What on earth was that all about?' Laurence glared at him. 'In the middle of a business meeting. Have you lost your mind?'

'Maybe. But I had to say it. I've tried and tried to tell you. You wouldn't listen.'

'Oh, son.' His mother touched his arm. 'I'm so worried that you're making a mistake.'

'I'm not. Victoria was the mistake. She might have seemed like the right choice for you, but she wasn't for me.'

'He's right.' Eloise smiled at their parents. 'I'm glad I married a good man before you chose anyone for me, because there's no point marrying anyone if you don't love them.'

'What is this nonsense?' Laurence stared at the two of them. 'Love can go hand in hand with business.'

'Yes, Dad. It can.' James sat on the edge of the table with a sigh. 'You and mum have shown us that. But it works because the love came first. You and mum have had that from the start. I'm not prepared to do it the other way around. It's too risky. What if Victoria and I had tried only to realise we didn't really like each other until after we were married? How messy might a divorce have been?'

'Yes.' Sherri frowned. 'That could have been worse.'

'The bottom line is – I love Dagmar. I want to be with her, and I want to honour my promise to save the Cosy Bean Café.'

Laurence's brow furrowed. 'What is it with this girl?'

Sherri put her hand on his arm. 'Wait a moment. I want to hear this. How will you save the café? You can't use the fund, we've told you—'

'I know that.' James pulled away from her. 'I have another plan that doesn't involve anyone's investment but my own – even though it would be a lot nicer if you were all emotionally invested.'

Laurence shook his head. 'I'm not sure about this.'

'You don't have to be sure. I'm sure and that's enough. I have my own life to lead. Is my happiness not important too? I've spent long enough trying to find someone "socially acceptable", and I know that's what I promised you, but please, release me from that and let me and Eloise show you we can run Duchan

Fayre perfectly well together without needing to be attached to a big name. Let's make our name big.'

Sherri came over and put her arms around him. 'I'd like to see that happen.' She moved on and hugged Eloise, then glanced at her husband. 'Can you release him from the promise?'

Laurence grunted and looked away. 'I suppose so, though I'm not at all convinced.'

'Then let us show you, Dad.' James let out a breath. 'We won't let you down.'

'Indeed, we won't.' Eloise smiled and made a mini salute. 'So, tell us, how do you plan to save the café?'

'Well, I own that piece of land at the top of Loch Briar,' James said. 'I was going to sell it to raise the capital, but I'm too late with that. So, I'm going to offer them the land to build a new café. The number of people walking past is one of the things that put me off building a house there, but it would be ideal for a café.'

'Nice.' Eloise nodded. 'I'm sure they'll appreciate it.'

'I need to talk to them about it first.' It would only have to be a simple building. A log cabin even. A place like that right next to the loch would be really popular and very quaint, but if Dotty and Dagmar didn't like the idea, there was no point even thinking about it.

Eloise hugged him, and his heart felt lighter.

'Just don't go throwing money about.' Laurence frowned. 'You shouldn't let business be ruled by your heart.'

'Why not?' James held eye contact with his father. 'After all, you just told me love and business can go together. And this time, the love's already there, so hopefully we're already partway there.'

CHAPTER THIRTY-ONE

Dagmar

'It was very nice to meet you. And I hope you enjoy having your hair done,' Grant, the church minister, said.

'Thank you.' Dagmar shook hands with him. He was a lot younger than she'd expected. She'd thought he was a man of her mum's age – one that her mum had a bit of a crush on. But he looked more around her own age. He seemed to have amassed quite a following of women around her mum's age though, and they'd been helping him prepare the church for a coffee morning that weekend.

Although Dotty was obviously upset about the café, Dagmar understood why she still wanted to come here today. These were her friends and her support group. They were all concerned about her and eager to help out.

'And remember,' Grant said to Dotty. 'Drop in anytime if you need a chat.'

'Thank you.' Dotty patted his arm and smiled. As they made their way outside, she leaned into Dagmar. 'He's caused quite a scandal just by being single. So many people want to help find a wife for him.'

Dagmar shook his head. 'Oh dear. I hope they leave him to find someone for himself – assuming he even wants someone.'

Dotty chuckled. 'Indeed.' She checked the time on her phone. 'That was so lucky the salon had a cancellation. I feel like it was meant to be. Like a sign of hope.'

'Yeah.' Dagmar had done her best not to think about James while she'd helped her mum. She'd had a missed call from him earlier, but when she'd called back, the line had been busy. If only she knew what was going on. Were his parents keeping him busy so that he couldn't speak to her?

Dagmar and Dotty made their way down Kirk Lane, a narrow road with some cute but higgledy-piggledy houses on it towards Glenbriar's main street.

'I think Kristi and Caitlin live around here somewhere.' Dagmar scanned around. 'I'm pretty sure Kirk Lane was the address Caitlin had on her job application.'

Halfway up the main street was the hair salon named Cutting Edge. It had a neatly presented whitewashed front with fake plants at the side of the entrance. The hum of hairdryers and soft chatter greeted them as Dagmar opened the door. This was Dagmar's first time in a hairdresser, and she was sure the little flutter in her chest was more nerves than excitement.

'Hello, hello.' A smiley stylist greeted them, her dark hair pulled back in a messy updo. 'Are you Dagmar?'

She nodded.

'I'm Hayley. I'll be fixing your hair today. And are you her mum?'

'I am.' Dotty smiled at her.

'Would you like a coffee while you're waiting?'

'That would be lovely.'

'What about you, Dagmar?' Hayley smiled at her.

'Yeah, thank you.'

'No worries. I'll get Collete to fix them up.'

Dagmar relaxed as Hayley undid her plait and combed out her long hair.

'Your hair is stunning. What is it you'd like done?'

'I still want to keep it long, but it just feels drab sometimes.'

Hayley smoothed it through her fingers. 'I could take a few inches off it, and it'll still be a lovely length. We can put some toning conditioner through it to give it a lift and I can style it any way you like.'

'I'd love some curls. Not frizzy ones, but those loose ones.'

'I can do them, no problem.' Hayley beamed at Dagmar in the mirror. 'I think I've seen you before. You work at Glenvorneth, don't you?'

'Yeah. Do you know it?'

'Ophelia is a good friend of mine.'

'Ah, I see. Well, maybe you can do me curls like hers. She always looks amazing.'

Hayley chuckled. 'Yes, she does. I'll fix you up and you'll look just as fabulous.'

It wasn't an idle boast either. A couple of hours later, Dagmar hardly recognised herself. She tossed her head this way and that, admiring her new look. Dotty looked at her with a broad smile.

'You look wonderful.'

'Thanks, Mum.' Dagmar felt her phone buzzing in the back pocket of her jeans. She pulled it out and her heart leapt at the sight of a message from James.

'Finally.'

'Is it James?' Dotty pressed her hands together like she was praying.'

'Yes.' Dagmar opened the message.

JAMES: So sorry I keep missing you. Are you still at your mum's house (Ophelia told me where you were)? I really need to see you. I've got so much to tell you. xx

Dagmar drew in a breath, then showed the message to her mum.

'There you go,' Dotty said. 'That all sounds good.'

'I wonder what he wants to tell me.'

'Then message him back.' Dotty took hold of her upper arm. 'Quickly.'

'Ok.' Dagmar pulled in a deep, cleansing breath before tapping out a message. Hopefully whatever he had to tell her was good news.

DAGMAR: I'm not at mum's house. I'm in town just now but could meet somewhere.

She'd barely sent it when a reply pinged in.

JAMES: I'm also in town. Any chance you could meet me at Loch Briar, near the start of the trail to Heather Glen? There's a place with construction fences around it. I'll wait there. xx

Again, Dagmar showed the message to her mum. 'Why would he want to meet me there? That's a weird location for him to be in. I thought he'd be at work.'

'I'll drive you there right now.' Dotty took her hand. 'Come on. Let's go.'

Dagmar barely had a moment to think about it before she was back in the car whizzing towards the top of the town, where the road turned onto a track that led to a small car park. This path was incredibly popular with walkers and cyclists, joining up a riverside path with another that skirted Loch Briar. James had told her ages ago he owned land here. It was a beautiful location, but she understood why he didn't want to live here. The plot was fairly small and was on the crossroad section of the path.

Dagmar's thoughts were wandering, partly because nerves were jangling her stomach so hard she couldn't focus. She was so desperate to see him again. It felt like she hadn't seen him for ages, even though it was only a few days.

'On you go.' Dotty patted her on the leg. 'I'll wait.'

Dagmar leapt out of the car and headed over to the patch of land surrounded by construction fences.

James was standing near the fence, his hands deep in his pockets. He looked up as she approached, and his eyes widened. Her heart pounded in her chest.

'Dagmar.' He marched over to her and opened his arms. 'My god, I've missed you.' He pulled her into a hug, and she returned it instantly, melting into his warmth. 'The last couple of days have been crazy.'

She glanced up at him, sweeping her hair behind her ear, remembering how different it looked.

'You look incredible. I mean, you're always beautiful, but your hair...'

'I had it done.'

'It suits you. You're an absolute knockout. But I thought you were ill.'

'I had a migraine this morning, but it wore off and Mum persuaded me to go out. I was so distracted wondering what was going on.' She gave him a vague smile. 'Why did you want me to come here? What's been happening?'

He let out a sigh. 'I'm so sorry. Everything hit all at once. I was trying to sell this land to raise capital, then I got your message that the building had been sold, and my parents kept arranging meetings with Victoria and the countess.'

'And are you and her—'

'She and I are nothing. I told you. I only want you. Now she knows that, so do the countess, and my parents. I told them all at the meeting this morning.' His eyes were steady on hers. 'They know my wishes.'

'And what are they?'

'I want to make a fresh start. With you... if you'll have me. I have an idea for this land too. We could use it to build a new Cosy Bean Café on. I'd love for your mum to see it too. We can work together to make it happen.'

'Are you serious?' Her voice was barely above a whisper.

'Of course. I'd do anything for you.' He tightened his grip on her. 'Because I love you. I love you so, so much. I want a life with you and the horses. That's what matters to me.'

'Oh my god.' A rush of emotion galloped through her, and she threw her arms around his neck. 'That's what I want too. I thought I was being crazy.'

'If you are, we can be crazy together. In fact, I want us to do everything together.'

'Same. It's been torturous not seeing you the past few days.'

'Agreed.' He threaded his fingers into her hair and dipped in, placing his lips on hers. She smiled, remembering how wonderful it felt to be in his arms.

'What about your parents?' Dagmar pulled back. 'They don't want me seeing you.'

'I've sorted things with them. It might take a while for them to come around, but I've told them how I feel and if they respect that, then they'll accept you. But don't worry, you're more important to me than their opinion and I will fight for you.'

Dagmar smiled and sucked on her lower lip. 'I was so worried, but it feels like a huge weight has gone.'

'I have something else for you.' His words fell softly on her ears. He reached into his pocket and handed her a small package.

Stepping back, she took it and unwrapped it, her breath catching when her eyes landed on the little black Schleich horse inside. 'Oh, my god. It's my horse...' She looked up at him. 'Where did you find it?'

'By some miracle, my sister still had it. She even remembered it was yours. I wish I'd been able to return it to you years ago.'

Dagmar clutched the horse to her chest. 'Wow. I never thought I'd see it again. Silly really to have cared about it this long, but it was my favourite.'

'And you were mine.' James stroked her face. 'I wish I hadn't followed the crowd. I wish I'd followed my heart instead. If I had, we might have dated back in school.'

'I think I like you better now,' she said. 'You've grown up.'

'I hope so. I've been on the wrong path for a long time. It's time I got back on track.'

She nodded, a smile breaking through. 'Then let's make a new start together.'

He pulled her close, pinning her up against him, a smile filling his face. 'That's the best thing I've heard for a very long time.'

Dagmar beamed at him, then looked around. 'My mum's in the car. Should I call her to come and see the land?'

'Definitely.'

Dagmar leaned up and kissed his cheek. This was the start of a whole new chapter in her life, and she was ready to embrace it.

Epilogue

James

Some Weeks Later

James stood on the plot of land by the loch, hand in hand with Dagmar. The sun was out, and it was warm. Brann and his team were raising the walls of the cabin that would soon house the new Cosy Bean Café.

'This is going to be wonderful.' Dotty's eyes shone brightly. 'I can't thank you enough.'

'Don't thank me.' James patted her on the back. 'Just keep making the best pastries in town.'

'I'm dying to taste them,' Sherri said. 'So's Laurence. He's very partial to a cinnamon Danish.'

'Indeed I am.' Laurence gave James a stoic nod. 'This looks like a solid investment, after all. You know I had my doubts, but you stuck by your guns, and it's paid off.'

'I decided to go back to the way you used to be – and judge people on their qualities, not their bank balance.' James eyed his dad, catching his sister grinning as she sorted baby Alfie out in his buggy.

'Yes, yes.' Laurence pulled a face, obviously not appreciating being called out, but James had had enough. If he and Eloise were going to make Duchan Fayre a successful legacy, it would be without the kind of snobbery their parents had adopted, though his father's attitude had softened considerably since meeting Dotty and Dagmar properly, and discovering they were nice people.

'I've got some champagne on ice for the dinner tonight,' Sherri said aside to Dotty. 'We're looking forward to having you over.'

James put his arm around Dagmar's shoulder and smiled. She returned it, her eyes glossy and bright.

'I have some good news to share too.' Laurence rubbed his hands together and leaned closer to James. 'We spoke with the countess of Dairvin, and she's agreed to keep the sponsorship deal with Duchan Fayre going for next year's horse trials.'

James huffed out a laugh. 'Well, that's something.'

'I think Ophelia helped,' Dagmar said. 'She's got a way with the countess, and I think the countess respects her, as Ophelia is one of the few people who stands up to her.'

'That was nice of her,' Sherri said. 'I thought she was a bit bolshy when I first met her, but she's actually just good at business.'

'Yeah. She can be a bit scary sometimes, but her heart's in the right place.'

'How's the new girl working out at the stables?' Sherri smiled at Dagmar, and James breathed more easily to see these pleasant interactions.

'She's great. She's Brann's daughter, you know?'

'Is she? Gosh, he must be older than he looks.'

'I think he is.' Dagmar smiled. 'And Caitlin is such a hard worker. It'll be a relief not having to work such long hours, and she's so enthusiastic. She still has to wait for her exam results to see if she can do the training she wants, but even if she doesn't, we have a plan to get her on another course. So either way, it should work out.'

James nodded, his heart full to burst. Now they could focus on their shared dream and find a new place to live. Somewhere they could keep horses of their own. He squeezed Dagmar's hand. This was the best feeling.

'Here's to a fresh start.' He raised an imaginary glass.

'And lots of cakes,' Dotty added.

Everyone laughed, raising their own pretend glasses.

Later that day, James and Dagmar made their way back to the stables before they were due at his parents' house for dinner.

'Shall we go for a quick ride?' James asked. 'I miss being in the saddle.'

'Sure, why not?'

James winked at her. Their first few months together had been such a whirlwind. They were adjusting to new ways and the joy of seeing each other almost every day.

They led the horses out of the stable and mounted up, heading towards the bridle path. James finally had the woman he wanted by his side. She was the one he'd like to marry and, when the time was right, he would ask her, but for now, they were just enjoying life together.

As they rode side by side, James grinned. It was kind of a permanent feature on his face these days. 'You know' – he glanced over at Dagmar – 'starting riding lessons this year was possibly the oddest thing I've ever done. But also, one of the best. Not only did it reconnect me with you, but it gave me a new thing to enjoy. I can't imagine life without horses and riding now.'

Dagmar's eyes sparkled. 'That's music to my ears. I never thought I'd meet anyone who'd like horses as much as me.'

'I love them... Not as much as I love you, but then, I don't love anyone else that much.' He winked. 'There's something incredibly freeing about being on horseback. It's become a part of my existence.'

Dagmar smiled. 'You've taken to it so well.'

'Riding lessons were the best investment of my life so far.'

'Come on.' She and Zephyra trotted off. Conker waited placidly, and James felt that wonderful affinity with him he'd had from the start. He urged Conker forward and Conker set off, his hooves beating a satisfying rhythm on the ground. James focused on the motion, finding his balance and attempting to rise in the stirrups like Dagmar, though it would take more practice to get it right, and he'd probably never be as elegant as her.

'You're doing great,' Dagmar called.

James laughed, moving up beside her. He slowed to a stop. 'Would it be dangerous for me to lean over and kiss you?'

'Yes.' She glanced around. 'But I could do it.' She pushed out, and he leaned in and kissed her.

'I love you so much,' he said as she moved safely back onto the saddle.

'And I love you. I never thought I'd say those words to any-one... Well, except my mum. But I really do love you.'

'You're the best thing that's ever happened to me...' He squinted into the canopy of trees above where sunlight was spilling through, and he shielded his eyes. 'And I feel like this afternoon is the perfect time for us to ride off into the sunset together.'

She reached over and took his hand. 'Then let's do it.'

With a shared smile, they urged their horses forward, walking along the bridle path towards the stables and a new and exciting future.

The End

MORE BOOKS BY MARGARET AMATT

Scottish Island Escapes

1. A Winter Haven

2. A Spring Retreat

3. A Summer Sanctuary

4. An Autumn Hideaway

5. A Christmas Bluff

6. A Flight of Fancy

7. A Hidden Gem

8. A Striking Result

9. A Perfect Discovery

10. A Festive Surprise

The Glenbriar Series

1. Stolen Kisses at the Loch View Hotel

2. Just Friends at Thistle Lodge

3. Pitching up at Heather Glen

4. Two's Company at the Forest Light Show

5. Highland Fling on the Whisky Trail

6. Snowdown at the Old Schoolhouse

7. Starting Over at the Crafty Bee Barn

8. A Surprise Proposal in the Rose Garden

9. Cutting it Neat for the Wedding

10. A Classy Affair in the Country

11. Mix Up under the Mistletoe

12. A Fresh Start on the Bridle Path

13. Last First Kiss at the Village Church

14. Fight or Flirt on the Scenic Route

15. Love Match on the Road Home

Love on the Edge – Barra Series

Acknowledgements

Thanks as always to my husband, Ian, for supporting my dreams and helping me think up some of the place names in the book (as well as all the bonkers ones I'll never use but are good for a laugh!). Also to my son, whose interest in my writing always makes me smile. Although romance books aren't exactly his thing – he keeps asking me to add outer space elements or at least elves – he's always ready to cheer me on!

Throughout the writing process, I have gleaned help from many sources and met some fabulous people. I'd like to give a special mention to Stéphanie Ronckier, my beta reader extraordinaire. Stéphanie's continued support with my writing is invaluable and I love the fact that I need someone French to correct my grammar! Stéphanie, you rock. To my lovely friend, Lyn Williamson, thank you for your continued support and encouragement with all my projects. And to my fellow authors, Evie Alexander and Lyndsey Gallagher – you girls are the best! I love it that you always have my back and are there to help when I need you.

Also, a huge thanks to my editors at Leannan Press!

Of course a huge thank you goes to the readers who continue to support me in so many ways. I appreciate each and every one of you and hope that I can keep bringing you more books to enjoy! Big love.

Margaret XX

ABOUT THE AUTHOR
Margaret Amatt

Margaret has told and written stories for as long as she can remember. During her formative years, she spent time on long walks inventing characters and stories to pass the time.

Writing books is Margaret's passion and when she's not doing that, she's often found eating chocolate, walking and taking photographs in the hills around Highland Perthshire. Those long walks still frequently bring inspiration!

It's Margaret's pleasure to bring you the **Scottish Island Escapes** series, **The Glenbriar Series** and the **Love on the Edge — Barra** series. Each series features interconnected stories for those who enjoy inhabiting Margaret's world but each and every book can be read as a standalone if you'd rather dip in and out.

You can find more information about Margaret on her website or by signing up for her newsletter

www.margaretamatt.com